Flaw in the Master's Ring

BRIAN PHILLIPS

Edited by Kelly Byrd

DEDICATION

To my brother Joe, who proved that if you keep asking "is it done yet," it may eventually get done.

ACKNOWLEDGMENTS

I would like to acknowledge the inspiration and fun I gather every year at RavenCon! I encourage anyone involved in writing fantasy or science fiction to join us in Williamsburg Virginia!

WHERE IS BROTHER QUIET?

Wine sloshed around the rim of a smoky-green glass. Placing a pale hand on the stem, Brother Quiet lifted the glass to his lips and took a long swallow. The Rat offered him a spotless white cloth, hoping to stop the slight dribble running down his chin from dripping onto the table.

"It's fine." Brother Quiet said, annoyed with the fastidious nature of his host.

"I'll tell you when it's fine. Right now, you are in an alchemy shop eating cheese and drinking wine, surrounded by concoctions that could burn all of Home's Hearth to the ground, taking us along with it. Spills are not fine here, especially when they involve alcohol, naphtha, or any number of other flammable liquids."

Brother Quiet had lived in the relative safety and shelter of the sewers for years. His manners had not improved with the experience. Nor did his recent conversion by the Takers improve social skills. The Rat sighed. Sometimes no other options presented themselves and he had to deal directly with the newly Taken. He pulled his hand back, bringing the untouched cloth with it.

"Right." Brother Quiet jammed a wedge of white soft cheese into his mouth, purposefully spilling just a few white specs on the table. The Rat didn't react. Instead, he connected with the thing that now lived inside Brother Quiet, simply encouraging it to notice his annoyance and hopefully, bringing Brother Quiet to heel.

In a few moments, he had his wish. Brother Quiet took a final sip of wine, emptying the glass in a single swig, then leaned back in his chair, calm and peaceful.

"Are you finished?"

He looked down at the plate, oddly confused about why he had cared so much about the cheese just a few moments ago. He'd forgotten what point he was trying to make.

"Sure. Let's get to it."

The Rat took out a small journal from beneath the table, then he reached over to take up a bottle of ink. Using a short knife he carried for just such a purpose, he sharpened a feather quill, opened the book, and scribbled a few lines of a language that hadn't been spoken for a century.

"They made me the keeper of the goddess's bath."

The Rat's eyebrows raised in surprise. "That's an honor if there ever was one. But that seems a little close to Phyllicitus for comfort. She might identify you if given a chance."

"Luck is with us there. She has been staying at the Garden lately. The other Priestesses tell me that she's been sad and wanted to spend some time seeking pleasures."

"Do you believe them?"

"Not really. One of her favorites is back from some journey. Sister Hope tells me that the goddess and this Aileen person were once very close. I think Phyllicitus is trying to mend some kind of bridge with her. It could take a while."

"Aileen eh? The same one that allied with the Necromancers?"

"That would be her. I get the sense that her alliance with

those forces is still very much intact."

"A pity. I was hoping to avoid that kind of confrontation. I've noticed there are a few necromancer masters in town. I wonder if they are together."

"No idea."

"They also seem to have captured one of us, some woman. I'm sure there are experiments going on every night. I feel for the poor soul they have in their grasp."

Brother Quiet didn't respond to that. His soul had been taken from him just a few short days ago. He found it difficult to sympathize with others in a similar bind.

"So, there it is. I'm trusted. I have access to her baths and her apartments. Your plan is going splendidly I'd say."

The Rat corrected him, "Their plan."

"Their plan, your plan, it's all the same, isn't it?"

The Rat stopped to scratch down a few more words into his book, then to scribble a quick glyph on the upper corner of the page.

"So now what?"

"Now what? Now it's the easy part. We assemble all the Taken in Home's Hearth, sneak into the baths after dark, and take her."

"Take her? The goddess? We will be lucky to avoid discovery the instant she returns."

"That's why we are going to do this on the first night she returns. You will avoid seeing her at all costs, then you will unlock the wards that protect the baths."

"Unlock wards? How?"

"Please, I'm an alchemist. I'll have something for you. Don't worry."

Brother Quiet nodded. "Just curious, what are we going to do with her? I mean, well, she's a goddess after all. We can hardly kill her. Even if we did, what would it accomplish?"

"Luckily, that isn't your problem. We just need to get hold of her. Leave the rest of it to our Taker friends. There are other forces at play here, forces it would be best to remain ignorant of."

He nodded. The Rat could feel Brother Quiet trying to struggle against his Takers. It would be a valiant attempt, but it was doomed to fail. Once taken, release became impossible. He enjoyed watching the doomed struggle. Brother Quiet's pristine face betrayed none of the anger and desperation that lived deep in his soul.

The Rat smiled across the table. He picked up the clean cloth and used it to remove the last of the ink from his quill. Then he turned and picked up a clean wine goblet. Images of ravens were carved into its surface, giving the illusion of a line of birds in flight. He reached over and poured a full measure of wine into the cup.

Sitting back, he opened his senses to the Takers. He could feel every desperate emotion that Brother Quiet was feeling. Guilt, hate, and sweetest yet, despair. The Rat let out a small sigh of pleasure and began to sip his wine while watching his entertainment.

ARGUEMENT

"Junk. It's all junk."

Piles of clothing, charms, wine bottles, and letters surrounded him as Miller tried to pack for Aileen. He was sure the Gardens would have every comfort she needed, especially when the goddess was sponsoring her. Some things gave her comfort though. Miller wanted Aileen to have those right now. Somehow, he felt it was important. He left behind other things Necromancers used, cursed daggers, scrying bowls, poisons.

A large green bag stood open on the floor, half filled with shoes, dresses, clean undergarments, a rainproof cloak, and bathing supplies. He wrapped a gift in wax leather to protect it and placed it in the bag as well.

"Here comes crazy," Cerna warned from his post. Miller sped up, ceasing his careful considerations of what to pack and simply thrusting in wads of whatever he could reach quickly. He pulled the cord tight to seal the bag then tied it off.

The door opened. Franz came in first, holding a crate against his chest, struggling beneath its weight. Master Darjeeling followed three steps behind holding a broken tree branch in his hand. It tapped on the floor as Darjeeling walked as if he were searching for something.

Miller didn't want to be noticed, so he kept quiet. That tactic didn't work. Franz waved over to him. "Packing up? Are you leaving?"

He shook his head. "No. Mistress Aileen is staying at the Gardens tonight. I'm just bringing some things."

"Really?"

He nodded, gazing down at the pile of supplies.

"I guess you can't take the priestess completely out of someone, eh?"

"I don't think I can comment on that." Miller offered a nonchalant shrug.

Master Darjeeling swatted Franz on the side of the head with his branch. "Watch what you say."

Franz looked back, surprised. Darjeeling strode forward brandishing the branch back and forth as if it were a sword. "You are talking about a full Master of the White Hand. Do you dare speak ill of her?"

Franz blanched. Stepping back, he fell to his knees. "Please Master Darjeeling, I meant no disrespect."

"You are a toad and a liar Franz." A broad smile broke out on Darjeeling's face. "That's why I like you so much. Get up. Help the lad with that bag. Be useful." Franz set down the chest, then reached forward to help Miller with the bag. Before he could touch it, Miller pulled the bag away. "No, I've got it."

Darjeeling resumed tapping on the floor distracted with his own stick. He began to walk around the magic circle, tapping the floor as he stepped. Brita looked out of her tent, wondering what was going on.

"Is there something amiss Master Darjeeling?" Miller asked.

"Sure. The world is preparing to be eaten, and I haven't even gotten a bath yet. What is right about that?"

Miller stood there confused by his answer for a moment. The man was barely sane.

Then he remembered Brita's earlier words. Bees. Bees were in Ebber's head. Bees are in Darjeeling's head. He stared at Darjeeling a little closer. His gait wasn't completely straight, his eyes hunted along the floorboards for some unseen thing.

Was it unseen? Or was it only unseen to everyone else? Everyone who wasn't taken.

His heart sped up. A Master of the White Hand, Darjeeling's skills of alchemy were unmatched. His skills of mental domination and mind invasion were also dangerous. At any moment, Darjeeling could snatch all the thoughts from Miller's mind, examine them, and then return only the ones that he thought fit. Miller started to worry. Could Darjeeling sense his fear? His doubt? His worry?

If so, what would he do about it? Apprentices were useful, but they could be replaced. A single master like Darjeeling, assisted by the Takers, could lay waste to dozens of magicians, within the White Hand and without. The thought made him shudder.

He could feel fear rising in his gut. His hands began to shake on their own accord.

"Are you well?" Franz asked, staring at him from a few steps away.

Miller shook his head. "I've got to get this to Mistress Aileen. She will be disappointed if I am too slow."

Franz nodded his head in sympathy. "Go then. Don't disappoint your Mistress."

Miller hefted the bag upon his shoulder. Brita gave him a coquettish wave as he opened the outside door and walked out onto the street. The sun cast off rays of fading light as it began to pass beyond the horizon and the air felt pleasantly cool. He walked away from the New Pony thinking of ways that he could guard his thoughts against who could use crafting to read his mind, someone like Master Darjeeling. He remembered his early days in Mistress Aileen's service and the lessons she taught him.

There was a contraption, a tool that she had shown him. It was a simple wooden stand consisting of two steel rods held up by blocks at either end. Six heavy metal balls hung by two strings each tied in place to both rods. He remembered pulling a ball back then releasing it. When the ball swung it struck another, sending it into the next ball. After a few moments, all of the balls would move in unison. She used this to teach him the first of the disciplines. Mistress Aileen didn't need to command him to watch the machine, he was fascinated by it. It moved without magic, without springs or other propulsion. It moved and moved, slowing only slightly every time a ball struck another.

He wished he had that contraption now. He wondered if he could use the disciplines to guard his mind and if such a device could help him sharpen his defenses. He recalled Mistress Aileen would inject thoughts, making him smell rotten meat, old fish, and every other disgusting odor she could recall. He had used the device to concentrate on, to weed out those thoughts that were forced into him. From the beginning Mistress Aileen had taught him to defend his mind. Now, in hindsight, he had to admit that she had been entirely correct with that caution.

He walked through the streets of Home's Hearth toward the Gardens. Passing by his favorite bakery. He stopped to buy some berry muffins and a sweet cake for her. He wasn't sure how she was feeling, but such gifts always gave her cheer. From what he could tell, she could use some cheer.

When he arrived back at the entrance of the Gardens, Miller's stomach was complaining loudly. He hadn't had a full meal in since the previous day, and the smell of the freshly baked treats filled his nostrils with desire.

One of the escorts at the entrance stepped forward as he approached. She was tall, athletic, and had long blond hair. She didn't wear a dress. Instead, she wore a strange leather outfit inspired by historic armor. Where the hard-boiled leather breastplate should be, she wore a clingy leather top. Her face was painted in different alluring shades of color, highlighting eyes of the brightest blue.

"I'm sorry, I don't recognize you. This place is only for members. We're also having an event tonight. You'll have to come back tomorrow during the day."

Miller breathed out in frustration. "It's fine. I'm here to see Mistress Aileen. She is staying with the goddess. I'm expected."

The escort's right eyebrow raised, giving her the look of someone who didn't quite believe what she was hearing.

Miller continued, hefting the green bag. "Seriously, this is important. I'm not trying to sneak into your party. I just need to drop this off, have a few words with Mistress Aileen, and I'll be on my way."

She offered him an apologetic smile. "Phyllicitus is at the event, so she won't be seeing you any time soon. Perhaps you could return in the morning? I can have that bag sent along to Aileen if you wish."

There was no use in fighting it. Making an enemy of the Gardens would do little for his task. He offered the bag to the woman. "Please tell her that I will return in the morning. I should be here just after dawn."

She smiled again as if Miller didn't understand something very basic.

"Do yourself and your Mistress a favor. Don't arrive until just after the lunch hour. Expect them to sleep late."

He was being dismissed. There was nothing else to be done. He offered a polite bow and walked back the way he had come. The two-tracked path quickly grew darker as the sun began to set. Black shadows cast by the high trees obscured the trail ahead. He knew that the streets of Home's Hearth were only a short walk away, ten minutes at most, but the dense wood gave an illusion of isolation.

His mind drifted back to the disciplines. Could they defend against Darjeeling's crafting? He knew only a few spells that affected the mind, and he doubted that anything he did could stop a Master of the White Hand. He began to focus on the disciplines as he walked.

Calm, the first discipline, keeps fear at bay during the worst of times. Miller evaluated how it might help and came up with nothing. He thought about focus, the second discipline that clears the mind of all things not important at the moment. He wondered if the focus discipline might help as well. Alertness, the third discipline, heightened the senses and prepared one for surprises. Peering into the darkness, he thought a little alertness would be a good thing right now.

He focused his mind on the third discipline. Every sound began to register to his ears, and to his mind. He focused on whatever animals might still reside in the woods. His vision began to pick out shapes in the darkness. Thick trunks jutted upwards sprouting thick canopies of leaves. A rectangular memorial stood away from the trail in silent testament to someone who had long passed.

Then he saw the shadow. It was a person standing only three paces into the wood. They stood perfectly still, observing him.

A chill went up Millers' spine. He reached for the dagger hanging at his side. There was little chance that he would be attacked in the confines of the Garden, but he was close to the city streets now. Anything could happen.

"Show yourself," Miller announced as he stopped on the trail. He pulled his dagger from its scabbard a finger's length. A few heartbeats passed before the figure walked onto the trail. He wasn't merely standing in darkness; he was shrouded with it. As he moved, Miller could see shifting patches of black, obscuring and masking his face along with the rest of the body. Only hints of clothing would peek through, and then only for a moment.

Miller pulled the dagger entirely from its sheath.

"That's a good lad." A voice said from the darkened figure. Miller recognized the voice.

"Master Easter?"

The swirls of darkness began to dissipate. Five short breaths later, the swirls were entirely gone. Master Easter stood there with an embarrassed look on his face. Standing two hands shorter than Miller, Master Easter wore a luxurious cloak wrapped around his shoulders tightly, even in the warm night.

Miller stood there, unsure what to do.

Easter's well-mannered voice came out smoothly, patient, amused.

"Are you going to keep pointing that at me? Or do you just want to skip to the part where you do the stabbing?"

"What?" Miller looked down at his knife. "Oh, sorry." He quickly returned it to its scabbard.

After a moment of silently staring at each other, Miller asked, "Were you waiting for me?"

Master Easter shook his head. He seemed to grapple with his next words. "I was hoping to have a conversation with Aileen, but the Garden is closed to visitors."

"So, you decided to hide in the bushes?"

A smile broke out on Easter's face. "What can I say? I've got nothing better to do."

Miller offered a short formal bow. "I guess I should leave you to your bushes then. Sorry for interrupting your bush time."

Easter's eyebrows raised in mock surprise. Miller wondered if he was insane by not being more respectful to Master Easter. He was too tired to worry right now. There were too many important issues at stake.

"No, wait," Master Easter said, walking out of the woods toward him, "Walk with me for a bit. I'd like to hear about your research with Brita. Any ideas yet?"

Miller felt like he had just stepped into quicksand. How could Master Easter know of his suspicions? Was he in league with Master Darjeeling? He was caught in a trap of indecision. It could be a lethal mistake sharing his suspicions with Easter before he talked with Aileen.

But if Master Easter was unaware of Brita and her bees, the Order, and quite possibly every human in the world, could be in danger. Sometimes choosing the right path was easy, even given the risk.

"Sure. I'd like that."

SUSPICIONS

A few minutes of walking brought them out of the dark trail and onto the well-lit streets of Home's Hearth. The sun was in the final moments of its journey through the sky as a red sunset shown against the far clouds. Miller watched as a half dozen torch-boys sped through the streets lighting every street lantern they found.

Easter nodded with satisfaction. "This city has recovered nicely since Phyllicitus returned." She had been back for three years, Miller noted, yet Easter continued to talk about her absence and eventual return like it was yesterday.

"I've noticed. How does she do it? I remember this place being on the edge of chaos just a few short years ago. But The goddess hasn't cast a spell, or even given a speech."

"She is a God. She doesn't need to do anything. Gods personify some kind of aspect. That aspect frequently shows itself as a part of human nature. Sometimes the aspect is part of the natural world. For Phyllicitus, that aspect is love. All who come near her are subject to love. Think about it."

Miller had known human gods found a way to transcend their human limitations, to become something more. He had never thought about what that meant though. "So, a god becomes what? Some kind of cause?"

"You could think about it that way. Humans becoming gods can get more nuanced. Everyone can have a cause, but a god becomes the cause. They tie themselves to that aspect until their identity and the aspect are one and the same."

"How do they do that?" Miller had never heard of such a thing.

"That's the thing. The gods don't know either. Somehow the identity of a person has power in this world. All varieties of crafters have been trying to understand the universe and it's rules of magic through the ages, with only small success. How do you change your very identity? Nobody knows. We have plenty of histories, even interviews, that tell us the same story. One day a person wakes up, and they understand the world differently. They transform from humans into gods."

"Is that how the First Gods work? An animal wakes up and is super powerful?" Miller thought about the Raven God. He had seen it once while traveling with Mistress Aileen. Facing that First God had been terrifying. He had felt the Raven God could peer into his soul, his destiny.

Easter chuckled. "Everyone asks that. I think the First Gods are an entirely different matter. Not only do they interact with the identity of animals, but somehow they interact with its environment as well."

"Environment? Like the air and the sea?" Miller said.

"Yes, and more. The First Gods seem to be part magic and part nature. It's as if they were made of the stuff that created the universe before magic was separated from earth and stone."

"But people have magic. Aren't we made of that same stuff?"

Easter smiled back at him, "That's the dilemma that we have been arguing about for centuries. Where is the root of magic? Is it the earth? Is it something beyond?"

"It can't be just the earth. There are other worlds and cracks between them. I have seen them."

"And did magic work there?" Easter asked with a playful note in his voice.

"No, and yes. There was magic, but it wasn't the same," Miller replied.

"Then what was it?"

"I don't know. It was different than what I knew."

Easter nodded in silent agreement, pondering the workings of the universe, and how the First Gods came to be.

They walked on a few more minutes in silence before Easter changed the subject.

"So let's talk about Brita, shall we? While I always enjoy a good discussion of the Gods, let's focus on our immediate project." Easter began.

"Sorry. Brita. Truth be told, I haven't had more than a few hours to work with her. Back at the other inn I wrote fifty pages of observations. Here, with all the activities going on, I've barely accumulated ten."

"Yet now you carry your journal with you. Before you left it for any of us to read. Did something change?"

At that point Miller knew that his secret was out. Easter had noticed his defensiveness, hiding his sources from Franz and Darjeeling. There was no additional harm in confiding with Easter. If Easter was deciding whether to kill him or not, odds are he'd already made up his mind a long time ago.

Miller took a deep breath before starting. "I'm not sure what to tell you. I came across something, well, odd. It could be coincidental, but it might be a clue. I'm not sure yet."

"Are you going to keep me in suspense all night? Out with it." Easter said.

"Do you remember the battle at the tower? Brita had been brought into a group of Taken."

Easter nodded. "The tower? That was a fight. I'm glad we got there in time."

"Barely in time." Miller said.

"Barely." Easter agreed.

Miller continued. "Brita told me about one of the possessed she traveled with named Ebber. He apparently was been possessed twice. The first time was like what we saw three years ago. He was a mindless thing that roamed the lands intent on murder. The second time, he became some sort of agent for the Takers, yet his self-determination and autonomy had largely been restored."

Easter nodded. "I remember you mentioning this," he urged as he waited for Miller to continue.

"That isn't all. This Ebber person seemed quite insane to her. Somehow, the method that allowed these possessed by the Takers to communicate with each other wasn't functioning right for this Ebber. Brita told me that she couldn't feel his emotions like she could other possessed. When she tried, it felt like a beehive was buzzing in her head."

"I remember that conversation as well."

"I spoke with her yesterday. She told me that she felt that same buzzing feeling again."

Master Easter blinked. "When she was out in the carriage?"

"No, in the New Pony."

He continued the walk another twenty paces before he stopped and asked the question. "Do you think there are possessed in Home's Hearth? Could one have simply walked by?"

"I'm not sure. So far the goddess has been able to keep the Takers out, or at least keep the hidden. I have to assume that the Takers are trying to get in though. But in any case, it wasn't someone walking by. She named the source."

"Indeed? And what is that name?"

Fear began to bubble up through Millers guts as he said the name. "Master Darjeeling."

"What?" Easter took a step back. His surprise was obvious.

"Brita told me that Master Darjeeling had the same buzzing coming from his mind as Ebber did. I don't think we can dismiss the chance that the Takers have made some inroads on one of our own. It makes sense for them to try. And if you haven't noticed, Master Darjeeling is barely sane as it is."

A wide grin broke out on Master Easter's face. "Oh my boy, I thought you had something for a moment. I hate to tell you this. Darjeeling didn't go mad by being possessed. We did that to him."

"The order did that to him?"

"All masters go insane in the end. We all know that as soon as we gain our ring. Darjeeling is special though. He lost touch with reality early."

"What happened?"

"I thought Mistress Aileen or Mistress Sword would have filled you in, given that you have lived in proximity to Darjeeling for the past few years."

"Mistress Sword and I don't speak much anymore," Miller said coldly. "And Mistress Aileen doesn't like to involve me with other masters."

"Wise of her," Easter paused before he continued, "So here is the short version of Master Darjeeling's madness." Easter started to walk again as he began the story. Miller had to skip a few steps to catch up.

"It was a few hundred years ago, two hundred and sixty if memory serves, Darjeeling had just gotten his ring. He decided to investigate the Takers, and try to discover where they came from. We had been unable to stop the Taker advances. We thought they were a rival group of wizards at first. Darjeeling thought that perhaps the Takers were some form of spirit and wanted to at least communicate with them. We had thought if we could find out why they continued their onslaughts, then we could stop them."

Miller refrained from interrupting. It was rare to get this kind of a story from a White Hand master.

"Back then, there were two schools of thought in the conclave. One group of cabals wanted to communicate with these Takers and discover their nature and intent. The hope was that we could reach some kind of arrangement with them, or at least find a weakness. Master Darjeeling, an alchemist of great renown even then, came up with a potion that should have allowed him to communicate with them, perhaps even discover how the Takers controlled their victims."

Miller nodded, agreeing with the tactic. Against an invisible enemy, any effort to gather information was a good idea.

"It didn't go so well. It turned out that Darjeeling's potion worked better than he had hoped. These Takers didn't communicate with words. They used powerful emotional drives to control their victims. Darjeeling was unprepared for that. The mere act of listening to Takers broke something inside him. Madness came on instantly. When the potion wore off, the connection was gone but the insanity wasn't, the damage was done."

"But the potion formula? Has anyone tried to improve upon it?"

"Sure. There have been eight attempts since then. Every one of them was unsuccessful. We gave up after we lost those masters. That plan has been mostly abandoned."

They turned a corner. Tall manor houses made of brick and marble decorated the sides of the street. A group of men struggled to remove a tree from one of the landscaped yards before the sun disappeared.

"So what about the other plan?"

"That one is more of a long-term effort. It's still in progress."

Now Miller was interested. "Is that plan to come here? It doesn't seem like much of a plan."

"No, nothing that simple." Easter waited a moment to consider what he was going to say next. "You are probably going to get drawn into it anyway. Aileen has been involved on the periphery of it."

"She has?"

"Do you remember the three-month trip that she took last year?" Miller remembered that summer well. He had been left behind to craft magical items for Aileen. At the time, he thought he was lucky to have been left behind. Now he felt like he had been left out of something much more important.

"Sure. I crafted a silver brooch for Aileen. She still has it."

"Well, she had to meet up with Hermagon's coven. They have a lair where they do their work. It's far from civilization and quite hard to get to."

This discussion was so vague that Miller was starting to have difficulty following the point. "What is their work? It's far from town so I assume it's something dangerous."

"Oh yes, quite dangerous." Easter abruptly changed the conversation. "Do you remember when we were talking about the Gods? The First Gods? The gods of man?"

"Sure. The First Gods are gods of nature. They exist as avatars of natural forces. The gods of man are people who have transcended their humanity by somehow embracing an aspect." Miller said, almost by rote.

It didn't take Miller long to make the connection. His voice rose in surprise. "Is Hermagon working with a god?"

"Sort of. It's a little complicated. What I'm about to tell you never leaves your lips outside of the order. Do you understand? The penalty will be dire. If you tell anyone, even your little Eisenvard friend, then you will die, they will die, and everyone they've spoken to since you talked to them will die." Easter said.

Ice ran down Miller's back. It took him a moment to reply.

"Maybe you shouldn't tell me."

"Oh, I'm going to tell you. Especially since you have a tendency to talk to outsiders. You need to know. Also, you will see some of Aileen's activities firsthand. It is important that you don't talk about some of those either." Easter said.

"Alright, but why isn't Mistress Aileen telling me this?" Miller asked.

"Not sure. But here it is." Easter glanced around carefully, then waved his hands using the sign of winds. He felt the channeling as the sounds of the city snapped away leaving absolute silence.

"When Darjeeling volunteered to take his potion, another of the masters used his skills at future telling. He saw a vision of

Darjeeling's failure. He predicted accurately but told the conclave that the experiment must continue because it would bring about an event that would protect the world from the Takers, perhaps even lead to their defeat."

"So you let Darjeeling get like that? On purpose?"

"Keep your eye on the big game. Darjeeling knew what he was getting into, just not the consequences."

Miller nodded, eager to hear the rest of the story.

"That master saw a vision of what was to come. He said that a new god would come into the world. That god would come from the Order of the White Hand."

"What? A necromancer god?" Miller took a few moments to process this idea. Humans became gods frequently enough that on the surface, the idea didn't seem impossible. A necromancer god would be a completely different matter. "Forgive me, but that doesn't seem like a good idea for anyone." Miller said.

"Exactly. Most of the conclave felt the same way. But at the time, the Takers were making headway everywhere, so the conclave voted. Against my advice they decided to launch an effort to grow our own god. Master Hermagon has been leading that effort since."

"So how did Mistress Aileen get involved?"

"It's complicated. She said a few things critical of the idea during a conclave meeting, and essentially volunteered herself to check up on Hermagon's progress then report back. You know what the reward is for doing a good job, don't you?"

He did. "More work."

"Exactly. So Mistress Aileen has been tasked with inspecting progress and reporting back every year. The new god is real, and it is growing steadily in power. Soon Hermagon won't be able to hold it in. The god of necromancers will escape into the world."

"Isn't that a good thing? Won't it fight the Takers?"

"It would have been if this god wasn't completely insane. Hermagon succeeded in growing one but failed utterly in growing one that was a force for good, or even for order. This thing is evil, broken, chaotic, and wrong. Very soon, something will have to be done."

"How are we supposed to do something? It's a god."

"You see the problem. Right now, we observe. We look for ways to inject some compassion or logic into the system, and we try to keep the Takers at bay. If this new god arrives to battle the Takers, it will probably destroy most of the people in this land in the process. A god of necromancers will have a use for dead bodies."

CERNA'S DUTY

A knock came from the door at the New Pony. It was light, almost hesitant. Cerna looked up from the crossbow he was polishing. He scowled as he set it down on the table. Brita crawled out of her tent that stood in the middle of the magical circle. Given the charms of warding that decorated the interior of the room, visitors had become rarer.

"Who knocks here? Really?" Miller asked, his eyes cracking open as he awakened from his nap. He stretched his arms out, trying to uncouple himself from the wooden chair.

Cerna stretched back the bowstring and hooked it on the metal notch. He walked to the dirty window that stood adjacent to the outer doors and looked onto the street.

"I can't see them."

The light knock sounded again. Cerna scowled and walked away from the door, standing three paces back, he leveled the crossbow at the entrance. "Care to answer the door?"

"Are you kidding?" Miller responded.

"Let me rephrase this, answer the door. I've got a crossbow. You don't want the crossbow to get ambushed first, do you?"

Miller stood from the chair and moved to the side of the door, and carefully opened it, staying out from between the pointing crossbow and the entrance.

"It's a little girl!" Brita exclaimed, "And she's so cute!"

A girl stood in the doorway. She looked to be seven years old. The girl's red hair lay across her shoulder, tied into an elaborate braid. Her dress was made of faded green linen. She had begun to grow out of the dress as well as the worn shoes that she wore.

"Hello." The girl said shyly.

Miller crouched down so he was eye level with her. "Hello to you. Are you looking for the New Pony Inn? Or are you lost?"

Her hand sprung forward from her side. Miller panicked, imagining Cerna shooting the girl with his newly polished crossbow. The girl held a folded piece of yellow parchment wedged between her thumb and forefinger.

"Sent here with a note I was." The red-haired girl mumbled.

Miller gazed at the note. A single word was written in bold black ink on its surface. The note was for Cerna.

Miller stood from his crouch and moved into the entranceway. He pulled the note from her hand and unfolded it. The script was thin and delicate, much like an educated lady or a practiced scribe might write.

Scowling, Cerna lowered his crossbow and moved forward, snatching the note from Miller's hand. Cerna began to read the paper as Miller returned his attention to the little girl. She stood there, palm outward, patiently waiting for something but she was unwilling to ask.

"Were you told that we would pay you?"

The girl's face turned red as she nodded. Miller calculated how much such a delivery usually cost, then removed two copper coins from his pouch for her fee. He glanced over at Cerna's face, watching him smile as he read the note. Miller added another coin then set them in the little girl's palm.

She spun and bolted from the room, yelling back a cheerful "Thank you!" as she arrived onto the street. The girl kept running, part skipping, part desperation to be away.

Runes decorated the walls in the main room. They were enchanted to drive away any unwelcome visitors, to resist magical streams, and to interfere with all casters not trained in the correct White Hand disciplines. Miller couldn't help but feel some affection for the little girl who overcame her fears enough to pound on their door.

"Brave girl." Miller commented.

"Yeah, brave girl." Cerna agreed, distracted by his note.

"I liked her. I wish she would have stayed a bit longer." Brita supplied, pouting from within the magic circle.

Walking over to the fireplace, he used his feet to kick over a log. Sparks erupted in the hearth. Miller bent down and picked up a new log, placing it in the fireplace. He walked to the cooking area and collected a half dozen eggs along with an iron pot. He filled the pot halfway with water. By the time he returned to the fire, flames were roaring from the newly placed log. He set the pot on the fire and set the eggs aside.

Brita and Cerna had started talking while he was away.

"I think you should go." Brita said.

"I can't. Easter would not be happy with that."

"It won't take that long, probably less than an hour. I think she likes you."

Cerna glanced Miller's way. An unasked question danced in his eyes.

"What?" Miller asked.

"I'm thinking about going out in town."

"I figured, judging by that last bit of conversation."

"How much did you hear?"

"Not much, but enough. It sounded like you made yourself a friend."

Brita giggled, "She seems friendly, that's for sure! Didn't you read the note?"

Miller shook his head. "Only the first sentence. It seemed a little personal."

"Personal! I'll say!" Brita began to laugh outright, losing herself in the humor of it all. "It pretty much asked him to come by and take her clothes off!"

"It did not!" Cerna objected. "She just likes me, that's all. Wants to get to know me. I get the feeling that her father is a little controlling if you know what I mean?" Cerna flexed his muscles, showing his massive shoulders to both of them. "Look upon a marvel of manhood! You can't blame her for being interested."

"You can't be serious. You're going on a date?"

"Just a walk around the market. I'll pick up some cakes and beer while I'm there."

Brita yelled out "Cakes!"

Miller shook his head. Of all the weaknesses he expected from Cerna, a weakness for women wasn't one.

LESSONS

Miller wandered the dark streets of Home's Hearth, exploring the empty side streets and closed markets. Cerna had gone to visit with his new lady friend, and Brita lay asleep within the protective circle. Easter had returned for the night and Miller decided to take advantage of the opportunity to walk about town and do some uninterrupted thinking.

He had been in Home's Hearth for a week and none of his efforts involved identifying Takers or finding their new servants. There seemed to be a lot of important things going on with a lot of important people, but none of it resulted in any gains.

Miller's thoughts dwelt on his conversation with Easter. A god of necromancers terrified him.

What could he do though? Miller thought about the resources he had available, and the challenges he faced. He needed to discover how these new possessed victims of the Takers could be identified and perhaps even freed from their yoke. The frenzy of activity at the New Pony made this almost impossible. As long as competing masters were present, their individual agendas would dominate everything else.

He needed help.

He did have a willing partner in Chamise. Her raw magical talents could be useful. Also, her odd alliance with the remaining Eisenvard could give her impact outside of the magical problem at hand. Sometimes strong arms and sharp steel could solve problems when magic failed.

Brita continued to be a source of hope to him as well. She was Taken, but remained aware enough to offer clues, if only he could decipher them.

The priests weren't very useful. Phyllicitus seemed to have abandoned them, offering little support. The White Hand masters were distracted. Even the apprentices were unreliable, being embroiled in the plans of their masters. To make matters worse, one of the masters, Darjeeling, might have symptoms of Taker possession and none of the other masters would take it seriously when he brought up that point.

He knew that there was no way his mission could succeed if things stayed the way they were. He wondered how Aileen faired. She had sent him here with little explanation, and he hadn't seen much of her lately. Miller looked forward to another of their long conversations, even as he doubted it would happen anytime soon.

A soft rain began to fall, decorating the streets with a slick sheen of droplets. As he stepped across cobblestones, he realized why he was out there. The New Pony was part of the problem. It was a hub of activity. He thought about the experiments, interviews, and spells he needed to weave together to do his task. None of it was made easier by the New Pony. It simply had to go. He needed to find a new location, one without masters, apprentices, or clashes between the Order and the Temple.

He walked. He found deserted craftsman halls and market shops that looked prosperous and thus would be unavailable to his needs. He moved between stables and wine shops. He stopped at every inn he found, asking about old abandoned buildings that he could rent or simply occupy.

Home's Hearth was where Phyllicitus lived. There were no corners that were less fortunate, no hovels that had experienced better times, and no places abandoned to the ravages of time. Miller wondered how the masters ever got the owners of the New Pony to agree to their presence. The power of Phyllicitus seemed to bath the entire city in hope and prosperity.

It dawned on him why the Temple didn't want the Order in the city at all. He was sure the masters had done something dark to get the New Pony. They used the same tactics over and over. Easter would be reasonable, offer money and give promises. If that didn't work, then the masters might opt to convince them using their darker arts.

Were the masters better than the Takers? The thought disturbed him and he dismissed it. Thinking on that, analyzing how the masters did business, made him wonder why he had ever volunteered to get involved in the first place.

He arrived at the entrance New Pony. The horizon glowed red with the light of early morning dawn. With some regret, he mounted the stairs and reached for the door. Walking inside, he passed by the sleeping forms of Franz and Darjeeling. Franz jerked awake as Miller fetched his wool blankets and laid them upon the floor directly next to Brita's protective circle.

Franz raised both his hands in front of him palms up in a silent question. Miller responded with a nod and a wave of his hand. Miller hoped that his presence would give some comfort to Brita. Right now, she was his only link toward success. If only he could unravel the riddles she spoke, there might be a key.

Miller awoke after sleeping for three hours. Brita had come out of her little tent and sat on the floor across from him.

"Where were you yesterday? You were out all day and night."

She stuck her lower lip out in a pout. "You weren't out making friends, were you? I was all alone here."

Miller shook his head. "You weren't alone."

She nodded. Her expression changed to a frown. "I'm never alone, am I? I'm always with the Friends."

He gestured back toward Franz's empty blankets and the empty sleeping pallet that Darjeeling had occupied last night. "There were at least two others here."

"As I said, I'm always with the Friends."

Miller froze, realizing what Brita meant. He looked around carefully, noting the state of the inn, how their gear had been rummaged through and thought about what that could mean.

"Where's Cerna? Isn't he back yet?"

"Oh, Cerna? He went out on an errand a while ago. I think he's still out walking with that Hazel woman."

Miller shook his head. When people in Home's Hearth said two people were 'out walking' they usually meant that more was going on besides walking.

"Didn't Master Easter tell him to stay and guard the inn?"

"I think so."

"So why did Cerna leave?"

"I don't know. Maybe he's had enough of doing what he's told. He can be grumpy like that."

Miller had a hard time believing it. Cerna was Easter's man. If Easter told him to stay and guard, he wouldn't care about anything else. He would stay and guard.

Miller stood up, gazing about, trying to take in the entire room. Newly carved runes decorated wooden beams that spanned the width of the room. Each of the runes was formed to channel power around the structure, keeping magical forces contained within the inn. This included both friendly spells like a Priestess might use or unfriendly ones. It was less a defense against rogue spell-casters than a wall of privacy between the inn and the temple.

"What's wrong?" Brita asked.

"I'm not sure. Cerna wouldn't just walk off." Apprentices

survived by paying attention to details. Somehow, he had begun to feel that this might be more than a test than he was ready for. A feeling of unrest and suspicion crept into his bones as he noticed how Darjeeling's, Franz's, and Easter's things disappeared from the inn, yet the pile of Aileen's gear remained untouched. Miller walked over to the neat stack that he had organized just a day ago. It lay where he put it, untouched. Nobody wanted to take a Master's things, after all.

For a moment, he wondered who had moved the pile of gear. Probably Franz, he thought, that was the kind of thing apprentices were normally tasked to do. He must have worked quickly though, Miller thought.

Brita spoke from within the circle, interrupting his thoughts. "Someone is coming."

He couldn't hear anyone approaching. "How do you know?"

She twisted her face and bent her head to the left. She looked as if she were experiencing intense pain. Her voice was high pitched, forced, and broken. "You know. A girl just knows these things."

Miller took five quick steps toward the front of the inn, looked out the window, then quickly retreated back.

"There's a crowd of six people heading our way. Some woman I don't know is leading them." He walked quickly to the pile of gear he had just been examining. He moved two large bags, a pile of woolen blankets, and a saddle off the pile to expose the brass embossed hilt of Aileen's war-sword. Its blue scabbard lay tied in black leather strips covering the original goddess symbols. Miller had made that sword three years ago; he knew it well. Snatching the sword up with his left hand, he spun toward the circle.

Brita pulled on an oiled coat then began picking up her few possessions. Miller walked over to the circle. It protected the population from her. It also imprisoned her. Miller's mind raced as he struggled to come up with a way to free her without exposing her to the innocent and undefended residents of Home's Hearth.

The back door slammed open. A man holding a short spear entered the room. His shoulders were almost as wide as the doorway, covered in chain mail. He had to turn his body at an angle to pass through the doorway. Whoever he was, he was strong and had come to kill someone.

Miller didn't bother talking. The enchantments inscribed in this place would require significant magical power to overcome. These invaders weren't from the temple. They weren't a group of random thugs. Miller drew Aileen's sword.

Miller remembered when Aileen had asked him to build this enchanted weapon. It had to be lethal to the Takers and tuned to Aileen's own magical flows. Creating the blade had taken him two years to forge it, six months to season it, and a half second to pair it to Aileen. Now it was awake with her power, surging blue sparks along its blade as currents of raw lightning cascaded along it. The smell of burning wood began to fill his nostrils as he gripped the hilt tightly. Any other Master of the White Hand would have built a curse into the blade to kill or enslave any who touched it. Mistress Aileen hadn't. Instead, she had opened it's power for him to use and then required him to learn its secrets, to share its power. After all, he was as much Aileen's possession as the sword was.

The man stood stunned at the door, unsure of how to proceed in the face of lightning. His arrogance and swagger deserted him. Brita began to scream in terror as the harnessed lightning snaked across the floor near her. The lighting would strike down anyone it touched, man, beast, or possessed. Only the magical circle would save her from its wrath. The lightning was made to rip the Takers from their hosts, leaving their dead bodies to the mercy of a peaceful afterlife. It was the mercy that a priestess of Phyllicitus would show if she were a necromancer.

A woman dashed into the room. She held a leather bag in one hand and a long dagger in the other. The woman screamed out in a frenzy, calling for help. Five others rushed in behind her.

Brita called out in terror. The sparks snaked closer to her

legs, near the edge of the protective circle. There was no use talking, no use negotiating. Miller nodded as he remembered what Master December had told him once. "Sometimes you just had to get dirty."

Miller saw the trap. The brutish warrior stood in the way of his retreat, blocking the door. The other five warriors charged in to take him down. He could easily cut past the lone man blocking the rear, but he would have to leave Brita to do so. It would be so simple if only he could be a little more cold-hearted. He couldn't.

Spinning toward the back door, he leaped at the armored man that blocked him. The man thrust his spear toward Miller's heart. Miller barely managed to parry it aside, stepping into close quarters. He grabbed the wooden shaft of the spear with his bare hands for just a moment, then touched Aileen's sword against the man's metal armor.

Waves of blue power cascaded along the blade, pouring into the armor. Sparks exploded as metal transformed into slag and the underlying padding caught fire. The spearman tried to pull away, but it was too late. By the time he fell to the ground his body had been consumed by the lightning; only charred ash remained.

He quickly looked back. Brita had stopped screaming. She stood at the edge of the circle, trembling as she awaited the five warriors. The woman in the lead ran towards the edge of the circle opening up her bag. Miller didn't wait to see what its contents were. He thrust his sword toward her, the circle, and the open front entrance. Pouring all of the sword's remaining energy into his nature channels, he engulfed the room in lightning.

Waves of blue sparks and cracks of storm power exploded in the room. The lightning washed over the protective circle like it was a dome. Brita stood paralyzed with fear as the wave of death washed over her head. When it spilled into the midst of the attackers she began to scream. A thunder-stroke exploded in the room, its sound rendering him deaf. Two of the attackers fell on their knees, another was simply tossed through a wall leaving a man-sized gap behind.

The sword's power began to falter. Miller had used up too much, too soon. It would need time to recover. He felt a knot in his stomach as he realized what he needed to do. None of these were people anymore. They were all Taken. If he let them get away they would simply claim more lives then gather more bodies to their cause.

He dashed around the edge of the circle. His sword found the throat of a young man who was struggling to regain his feet. The weak spark was less than he had wielded previously but it was enough to send the young man into convulsions as the blade cut through him.

Miller didn't wait for them to strike back. Instead, he released Aileen's sword and let it fall to the floor. He began reciting words of darkness, releasing his channels to push back the power of light and bring about the night of the void. It wasn't quick enough. The woman who led the attack struggled up, then dragged herself forward. She grabbed Miller's leg and hold him firm. The remaining two attackers struggled to their feet as the blue sparks faded away.

He quickly abandoned his spell of darkness, moving on toward a new spell. He opened his body channels in an effort to gain enough strength to break free. As the sparks faded away the next threat emerged.

The closer attacker, a young man wearing a leather breastplate, pulled out a knife and cut away his sleeve. He staggered closer to Miller and extended his bare arm forward. Then he did something that surprised Miller. The attacker used his knife to cut his own wrist, spraying blood across the floor, across Miller's shirt, across his face.

He began to panic. It was infected blood. He stepped back. Miller tried to pull off his shirt and get the blood off of his skin. He didn't know how much time he had. It couldn't be much though.

Then another form entered the room from the main

entrance. Wearing a dark hooded cloak, the figure began to laugh at the scene. Pulling back her hood, Mistress Sword stood there behind the attackers.

"Not impressive apprentice, it really isn't."

Reaching above her head, she snapped her fingers and the world exploded

SWORD AND FIRE

Thick odors of burning incense filled the room as Mistress Sword looked out the window. Midnight passed by an hour ago. She stayed awake in the hopes of being contacted Master Hermagon. A century-old skull lay in the fireplace, flames devouring its surface. Runes decorated the surface of the skull, transforming flames into magical flows. She looked forward to the meeting tonight. The cabal sent her here with little clarity or purpose. There wasn't much going on in Home's Hearth so far. It hardly seemed worth her time to be here.

She glanced across the room at her high-backed chair. Clothing lay on the seat cushion, folded neatly, ready to return to the owner. Aileen had left a few of her things here. Only two days had passed since then and Sword continued to think of her. Memories of their night filled her with joy, excitement, and a little regret. All priestess were trained in the arts of pleasure from a young age. Someone learned in the ways of the temple could experience and give love far beyond what others could do.

That training worried Sword. She couldn't be sure if her connection with Aileen was truly special or if it was just an effect of her temple ways. In the short term, she thought, it would not matter much. Both of them were Masters of the White Hand and their lives would be long. Aileen was the first White Hand master, or mistress as she preferred to be called, to ever come from a house of worship.

She reached over for the bottle of light red wine. It blended different grapes into a gentle set of flavors. She preferred to have her apprentices pour wine and make a fuss over her. Tonight was private though.

She glanced at the skull to check on her meeting. One of the runes had begun to burn with power. It would not be long before her guest arrived. Glancing over at Aileen's clothes laying on the chair, she grinned. She didn't think it would be wise to leave that laying around when her guest arrived. She picked up the seat cushion, gently set the cloths under it, and replaced it. Then she sat down on the chair and began sipping her wine. Within fifteen minutes another of the runes began to glow. She poured herself more wine.

Her guest arrived in the middle of her third glass. The final rune began to glow. She felt the magical flows shift. Smoke from the fire no longer went up the chimney. Instead, it flowed into the center of the room, pouring into a slowly forming cloud of dark gray. She watched it form as the moments passed. The cloud grew more and more solid until it took on a shape.

It looked like a man, slightly shorter than her. Details of the man began to emerge. His arms hung from loosely from his side, as if ready to react to anything, yet unwilling to commit, to give away his intentions. A short pointed beard stuck out from his chin. The smoke grew denser. Hermagon took shape in the center of her room. Smoke created his form, making him appear as he did in life, except he had no color except different shades of gray. Hermagon offered a slight bow to her as he took his final shape, a form of smoke with a thin tendril reaching back to the rune-encrusted skull.

Mistress Sword gained her master's ring three years ago and Hermagon still made her shudder. He was an old White Hand, powerful, with dark allies and spells that she might not ever fathom. She couldn't be killed by him, but she always trod carefully when she was near him. Tonight, she had three glasses of wine in her. Instead of bowing deeply to acknowledge him, she merely raised her glass in a toast.

"Welcome to Home's Hearth." Mistress Sword said, a small chuckle hidden at his expense.

Hermagon furrowed his brow, gazing back at her. His gaze normally cut into her. Now he stood here, a mere apparition of smoke, and it passed through her unnoticed. Sword started to like this smoke form of his.

"I can't stay long," Hermagon said, "the spell doesn't permit much time."

She nodded back, surprised that such a spell-caster would be so limited. She wondered if the time limit had more to do with the goddess's power in Home's Hearth than Hermagon's ability to cast. Even her own powers seemed dimmer since she had arrived. Phyllicitus clearly had an influence on the flow of magic here.

"Have you met with Easter and his priestess?" Hermagon began, applying disdain to the word priestess, showing his dislike for Mistress Aileen, or perhaps any woman Master of the White Hand. Sword nodded her head, ignoring the comment. Hermagon was old, his ways were old. She feared it would lead him into trouble. The world changed and marched on. It left those who would not change with it behind, even Masters of the White Hand, especially Masters of the White Hand.

"Their plans?"

"I don't think they have any. They brought apprentice Miller along, hoping he could work a miracle again. So far, no luck. Phyllicitus seems upset with Aileen. All her energy has been devoted to dealing with the temple. Easter is skulking around the shadows. I have no idea what he is up to, but I never do. Darjeeling is here as well. Were you aware of that?"

"I suspected. Darjeeling won't be a problem for us. He never takes positions he can't change when the tides shift."

"Position? This isn't about dealing with the Takers? That's what Aileen told me."

The smoke apparition shook its head from side to side. "Clearly not," it said with uneven voice, "this is all about the conclave this fall. You have been paying attention, haven't you?"

"Yes. Aileen is due to make another report to the conclave about your project. I know that."

"And that means she will be coming east to Godhome."

Mistress Sword offered a dismissive laugh. "Godhome is it? Seems like a fairly arrogant name for a hole in the ground."

The smoke shadow shrugged. "There is a god that lives there. I think the name suitable."

She took another sip of wine before she continued. "Does that mean that your project is nearing completion?"

"Yes, it will not be long now. Three years, perhaps five, and I will be complete. We will be done with these Takers once and for all."

A shiver ran up her spine. Aileen continued to fight against Hermagon in the conclave. She did not want his project to finish. While Aileen always said that she was being logical, Sword suspected that her opinion formed from her past as a priestess, not from her newly acquired position of White Hand master. The god that Hermagon had created may be the single most powerful casting the White Hand had ever accomplished. It began two centuries ago. The Takers were fated to eat the world if they were not stopped. So far, only Hermagon had come up with a plan to actually stop them.

Hermagon continued, "These next few years are going to be sensitive. This is the point in time where the cowards will back away. Easter may be my fiercest opponent. Sometime in the next few conclave meetings, he will make his move."

"Make his move?"

"Yes. Don't worry. Easter rarely does things directly. He will poison the minds of the other masters, drawing them in alliance against us. He has already begun the end game with Aileen. Don't fool yourself, she is just another of his tools in his campaign against us."

"But doesn't Easter want to stop the Takers as well?"

"Sure. He doesn't object to that. He seems to disagree on the method."

"Method? It hardly seems time to quibble about methods. If the Takers continue their onslaught, each one growing more and more deadly, then discussions of method become moot."

"I agree, of course. Easter's opposition surprises me, I admit. It was one of his own cabal that came up with the idea. Darjeeling saw the solution in one of his mad visions. He was the one who convinced me to go forward with this."

"Their cabal is split on this?"

"No, sadly. Darjeeling has slipped further into madness since then. Now he moves back and forth between sanity and complete lunacy. He saw a new god in his vision, one that would stop the Taken. This god will be beyond the ineffective humans that had discovered how to grasp godhood. Phyllicitus had had five centuries to stop the Takers and accomplished nothing. Little help has come from other gods. I suspect the flaw is in their humanity. This new god will not have such flaws. It will not be a self-centered foolish creature. It will be a god of the White Hand!"

Mistress Sword could feel her heartbeat with excitement. Hermagon truly believed in the superiority of the order. A new god would throw all the other gods down, enslaving or killing them. She knew that this new god would be a new thing, unseen in the world before now.

Hermagon continued, "I need you to stay close to Aileen and Easter. Keep an eye on this apprentice Miller. He won't be far from their plans. Stay close but unseen when possible. I need to be warned when Easter begins his counter attacks."

She grinned back at Hermagon. His orders were clear yet left plenty of room for her to play. She could afford to be pliable to his will, at least for now. She had no idea how the world would change when Hermagon's new god arrived, she just knew that he would be unable to control it.

She raised her glass in a toast.

"To   the   Necromancer   God."

A VISITOR

An oil-soaked rag moved across the length of the crossbow, cleaning away a small amount of dust and depositing a glowing shine. Cerna looked down, appreciating his work, his eyes following the swirling grain of the wood. The crossbow hadn't been used nearly as much as he had originally expected. Usually, when Master Easter asked him to do a task, the crossbow performed a lot more work.

He moved his hand from the stock to the curved lathe at the top of the device, applying the polish sparsely, unwilling to let too much oil soak into the bowed wood. Cerna looked down at an unacceptably large smear of oil that shone on the lathe's curved surface. He grunted, unhappy that the oil would soak in and possibly weaken its pull.

Laying down the oil-soaked rag and picking up a clean cloth, Cerna rubbed the oily area with the new cloth, pulling the excess fluid away from the bowed wood before it could soak in. He turned the crossbow over then carefully inspected the trigger mechanism. Satisfied with what he saw, Cerna used the clean cloth to wipe away a bit of stray oil that had dripped onto the hand-length metal trigger. He liked to have a well-oiled machine. He knew that he would likely need to use it soon.

Sun shone into the New Pony Inn through a narrow gap in the shutters. Cerna liked the sunlight. The inn filled with darkness when they closed the shutters tight. The weather had been perfect when the sun rose in the morning. A slight chill in the air gave way to warm weather and clear skies. The weather continued to be perfect as the afternoon arrived. Brita had asked him to open the shutters just a finger's width if only to let the clean air in. He had happily complied.

Birds chirped in the afternoon air. Cerna prepared himself for another gloriously uneventful day.

Shouts came from the street outside. Raising an eyebrow, he looked quizzically at Brita. She sat on a stool in the center of the magical circle, a tangled ball of yarn in her hand. She was trying to knit a blanket, but her skills weren't up to the task. She frowned back at him.

"What are you looking at me for?" She asked.

"Arguments in Home's Hearth are a rare thing. Is there any chance this might be your Taker friends?" Cerna asked while he re-attached the cable to the crossbow.

"I don't think so. I don't feel anything. But the magic interferes, you know?" She replied, gesturing at the surrounding magical circle.

The argument in the street grew louder. Cerna heard something about firewood, and someone owing money. He didn't like the feeling of this one bit. Easter had told him to stay alert for the unusual, and to be aware of any behaviors that could be considered odd. Takers weren't affected by the goddess's peaceful magic, Easter had told him.

Cerna put his boot in the stirrup of the crossbow. He pulled back the string, straining as he leaned back, and set the taunt string against the roller, placing it snuggly in the wedge that held the string in place. Squeezing the trigger would release the roller, freeing the string and propelling a deadly bolt toward its target. He picked up a bolt from where it sat on the floor and set it against the string, ready for its deadly mission.

"Do you think there is a problem?" Brita asked, a nervous edge to her voice.

"I always think there is a problem. That's why I'm here," Cerna said as he stood. He walked to the window and peered through the crack. Two people stood in the street arguing. One looked like a brute, as tall as Cerna and twice his weight. The stranger's huge gut was eclipsed by massive workman's arms and a scowl that could spoil meat.

Cerna knew the person he was arguing with. He had met her on more than one occasion. They kept running into each other in the street. She would normally stop and talk with him. Of course, he noticed, normally her father was present but today he was not.

Beware the unusual, Easter had said.

"Shite." Cerna swore. There was one thing that Cerna knew, Easter was always right. That simple fact was both comforting and annoying at the same time. This one time, he desperately wanted Easter to get it wrong.

Cerna paused, thinking hard about where this encounter could go. He owed Easter a debt beyond calculation. Easter had saved his son years ago and asked for nothing except a favor in the future. Now the future was here.

"There's nothing to do, but to do it," Cerna muttered. He turned his head and winked at Brita, "Take care now," he said as he walked up to the door. He opened it, stepped through, and closed it tightly behind him.

When he stepped into the street, the argument grew louder.

Hazel shouted, "Get away from me! I don't have your money. You have to talk to my father!"

Cerna didn't allow the big man an opportunity to reply. He held up the crossbow in one hand, pointing to the sky.

"Is there a problem here?" Cerna asked in a booming voice.

The large man snapped his head around to stare at Cerna. "Back away, you don't want any part of this," the big man said.

Cerna began to lower his crossbow, to point the weapon at

the stranger's heart. The lower the crossbow tilted, the less he wanted to do it. Cerna could only angle it halfway to his target before his will to aim it gave out. The goddess's magic continued to work in Home's Hearth, yet neither of these two seemed to be affected by it. Cerna wondered if they were somehow immune. He chased the thought from his mind. Easter had always said that when faced with a dilemma, always choose the simplest answer. He knew that one of these people were Taken, and they were moving on the New Pony Inn.

Releasing a long breath in frustration, Cerna decided to try being friendly instead of simply shooting the man.

"Look, this isn't helping you at all," Cerna began, "You need to talk to her father. You'll get your money. I'll even make you a promise. If her father can't pay their debt, then I will. Let's not be unreasonable."

The hulking stranger didn't hesitate. He brushed a handful of dirty unkempt hair from his sweat-covered face before he replied.

"All right then. We're done here."

Without another word, he turned and walked away. Cerna watched the stranger's back as he walked away, suspicious. Any conflict in Home's Hearth surprised him but resolving one so easily was completely unexpected. One of these people were Taken.

Hazel walked up to him and took his hand.

"Thank you so much," she said as she gazed up into his eyes. Her hands felt sweaty when she touched his bare skin. She must be nervous, Cerna thought, it wasn't warm enough to sweat today. This entire situation felt wrong to him. It was definitely time to repay Easter's debt, but he didn't want to die today.

"I'm so sorry that you had to see that. That man, Jackals, has been harassing us. We paid him last month, we really did," Hazel began. Cerna didn't have the energy to listen to her nonsense. The entire situation felt like an obvious ploy to get him out of the Inn.

He didn't worry though. Easter had left a few tricks behind

in case the Taken tried to gain entrance. He thought about Brita for a moment, then decided not to worry about her. Easter knew what he was doing, as always.

"Do you have time to go on a walk?" Cerna asked, hoping to pull her away from the inn. It surprised him when she replied.

"Yes, I have a few hours before I must return to father. A walk sounds lovely."

Hazel took a step closer and took Cerna by the arm. They began to stroll, trading stories about the town, about the weather, and shared gossip about some of the temple's more outgoing priests and priestesses. As far as last days on earth went, Cerna felt satisfied. He found himself enjoying her company. He liked her unvarnished down-to-earth attitude about life. Hazel wasn't a court lady. She was originally a farmer and it showed.

They turned the corner twenty minutes later. A ruined statue once occupied the center of the street, now a single pair of legs, missing a body was all that remained. Three years ago, this had been a statue of the Eisenvard commander. In his arrogance, he had built a statue in his own image, deep in the belly of Phyllicitus's city. She had it struck down three days after her return. Now Cerna gazed on its ruin, thinking about his own arrogance.

The goddesses' power was on him, there was no doubt. He thought about Hazel, then about Brita. If Easter could save Brita, then why not others? Why not Hazel?

"Are you alright? You look lost in thought," Hazel asked.

A deep yawn escaped Cerna's mouth. "I think I'm getting tired, no idea why."

"Do you want to go back?"

"I should. Duty calls," Cerna replied.

Hazel offered him a smile as she said, "It always does."

☐

RANGING

Brother Quiet looked back at the other two clerics following behind him. A path snaked through the tall grass. Trodden stalks showed the history of those who came before. Soon it would be harvest season and the farmers would come to collect their hay for winter's feed. A herd of cows stood blissfully unconcerned with their progress in the far distance. Cool northerly winds pushed the long waist-high grasses in a gentle dance, moving back and forth as if welcoming them to its field.

"Come on. We are almost there." Brother Quiet said.

Brother Davin smiled toward him. Excitement made him jumpy, he hadn't left the city for months. Sweat dripped from his forehead, running down onto his shirt. The moisture in the air was thick and palpable. It clearly wore on him.

"Thank the goddess." Brother Davin made no attempt to hide his discomfort.

Behind him, Sister Mercy struggled along. Her long dress had rapidly become a hindrance as she traversed the field. Green and brown stains now smeared the elegant material. She did not complain as she carried a heavy canvas bag filled with medical supplies over her shoulder.

Brother Quiet pointed at a tall brown barn that lay another twenty minutes ahead. "It isn't far. Keep up the pace, it's just another few minutes."

"Few minutes? Looks more like a death-march to me." Brother Davin's feet ached. He wore his wooden soled shoes to protect his feet. He missed his temple slippers.

Brother Quiet smiled back at Davin again, nodding at his apt humor. The irony of those words was not lost on him.

Brother Davin continued his complaints. "We could have brought a cart though. It would have worked well enough. For that matter, why didn't the locals simply put the sick family into a wagon and bring them to Home's Hearth? The field is large but entirely passable."

"I guess we can ask them once we arrive." Sister Mercy supplied, exhaling in a combination of exhaustion and frustration. "In any case, I'll be getting a hot bath when we return. I think I may have ruined this dress as well." She said, annoyance leaking into her voice.

They continued their journey in silence. Each step brought them closer to the barn. The barn had seen better days. They could see gaps between the tall roughly planed boards. The fallow ground near the barn had become overgrown during the years. No sounds of animals, or of sick families, came from within.

"This seems peaceful. Did we come to the right barn?" Brother Quiet asked before continuing. "Please don't tell me that we walked all this way for nothing."

"I'm pretty sure this is the place."

Sister Mercy started walking fast toward the barn door.

"Hello! Is anyone there?"

She left Brother Quiet and Brother Davin behind as she stepped forward. She grasped the door handle and swung it open. A single man stood behind it, just at the entrance. He was tall and thin with rangy black hair that may have been clean once, but not in his memory. He wore a thick wool coat that covered him from shoulders to feet.

"Are you sick?" She asked gently as she glanced up and down his body, looking for sores or other evidence of illness. The stranger did not answer, merely stood in the doorway looking down on her.

"I'm Sister Mercy from Home's Hearth. Do you need help?"

The stranger responded. His voice was gravelly. It sent shivers down her spine. "Yes, as a matter of fact, I do."

The stranger lifted his right hand from his pocket. It was covered with a black glove that shone with the reflection of the afternoon sunlight.

"You're dressed warmly for a hot day like this."

The man reached his gloved hand to the side. She could not see what he did, but when she saw the hand return it held a wine cup filled with some dark liquid.

Without any hesitation, he jerked his hand forward splashing the liquid into Sister Mercy's face. Her eyes exploded in burning pain. She screamed then began to wipe it away. The dark liquid coated her like water. The liquid would not come away. It stuck like syrup, only everywhere it touched her skin, it burned.

Brother Davin surged forward, trying to help her. He made it eight steps before a heavy blow fell smashed into the back of his head. Brother Davin's world swam as he fell to the ground. The shock of the blow cut through his skull as he struggled to regain his footing.

Someone grabbed his face. Brother Davin felt a cool liquid being rubbed onto his cheeks, against his eyes. Fingers shoved between his lips. He could taste the flavor of burnt lemons. He looked up through blurry eyes and saw Brother Quiet holding his head in place.

"Why?" he tried to say, but it came out garbled. Brother Davin reached for his magical channels, trying to use his inner flows to remove the liquid from his face. His channels weren't there. His magic had left him. His arms and legs began to disobey him, moving in spastic jerks on their own accord as he dropped face down onto the ground.

Sister Mercy screamed; her voice full of fear. Her body tightened up into a ball, forcing her face against her knees.

Brother Davin began wheezing, struggling to breath. He felt his lungs working harder, struggling to gain any breath. He saw people then, rising up from the fields. At least ten people surrounded him. He wondered why he hadn't noticed them before.

Brother Quiet grabbed him by the collar and forced him forward, pushing him into the barn. A huge tub stood there, filled to the brim with a foul-smelling liquid. Brother Davin felt the new ambushers grab him, then lift high, only to be gently set within the tub. They forced his head below the surface of the liquid. He struggled, splashing, wrestling with the ambushers. It only lasted a minute. The combination of the liquid and the lack of air ended his resistance quickly.

It was a strange way to die, he thought, drowned in a bathtub of goo. Then he felt something wrong. It felt like something was crawling inside his head. Somehow it could look into his feelings. It felt like someone was trying to whisper reassurances to him but he just couldn't make out the words.

Brother Davin could hear one thing though, even below the liquid. Sister Mercy's screams of terror cut through the dark liquid and into his heart.

The gates to the Eisenvard compound stood open, allowing any passer-by to view the resident Eisenvard in the flesh. Miller walked through the gates and saw a group of men massed in a human scrum, struggling against each other within a pile of bodies. Thirty people sparsely lined the sides of the field, cheering encouragement, imploring one person or another to victory. It took Miller a few moments to realize he was looking at a game of nets.

Miller paused to take in the scene. He saw two teams

struggling to reach the bottom of the pile and retrieve the ball. There were ten players on the field, and another thirty onlookers spread around the borders of the game yelling encouragement to each side as they struggled. Within three minutes the pile stopped struggling as a tall bearded man entered the field from the sides, pulling bodies from the pile, attempting to break up the chaos.

An odd feeling of freedom descended on Miller. Workmen had come to do some repairs to the New Pony Inn. While usable, it smelled of burned wood, and some of the support structures had taken damage when the Takers tried their raid. It hadn't gone well for them. Sadly, all they had left was a few bodies. Master Easter was trying to pull the souls back and talk to them. Miller didn't want to be an assistant in that process, ripping holes beyond the final black door and pulling damaged souls into this world. Instead, he decided to take his newfound free time and catch up with Chamise.

"Enough! You're done for lads! She's got it! Let 'er go!" An Eisenvard shouted, urging his teammates on to victory.

The men grumbled. Some called out objections.

"Not fair!" A man cried out, laughing.

"Too short! There should be a minimum height!"

Chamise crawled out from the bottom of the pile. She held a brown leather ball in one hand and showed a broad victorious smile on her face.

"No time for tears boys!" She cried, tossing the ball in the air.

Groans from the opposing team answered her taunts as the two teams began to gather and organize on their sides. Miller didn't want to interrupt them, so he merely stood in place watching the game.

The game riveted Miller's attention. He could not help but cheer. The ten players gave each other no mercy as they forced the ball to one side of the field then the other. Each team struggled to put the head-sized ball into a cloth sheet that hung from temporary poles. The final play came when Chamise snatched the ball from an opposing player, threw it down field to a teammate, then the player threw it at an opponent's head, bounding off end entering the net, striking the winning goal.

Half the crowd groaned while the other half cheered. Spectators rushed onto the field from the sidelines, laughing, celebrating. Miller gazed at the crowd, thinking about how the Eisenvard had always been a competitive group. Amongst their own, they were even more so. It was no wonder they seemed to always be looking for a fight, Miller thought.

As the teams broke up into a dozen different conversations, Miller took the opportunity to seek Chamise. She stood with one hand on her hip, the other brushing back her sweat-soaked shoulder-length blonde hair, arguing with one of the Eisenvard.

Miller recognized the man she was arguing with, Custrel Schaller. Custrels were a rank in the Eisenvard, almost a knight but not quite. A custrel possessed all of the weapons and armor that a knight would have, but none of the patronage. Schaller spotted Miller and waved him closer, beckoning him to join them.

Chamise turned to face him. She wore only a simple tunic, colored blue by a cheap dye. Streaks of that same blue dye decorated her bare skin as the sweat mixed with berry juices and marked her as its own. She stood, victorious in the nets game, and absolutely stunning in life. Miller was caught off-guard. He had traveled with her, even nursed her after being wounded, but he had never seen her with the taste of victory in her mouth. She stood like a warrior queen, proud, strong, smiling, beautiful.

His mind stopped thinking about all else. He tried to see her, all of her. His heartbeat faster. He didn't understand why he denied her. She seemed so perfect...

The White Hand would make an example of her, he thought to himself. If he ever reached out, ever gave her the semblance of love or even just intimacy, the Order of the White Hand would see her as an unnecessary influence. The order would remove her from the company of the living, if she was lucky. The order could inflict worse fates than death. He didn't know how much of an example they would make of her. Miller didn't want to find out.

"Where have you been?" She called out. Her exited voice like a song to his ears.

"Getting things organized." He walked closer. Schaller took a polite step backwards from his entirely too familiar distance to Chamise.

Schaller grimaced. "Have you spoken to your masters? Are we welcome back at the New Pony?"

Miller shook his head. "I've decided that we aren't going to use the New Pony. The masters, well, they all have their own agendas. I don't them want to get in our way. I've asked Mistress Aileen to secure another place for our work."

"Work?" Chamise asked. "I thought you were going to teach me some spell-crafting." She crossed her arms, preparing to go on the offensive.

"That is the goal. But in the process, you and I are going to get some work done."

She shot back a suspicious look.

Miller held up his hands in false surrender. "Don't worry. You won't be doing anything bad. I've got a young woman that needs some help. If you're game, I would like your assistance with some of her problems."

She continued with her skeptical look, tapping her foot to show her impatience.

"What did you expect? A classroom lecture? We're talking spell-crafting here."

That appeared to relax her. Her foot stopped tapping and she uncrossed her arms.

Schaller turned toward her. "Well, this isn't the kind of conversation that I need to be in. I keep hoping you'll step away from this talent of yours. I guess I'll just keep hoping."

He turned and walked away.

"I hope I didn't start any trouble," Miller began.

Chamise replied, her voice sad. "No, it's me, not you. No matter what I do, I'll always be the witch."

Miller couldn't argue. He simply nodded.

"Well, there are worse things to be."

She shot him a scowl.

"Like what?"

"A necromancer."

A grin split his face. Chamise barked a short laugh. "Dream on. That will never happen."

He offered a playful grin. "Are you sure? I would get an amazing reputation if I brought in an Eisenvard!"

Chamise's smile fell away. Her voice turned cold. "I'm sure."

Miller decided not to continue with this brand of humor. Instead, he returned to his reason for visiting.

"I've got permission to give lessons at The Gardens. They have a library that we can use. Does that sound acceptable?"

Her eyes widened. "Really? The Gardens? How did you get that?"

"Mistress Aileen seems to be back in favor with the goddess. Somehow she has some influence again."

"Really? What did she do?"

"No idea. Whatever it was, it seems to be working out for her. I'm sure it will cause problems further on though."

"What do you mean?"

He thought of Mistress Sword, of her near-insane attachment to those close to her. If Aileen had returned to serve Phyllicitus, or worse yet, if she had become intimate with the goddess, then there would be ramifications. Sword simply didn't have the willpower to walk away from such personal hurts.

"Don't worry about it. There is nothing either you or I can do about it. Instead, let's start by meeting at The Garden. I'm going to be there every day starting just before lunch. I'll stay until dusk. Can you come any time during the day?"

"I'll come all day if you'll have me."

Miller looked back at the group of men. While they spoke among themselves, all eyes were on Chamise and himself. Their short haircuts and proud words betrayed them all. They were Eisenvard, each one.

"What about them?"

She looked back at him, a sour not entering her voice. "I'm not an Eisenvard. I haven't been for a long time. Don't assume I'm back with them."

Miller had seen her in the game. He had seen her in battle. He remembered something that Master December had once told him, long ago. People are who they are. There was no use trying to change them unless you didn't mind breaking them at least a little.

Miller wanted to keep Chamise just the way she was. "No, that isn't what I meant. I didn't mean that you needed them. I meant that they seem to like your leadership. I advise against abandoning them. Let's think of them as a reserve that we can turn to if something goes wrong."

"Wrong? What do you mean? Aren't we just teaching a few spells?"

"No. I'm going to be teaching you about the Takers as well as the disciplines. I warn you; it will frighten the hell out of you. If it doesn't, there's something wrong with you." ☐

FIRES

The pen-tip scratched along the paper as Miller wrote in the journal. Brita had become talkative after Cerna left, excited at the prospect of courtship, any courtship.

He dashed an idea onto the page, 'Takers do not change their victim's basic identity, merely channel it in new directions.' Three years ago, victims of the Takers became little more than shambling slaves intent on killing everyone they encountered. Today the Taken could fit into the population without notice. The notion disturbed him. Taken people could be hiding in plain sight almost anywhere.

The sound of clomping boots came from the front door. Miller looked up from his journal expecting Cerna's return.

He saw the door latch begin to glow. Before he could stand, the latch melted onto the floor. He tried to sense the flow of magic by opening his elemental channels but found nothing.

The door kicked open. A pudgy middle-aged man stood there. He grasped clay pot by its protruding handle in his left hand. Dashing into the room, he opened the way for more men.

A woman came into the room behind him. She looked to be forty years old with long graying hair. She held a wickedly curved dagger in one hand and a cloth bag in the other.

He began to cast. Miller didn't like had just happened to the door latch and refocused his elemental channel to manipulate air. The first man took a step forward and tossed the pot toward him, flinging a stream of liquid in his direction. It sizzled as it went through the air, flying towards both Miller and the pattern on the floor.

He released the spell. The air in New Pony instantly became denser. New air sucked into the room from the outside. The wind pulled the burning liquid from its mid-flight trajectory into a spinning column that stood in the center of the room.

A third man entered rushed into the room. He screamed as he hefted a short sword overhead. Miller could see his brown hair atop his head, and his facial tattoo of a howling wolf. Miller used his open channel to lessen the air density between the new swordsman and the spinning column of liquid. The liquid shot across the open room and slapped into the man's chest. He opened his mouth to scream, but the sound never made it out. Before the next attacker could enter the room, the liquid ate through the charging swordsman's body, reducing his torso to a bubbling mass of bloody horror.

Three more men charged into the room. These men looked deadly. They seemed cut from a common mold, tall, muscular, and each with short Eisenvard-style haircuts perfect for use in wearing heavy armor. He didn't like the look of this. Miller backed away from the door until he was just outside the boundary of the magic circle. Brita stood calmly, unperturbed in the center of the circle. She wore a calm otherworldly look on her face as the men approached, almost as if she had expected them.

Miller wondered if these men were Eisenvard. That explained why they would use alchemy but not spell-craft. Of course, he thought, the same would be true of Taken. He glanced up at the protective runes decorating the ceiling. None of them had activated. Whoever they were, they had some power.

He didn't have time to re-channel magic. Instead, he tried to use the air to hold the men back. He pushed air and the wind blew. It slowed them for two steps before the wind died within the room. Miller cursed out loud. He didn't have enough airflow to stop them. The attackers sprang back into action. The first two attackers joined them to create a crowd of five. The woman grabbed Miller by the arm. The pudgy man who first entered the room reached down for his legs. Miller felt them trying to push him to the ground.

A sixth person walked into the room behind them. She walked in slowly, smiling. Miller knew that woman. She smiled with inner mirth as Mistress Sword looked across at the melee. She laughed, filling the room with sharp cutting humor.

"You don't have permission to be here. I'll have to ask you to leave." Mistress Sword called out to the crowd, ending her statement with a laugh.

The rearmost attacker, a fighting age man with half of his teeth missing, spun to face her. Mistress Sword began to laugh as she moved her hands to manipulate her spell energy. Miller felt the magic channels shift in the room as the White Hand master applied her willpower and skill to her crafting. The man no longer needed to worry about his partial set of teeth as he exploded in fire. Mistress Sword continued to laugh as the attackers realized their peril. Fire jumped from the burning man onto the attacker next to him, spread over the man like spilled water, and he lit afire as well.

Miller looked back and forth at all the attackers then realized his danger. Sword would kill all of them, but she might just burn the building down in the process. He glanced down at the magic circle. It continued to hold. Brita might live, but he would be cooked alive if this continues. He sat on the floor and began casting all of the fire protection spells that he knew. He channeled skin hardness, flame resistance, and almost finished a third before Mistress sword released one final laugh and the entire room exploded in fire.

Flame surrounded him. He glanced at the protective circle. He might be able to break in and use it from protection, but the fire could flow in to kill Brita then. He could feel burning on his skin, and his eyes stung with the smoke, but he wasn't on fire screaming in agony like his attackers now were.

The fire leaped from table to bar to humans with no regard to who they were. It burned everything it touched. Miller began to cough, and he knew he was in trouble. The flame might not attach to him, but the air was leaving the room. Only smoke remained. He moved toward the door but couldn't go forward. The pudgy man who grabbed his legs earlier still had them in his grasp and he wouldn't release Miller, even though he burned like an oil-soaked log the man kept his grip.

Miller tried to call out, knowing that Mistress Sword would do nothing to save him. He tried to channel, to move air into the room, but he couldn't do it. His head spun and he collapsed onto the burning floor. He looked above and saw the protective runes begin to glow. He coughed, hoping that the runes would douse the fire before he died of asphyxiation.

Great, he thought, here's another fate to add to my list, choking to death. The world faded away as the smoke thickened. A moment later he lay unconscious in the center of the   burning   hall.

RECOVERY

Light burned through his closed eyelids. It took Miller a full minute before he could get the will to open them. A bright ray of light shone into the room from curtained windows, each decorated with thin fabric and with sewn images of a stag hunt. A carved dark-oak table stood near him with a mug of water sitting near its edge. Three upholstered chairs occupied the opposite side of the table. A painting of a lion hung on the far wall, so wide it would take three paces to walk past it. Memories flooded back into his mind. He remembered this room. He was back at the Gardens. This was Phyllicitus's apartments.

A red blanket covered his naked body. It was soft and warm. He wanted to lay here for hours. He tried to remember what happened after the fire but couldn't. He was in Phyllicitus's care now. It was not the time to worry. He would deal with Sword when he got the chance.

"There you are. I was wondering when your soul would rejoin us." He recognized the voice. It was filled with concern and only slightly laced with humor. "Enjoy your time near the crooked door?"

His eyes went wide. Panic crept into his voice. "Did I die?"

"No. But you came close. What did you do to Mistress Sword anyway? This does look like her work."

He exhaled organized his thoughts. He didn't see any reason to avoid the issue.

"Mistress Aileen. I'm sorry to report that the inn has been attacked."

"I've heard. Don't worry, we got Brita out."

Nodding, he offered a weak smile. "Your blade?"

"Of course I got it back. Sword knows what is mine. What happened? We didn't find anyone else."

"I'm not sure. Brita and I were alone at the inn. Six people came in and just outright attacked us. Somehow they were able to circumvent our defensive runes. I assumed they were allied with the Takers, so I fought." He hung his head. "I didn't win."

Aileen walked into view from his left, wine glass in one hand. She pulled out one of the small chairs and sat. She wore a brilliant white robe with only a gold bracelet to add decoration. Reaching out, she stroked his smooth arm. "I'm glad you got away."

Miller gazed down at his newly hairless arm. He reached up to feel his newly bald head, then above his eyes where his brows used to be.

"I got burned pretty bad, eh?"

"Yes. She burned you pretty badly. We got you healed though."

"I thought I was dead."

A small laugh escaped Aileen's lips. "No, don't be silly. If you would have died, then this whole thing would have hurt a lot more. It turns out that getting a goddess to heal your wounds is a good idea. Don't worry. Your pretty hair will all grow back."

He struggled to sit up. His skin felt raw. Glancing down, he saw new pink skin on his arm and his foot.

Miller continued, "Mistress Sword interrupted the attack. I

don't think she cared whether I lived or died, but she wasn't going to let the Takers get what they had come for."

Aileen continued to gaze at Miller's body, newly regenerated from being burned. Miller gazed up at her quizzically, trying to fathom what she was thinking.

Aileen offered a kind smile back to him. "Don't worry about me," she said, "Go ahead on inspect everything to make sure all your parts are there."

All of his parts were there.

He offered Aileen a smile. "That was close."

"Sure. A little fire may have solved some problems in life though."

She offered him a glass of wine. He reached out to take it from her, but she didn't let it go immediately. For a few moments, she held on, running a finger across the back of his hand. She shook her head as if to clear her thoughts. "Sorry. When I'm around the goddess it gets a little overwhelming sometimes."

She gestured back toward Phyllicitus's inner rooms.

Miller had just gotten burned alive. His defenses were lowered and just wanted to live life. "I don't mind if you hold me."

His heart pounded. He couldn't believe he had just said that. Aileen released his hand, pushing herself further back into her chair. Her eyes were wide with surprise. "Let's not do this, especially now."

Miller felt his heart crack. What he had just done was enough to get him killed by any other master. He needed to remember that Aileen was still a Master of the White Hand, not some commoner. Confessing his inner feelings would be a very bad idea.

Bowing his head, he apologized. "I am so sorry. I think the near-death experience has rattled my wits."

He knew it was a bad excuse when he said it, and so did Aileen. "You had better get that under control. As a White Hand apprentice, I'm guessing that you will have a lot more of those in the future."

He sipped on the wine. It was light, filled with the flavors of spring. After staring appreciatory at the glass, he took a second sip before raising the cup to his nose and taking in a deep breath.

Aileen gave him a moment to get his thoughts organized.

"Any idea what that attack was about?" Miller asked.

"Other than it took place in Home's Hearth, under the goddess's control, with her in the city? No idea."

The thought disturbed Miller. What could overcome a god? How could that even be done? His knowledge of the Takers didn't come close to allowing him to predict their motives or even their capabilities.

"And the runes."

"And the runes." He agreed. "I suspect they may have used some crafting or alchemy to get past them. I have a few ideas on how to improve our defenses and prevent another of these attacks.

"We've got a few moments unto Phyllicitus gets here. We need to have all of our discussions about the Order quickly. She won't tolerate those kinds of talks in her presence. Plus, I don't need her getting more information than she already has."

"Can't we trust her?"

Aileen slowly nodded. "You're learning. We can trust Phyllicitus to be herself. She couldn't be allied with a group of necromancers and still be true to her nature. Those two things are at odds. She will need to make a choice shortly. I don't want her to get into a place where acting against in her own self-interest is against her self-image. That kind of thing never works out well, at least that's what Easter tells me."

Miller nodded. Thoughts of the gods made him uncomfortable. They were almost as much an enigma as the Takers were. Easter worried about the gods and especially about when they made decisions about who they were. The gods should be steady and reliable. Shouldn't they? If Easter was worried about that kind of thing, he knew that he should be as well.

He stretched, swinging his arms wide. Painful pinpricks danced across his newly regrown skin. He rubbed his hairless arm in wonder at how soft it was, how whole it was.

"The fire. How bad was it? What did we lose?"

Aileen shook her head. "Don't worry. As far as fires go, that one was fairly contained. I think we will need a few days of repairs, but our landlord still has an inn."

"And Brita?"

"We got her out. The circle protected her from the flame, but she got a chest full of smoke. Frankly, I'm amazed the circle held up at all. Good job on that, by the way."

He nodded back, accepting the faint praise. He could have made the circle stronger, but he didn't want to alert any passing crafters to their presence.

"What happened then? How did they surprise us? No one was there except Brita and I. Even Cerna was gone."

She nodded back. "Yes. I'm surprised it took that long for them to try something. They must have been waiting for Cerna to leave. We thought they would try something more subtle."

"That was pretty direct."

"Yes. That's why I believe the Takers are close to doing something. They wouldn't risk exposure if they weren't confident."

Miller stopped fidgeting with his skin and stood up. He pulled the blanket tighter around his torso and began to look for some clothing. In a few moments, he found a neatly folded long tunic made of finely woven red cotton. It was undecorated except for yellow threading around the neck. He matched it with a black pair of short trousers that ended just below the knee. Their black color offset the vibrant red, creating a pleasing, stylish look.

"So now what?" He asked as he walked back toward her.

"We have a survivor. I'm guessing Easter will want to talk with him."

"Talk?"

"Sure. Talk. Let's go with that if it makes you feel better."

"Doesn't matter how it makes me feel, does it? It would make me feel better if I knew where Easter was. He's been gone for at least a day."

"He has been in Home's Hearth. I expect he has been keeping an eye on The Gardens. Both he and Phyllicitus are staying there. That should attract some attention from the Takers."

Miller exhaled in resignation. "Is everyone in Home's Hearth bait?"

She nodded. "For this game, absolutely."

"What kind of plan is that?" He questioned with a hint of sarcasm. "All right everyone here is the plan. Let's all stand around and get possessed. Once we are all in their power, the amazing order of necromancers will come along and kill us all. Hooray! The good guys win again!"

Aileen looked down at the floor before she whispered. "Something like that, yes."

Miller became serious. "We both know that isn't a winning strategy."

"Do you have a better one? Somewhere in your experience, have you developed a stratagem for victory?"

He exhaled, willing his cutting rebuke away. "I don't have a plan for victory, but I do have one for a better chance at victory."

"And?" She raised her eyebrows in surprise.

"And we aren't going to get there by being targets."

"So?"

"We need to change our approach. Let's assume that the Takers are preparing for us. They know we are here. They've had years to prepare. They are in Home's Hearth for a reason."

Aileen nodded. "Alright. Let's assume an intelligent plan on their part."

"What do we know? We know that they don't use magic the same way as we do, and we know that they have a way to slip around some of our spells. We also know they come from between the worlds where magic flows differently."

She continued to nod, growing interested in his line of thinking.

"We also know that Brita has been taken, yet she has enough freedom to leave small clues for us. Given what I saw of their powers, I'm guessing that it has more to do with the place between worlds than anyone is willing to admit."

Aileen's eyes narrowed. She didn't agree or disagree, merely let him continue.

"So why would they come here? I'm going to make another guess. Given that their power is founded on something between the worlds, and the fact that The Gardens has an artifact that uses a similar type of power, I'm guessing they are here because that artifact is here, and that their plans may very well involve it."

"An artifact?" Aileen sounded confused.

"The design in the library. Didn't some priest of Phyllicitus create it based on old lore? Old like when there were no human gods?"

She nodded. "Stevenson."

"Yes. That was his name. I'm willing to bet that some kind of secret is hidden in that library."

She shook her head. "I spent six months reading every journal and letter that Stevenson ever wrote. I studied his lore. I found nothing."

"In any case, it still functions."

"Functions?"

Now it was Miller's turn to be surprised. "Yes. Functions. Have you never seen the magic it can do?"

"It can make someone very focused. Other than that, I've seen nothing."

"Do you think that isn't magic?"

She decided not to argue with him. "So what?"

"I'm thinking that the design in the library is a different kind of magic. Our casting is based on the flows and channels of power. What if the old lore wasn't? I can think of three different magical techniques that aren't either. What if the Takers are using that old lore to escape from our sight? To possess people? To take?"

"I'm not sure. And even if they did, what could we do?"

"Right now, we can sit in Home's Hearth and get attacked at their convenience. My plan would be to learn enough about the old lore to find some way to detect them. I'd like to find a way to create some kind of alarm or tripwire. It has to be possible?"

"Sure. But is it possible in a few weeks?"

"Ask me in a few weeks."

She nodded.

"After all, what else do I have to do? It isn't like the temple is giving me any resources. Right now, I have Brita and I have an old design in a library."

"And your plan is?"

"I'd like to move into The Gardens, away from the New Pony. I want to investigate everything Stevenson left behind. I want to experiment with the designs he created. I want to discover how to detect magic like that."

She nodded. "You have a small chance with that plan."

"I'll take any chance right now. I have none otherwise."

"What will you need?"

This was the part Miller was nervous about. "I'll need permission from The Garden and two rooms."

"Two?"

"One for me and one for my assistant."

She looked back toward him with suspicion. "Don't tell me you're bringing your little Eisenvard toy along."

"She isn't a toy. Plus, I made a promise."

Aileen paused to consider what he had just said. Promises were powerful things amongst spell crafters, even more so between masters. An unfulfilled promise left a gap in whatever defenses he might need in the future.

"Agreed. You will have two weeks. We will need Phyllicitus to agree though."

Before he could object, Aileen interrupted. "Because it's her city. We can't hide anything the Order does, and we should not try. We will hide nothing from Phyllicitus."

"And the temple priestesses?"

"Not   our   problem."☐

RETURNING UNANNOUNCED

Master December stared down at the crystal-clear water. Guards patrolled Home's Heath. Walking into the city would be difficult at best. He arrived at midday to the site of long lines at its entrance. The weather had become warm as he patiently waited in line amongst the commoners.

After all, he considered, he was just a commoner as well, wasn't he?

He thought about the challenge of entering Home's Hearth. The best disguise might be to simply fit into the crowd. That normally allowed almost anyone to avoid detection. This afternoon was different. Priestesses lay in wait at the city entrance. They smelled of sorcery, alchemy, and purpose. While no priestess could challenge him individually, with magic or otherwise, there were enough priestesses to threaten what he truly wanted, secrecy.

He walked away, retreating to find an easier entrance. Three hours of walking had yielded no more accessible targets. The Temple was on alert. He stopped to talk with a local man fishing near the river and gathered news and gossip. There had been a fire in the city and the Temple was stirred up searching for someone to blame.

Arson? Master December smiled at the thought. Home's Hearth could always use fire to liven things up. If there was a fire, then something wasn't working in Phyllicitus's perfect little world. Easter would be here. Darjeeling, Sword, and Aileen were here as well. Any Taken who revealed themselves with four masters present was either very confident or very stupid.

He decided to bet on both. Sitting at the river's edge, he paused to consider his next move. Easter could handle a Taker infestation without any help from him but something broke past the peace of Phyllicitus. Her peace was more than just some state of public good behavior. It was more than a spell or enchantment. It was the core of what the goddess was, and how she fit into the world. Anything that could break her hold would need to defeat her power as a god. December worried about what could do such a thing.

He thought about the type of power that would take. Could the Takers defeat an ascended god? It had happened before, but rarely.

It had never happened with one of the First Gods though, never in the history of the world.

He began to smile. Perhaps there was something interesting here after all. He stood again, wiping the grass from his breeches. Master December abandoned the riverside and returned to the outer markets.

###

"Hello, Friend." Master December said.

The workman looked over, surprised to be addressed by this new face. Sawdust coated the workman. He showed evidence of a long days works nearing its end. The workman pushed a small cart with the remains of the day's labor, a hammer, a half-used box of nails, a straight measure, and a bent saw. December had moved up next to him unnoticed.

"What's that?" The man asked.

December nodded reassuringly. "I was hoping that you could help me with a small matter. You see, I'm a bit out of sorts." Motioning to his simple thin shirt, torn breeches, and bare feet, he offered a smile.

The worker stared back suspiciously. December opened his hand to reveal three thick copper coins. As the workman gazed down, December released his crafting. Energy flowed through his heart channel, enticing the workman's flows toward him, toward his control. The workman felt a jolt of excitement staring down at the thick coins. It was as much copper as he would normally earn in two days of labor. For some reason, he no longer felt any suspicion or worried about any scheme. Perhaps it was the subtle crafting that December had cast upon him, or perhaps it was his natural greed.

"You see, I'm having some troubles with my brother. I need to send him this coat, and this bag of things." Gesturing down at the bag in his arms, he opened it to show the black leather coat. "I can't go into the city yet, as I have business down the road, pressing business, you see?"

The craftsman nodded his head, taking in the story. December had used this tale many times during the centuries. It worked eight out of ten times.

The spell combined its temptation with the pull of his coins. "What do you need me to do?"

The master necromancer smiled back at him. Feeling relieved that such a great man had taken an interest in him, the workman relaxed. The spell moved deeper into his heart, coloring everything with an aura of wholesomeness and trustworthiness. The spell made December 'feel right'. The spell lied.

"My family should be gathered at an inn, but I'm not sure which. I'd like you to take this package to the Temple Grouse Inn and leave it with the innkeeper. Tell him it's for his lost stranger. He'll know me and take it from you."

"And my pay?"

"Oh, I'll give it to you before you go. I have faith in you. You won't forget about me."

The workman nodded. For a moment the workman considered simply taking the things then dumping them in a refuse pile. He could simply keep the coins and walk away. But what would the goddess think of him? The task was so simple though, why should he do something so vile?

The power of December's flow pushed the workman to action. The power of a goddess pulled him toward virtue. The workman had no chance.

December handed him the bundle along with the coins. A thick leather coat, stained black, was twined about a bundle containing a pair of well-made boots, dark green trousers, a midnight-black cloak, and a tunic made of fine blood-red cloth. Patting the workman on the back, December siphoned off a portion of the man's aura and held it in his channels, just in case the man should be needed again. December left the workman standing by his cart, package in hand, wondering why he had agreed to this odd request so readily.

Wearing a smile, December walked away. The power of the goddess was almost impossible to defy in this town, he thought, but very easy to subvert to his own ends. The workman was doing good deeds for a stranger. No spell or goddess-power would identify that man as a threat. All December needed to do was to gain entrance to the city, then go reclaim his things.

He reached down to feel the handle of his new dagger sheathed at his side. He missed his old dagger. Soon enough, he would have it back. He walked off barefoot toward the river. It was going to be a long, cold, wet night.

December walked back along the cobbled streets and arrived at the outer market. It was busy with people making trades and buying things. The smell of meat pie and roasting fish filled the air as he entered the crowd, causing his stomach to grumble with hunger. He paused to enjoy the sensation. Physical desires came to him rarely now. He had learned to savor them when they came along.

The crowd pressed in on him from all sides. The villages outside of Home's Hearth bustled with activity. The increased scrutiny at the gates had made the outer markets much busier than usual. He allowed people to come close to him, close enough so he could touch their auras, and perhaps sip a tiny bit of magic from their souls.

He found an open area filled with a dozen carts. Each cart held different foods. Soup makers competed with bakers, who battled brewers and wine merchants. He saw a wooden sign advertised fine wine and fresh fruit. The merchant had thoughtfully provided five stools for customers. It would be hours before dusk and Master December had little enough to do until then. He sat upon the first stool, ordered a bottle of wine and began to pass the hours, slowly sipping on the wine, and the souls of passers-by.

The afternoon passed by, nearing evening time. Low clouds rolled in, hiding the blue skies behind their gray ceiling. The master necromancer felt more relaxed than he had in days. His stomach was full of wine. That, combined with his overflowing channels of energy, put him into a confident mood. He looked up at the sun to judge how far dusk lay. After a moment of consideration, he stood, abandoning the stool he had held all day.

The market had shed most if its crowds as night approached. Sadly, its wares had been largely devoured as well. Moving past nearly empty tables he found his first goal. An elderly man stood surrounded six goats. Each of them was tied to a tree. The man was tanned dark, testifying to his time shepherding the animals in the field. The exchange of six coins earned Master December a fine young goat. Dragging the goat on a leash behind him, the feared necromancer continued his conquest of the market to purchase a turtle, then a young kitten.

The market hadn't provided all of his needs though. Leaving

its confines, he led the goat along a dirt track, heading toward the sounds of metal striking metal. The sky was showing a hint of red as he approached the smithy.

Lanterns surrounded the work yard. Three smiths worked here, toiling into the night.

The goat pulled at his tether, jerking his hand forward. December didn't hesitate. Snapping his will into five channels, he bore down with his magic, driving any semblance of independent will from the beast.

It wouldn't be needing its own willpower anyway, at least if December had his way. The goat followed behind, tamely carrying two other cages without further complaint.

As he entered the work yard, a stocky young man called out. He was covered in the dust of coal and iron. The soot that covered him demonstrated the history of his labors, and perhaps the fate of all his remaining days.

The young journeyman spoke up. "We're done tonight, come back tomorrow."

"Really?" December replied wryly.

December had waited for this late hour on purpose. With the changing of day to night, December knew that he could hide any channeling within the magical noises that such powers made. The channels broiled near such things upset at how the earth was beaten and molded into shape. Softly channeling, he stroked the young man's need to be helpful. He reduced the journeyman's need to stand firm. December moved spirit along the flows between them.

"I've only come for an iron bar, one that could help me pry a few stones from the earth."

The young man started to answer back, trying to send December away again, when he suddenly had a change of mind.

"Over there." He motioned at a stack of twenty iron rods that lay upon a worktable.

"Thank you," December said politely as he walked over to pick out the largest rod. He left without paying. December turned back toward the small trail that led back to the river.

By the time Master December returned to the river shore, the light had completely deserted the sky above Home's Hearth. Clouds obscured the stars, and only Master December's comfort in the night allowed him to successfully return to his earlier location.

December remembered how the river flowed into the tunnels beneath Home's Hearth. Anyone trying to swim through the tunnels would be hard-pressed not to drown. There would be underwater obstacles, perhaps even magical wards.

He spent a moment seeking out magical flows and enchantments. The temple possessed priestesses gifted in magic, and they were on the alert. He had to make sure he could pass undetected. He searched for alarms, signals, and traps. Five minutes later he was satisfied there was no magical alarm.

Loosening his belt, he threaded one end of it through the turtle cage. Finally, he re-buckled it, fastening the cage to his side and keeping the turtle in easy reach. Walking along the riverbank, he picked up six fist-sized stones and placed them in his pockets, weighing down his tall gaunt form.

December pulled the goat after him as he walked into the river. Cold water ran through his pants as the water came to his waist. He sucked in a breath as the chill hit him. Pausing, he savored how his body rebelled from the cold, knowing that soon it would be much worse.

Releasing the goat near shore's edge, he pulled up his second cage. The kitten mewed within its confines, blissfully unaware of its own fate. The goat stood near the shore, motionless and without direction or will.

He opened the cage, reached in, and grabbed the kitten by the scruff of the neck. He held it tightly as he pulled it out. The kitten began to wail a pitiful cry, angry at its treatment. Master December ignored the kitten's cries as he wove flows between the three souls, small as they were. He tied the goat's dampened fear to the kitten, then slowly released his hold on the goat's will. It began to panic, screaming out its anger. The goat's legs would not obey it. It waved its head back and forth, then began to scream even more loudly. Pain ripped through its body. December channeled hurt, grief, and the feeling of ripping flesh through the magical flows. The kitten began to scream in terror as well. The goat knew it was going to die in pain, and the feelings rushed into the young kitten obliterating any other though.

Like an orchestral crescendo, the goat gave a final scream and dropped dead, blood spraying from its mouth and nose. The kitten began to scream as the goat's death throws entered its own heart. Death poured into the small furry thing as December turned away from the shore and walked into the depths of the river.

Ten steps later he was completely submerged. December walked along the bottom of the river, feeding on the kitten's horror, substituting his need for oxygen with the power of the kitten's terror. He didn't need to breathe. By the time the kitten's heart stopped beating, drowned in water and fear, he had reached the tunnel entrance.

Thoughts of Aileen ran through December's mind for a moment. He remembered how Aileen had been such a believer. She had been tied to the goddess and to the forces of good, whatever those were. She had begun so foolishly, believing all of Easter's high-thinking words. It didn't take long for her to grasp the truth. Sometimes good intentions were worse than evil acts, and without strength, all of it would fail.

December walked down the tunnel comfortable in its wet darkness. He had recently consumed the life force of a small kitten, and its life force was beginning to fade away. He considered finding another small animal when he saw the barrier emerge from the shadows. A metal cage had been set into the tunnel. It was large enough to block a man. Two minutes of effort with the iron bar left it ruined. He left it laying at the tunnel's bottom.

The effort left December weak, having expended all of his stored magic. He reached into the turtle's cage to touch it. A few seconds later the turtle had transformed into a rotting husk and Master December sucked enough life force to continue his journey. He moved through the tunnel to emerge into the dark night.

He stepped out of the river onto the shore. He was wet, fatigued, and safe within the walls of Home's Hearth. He spent a minute squeezing his clothing, trying to drain as much of the water as he could. Somewhere in this city, there were Takers, and they had found a way to get around the goddess's power. It wasn't so hard. He had just done it. The Takers didn't frighten him.

But Mistress Sword was here as well. Her allies, Hermagon's cabal, would be eager to test their growing power against this threat. If they released the god they had been growing, it could easily defeat the Takers.

It would also defeat Phyllicitus, the people of Home's Hearth, and possibly drain all life from the world. The Takers frightened all of the masters except him. Master December knew where the real danger would be found. It would be from the order itself.

☐

THE SUMMONS

It was late. Miller had slept four hours, returned to the New Pony, and retrieved Brita in a rented carriage. He instructed the owner to lock both doors with iron in a vain hope to stop any who might want to intercept them. He braved the dark empty streets without any masters or Eisenvard. He knew that the Takers had some way of communicating with each other and he didn't want to take any chances.

The journey turned out to be uneventful. Miller had over-prepared. They arrived in the dead of night. They encountered one watchman and three drunken revelers on their journey. They arrived at the Garden less than a half hour from when they had set out.

Aileen looked over at both Brita and Miller. They stood bleary-eyed in her the apartments at the Garden. Goddess Phyllicitus, after a quick glance at the happenings in her apartments, simply shrugged and returned to bed. Miller caught motion in her private apartment as she walked out to greet them. There were people in her private chamber waiting for her to return.

"You brought her here?" Aileen asked, surprise in her voice.

"I'm bringing her to the library. I just didn't want to get ambushed on the road."

Aileen's voice sounded amused. "You're afraid of ambush in Home's Hearth? With the goddess in residence?"

"I'm afraid of everything. I thought you knew that."

Her smile grew wider. "That's because you are becoming wise. The White Hand training is paying off." Her smiles were becoming more frequent. Miller could see the effect simply being around Phyllicitus was having on Aileen. He wondered why she didn't come here more often. It was like Aileen enjoyed the White Hand life.

"I liked it better when I was ignorant and could sleep at night," Miller replied.

"Didn't we all."

Brita waved at him, trying to attract his attention. He was just too tired to respond. The best he could do was to mutter a terse question. "What?"

Brita's voice came out in a whisper. "I didn't see Cerna. Where did he go?"

No one had seen Cerna in three days. He had just gone missing. "I hope he didn't get caught up in some trouble."

"Do you think he would run away?"

Miller doubted it. Cerna was Easter's man, through and through. "No."

Aileen spoke. "I'm sure we'll see him again. Hopefully intact and un-taken."

Brita gave a quick start as she inhaled, then put her hand in front of her mouth. "Do you think he could have been taken? Here?"

"I have no idea. I won't dismiss the idea though. It's probably the worst thing that could happen right now. But we'll have to trust Master Easter with his little secrets and plans, won't we?"

"You have a lot of trust," Miller said, "Given we are talking about Easter, his play might be to get Cerna taken, just so he can march him up to the temple and demand some kind of action."

"Trust Easter? Not really. I just don't have a lot of other options." Aileen retorted. "Plus, I've been dealing with Easter on-and-off for years. He can be cold, but he isn't despicable. It would have to be really critical for him to allow someone to be taken just to create a new pawn in his game."

"You didn't deny it." Miller said.

She nodded her head in silent agreement. Easter would trade any of them for an advantage. The question was, how much of an advantage?

They sat on the comfortable furniture and talked well into the early morning. Miller was unsure about his plan to teach Chamise the disciplines. He tried to get some support for the idea from Aileen, but she wouldn't commit. Miller shared his concerns about Master Darjeeling.

"I know Darjeeling is a little off, even for a White Hand master. Mostly, he's pretty harmless. But you've got to keep your eye on him. Something went wrong in him long ago. It would be best if you kept your eyes open when it comes to Master Darjeeling." Aileen supplied.

Miller continued. "Easter told me about his earlier attempts at contacting the Takers. I can tell there are some mental scars left over."

"Those scars have been there a long time. They aren't excuses. They aren't badges of heroism. Those scars are more like badges of stupidity. Easter and Hermagon encouraged him on that fools' route. Now he bears the marks and I wonder if he will ever recover." Aileen continued for twenty minutes, spinning tales of Darjeeling's history. He seemed to be the oddest combination of jolly uncle and friendless assassin.

Brita had lain down on the thick rug during the stories. Her eyes fluttered with signs of sleep.

Miller summarized his point. "But can we can trust him? I don't have any hard evidence, but the way he went after my friends gives me pause."

"Friends? Do you mean the Eisenvard? You've developed a liking to your witch-hunters, eh?"

Miller waved his hands back and forth in denial. "Let's not get carried away. While they seem a lot calmer now that they used to be, I'm sure they're an eye-blink away from putting any of us to the fire."

"Oh, the fire." Aileen shuddered. "Let's not do that. The fire is a bad way to go."

Miller was surprised. "Did you ever die in a fire?"

"No. I'm not going to either. I got to see one of the other masters die in a blaze. It was in Darjeeling's asylum, long before I joined the order. That was Master Fleet, and it didn't go well for him. He protected himself with barriers to flame, but it didn't help."

"Didn't help? Why not? Did his crafting fail?"

"No. It worked just fine. He forgot about the smoke. After a minute of not being able to breathe, he lost consciousness. Then his crafting dissipated. Then he essentially broiled inside the burning castle for two days."

A chill went across Miller's spine. The same fate had nearly happened to him just a few days ago.

"Sounds pretty bad, but he didn't experience all of the pain, did he?"

"Oh, that was the easy part. He was good and dead during all of that. The hard part came when his apprentice dug him out two weeks later and took his body back to camp. It took him four weeks to grow enough skin back so he could even try to return from the final black door. Then six weeks of screaming and tears. It was one of the worst returns I had ever seen. Even Easter said it was unusually rough."

Miller sat in thought, imagining how it would feel to be burned alive, then take two months to return to life only to experience all the pain of the fire, again and again, living through it for weeks until the skin grew back, only then would the pain stop. It didn't seem like the perfect eternal life the order promised.

"You people are gross," Brita said from the floor.

Brita had mumbled other garbled words her sleep. The charge struck home though. Miller had to admit to the disgusting nature of their calm conversations.

"Interesting," Miller said, gazing down at her. "That's the first time I've heard sleep talking from her."

Aileen motioned about the room, offering a sarcastic face. "Perhaps it is the goddess speaking into her dreams?"

"Perhaps." Miller agreed. He noticed how Aileen talked about Phyllicitus more, and had begun to speak respectfully, perhaps even worshipfully of her. The speed of her attitude change surprised him.

He began to think through possible connections between magical flows, the power of a human goddess, and the Takers. He simply didn't have enough information to make any leaps of logic or faith to solve this problem.

"So, about Darjeeling." Aileen interrupted his thoughts.

Miller looked up, meeting her eyes.

Aileen continued. "It sounds like you might need a little help there if only to ease your fears."

"I'll always take help. What do you have?"

"First, a little advice. Don't always take help. Sometimes the helpers are more work than the problem."

Miller nodded, thinking about Franz and Darjeeling.

"Second, you may not like my idea, but hear me out before you disagree." She motioned Miller to sit on the soft red chair next to her. As he walked over to take the seat, she reached back onto a side table and moved aside a thin cloth. It covered a leather belt pouch, travel-worn and scarred from use. Taking it up in one hand, she held it out for him.

"Go ahead, take it."

Miller reached for it, then froze in place. Channels were alive around it. Magical power danced around it. There was some kind of spirit tied to the contents of the bag, something that should not be in this world. The bag stank of necromancy. It had the feel of the grave.

"What is this?"

"Just take it." Aileen forced the bag into his half-outstretched hand. "I put Faust's spirit binding in here. It's just a collection of odd bits he used during life. He managed not to go through that final door, so I gave him a place to call home."

His throat went dry. "Oh, home. How lovely." It didn't feel lovely. Miller wondered what could be used to give Faust a home. In life, he was a torturer, executioner, and loyal friend to Aileen. Back when he was alive, Faust could be the best friend a man ever had or his worse enemy. The challenging part was that you were never sure which one.

Miller looked back at her; suspicion unhidden on his face.

"What am I supposed to do with this?"

"How about be a necromancer?"

Shaking his head, Miller continued his suspicions. "And why? What is this supposed to do?"

"If you were paying attention when I taught you spirit summoning, you will remember that this will allow you to call Faust from the beyond. Then once you have his help, you can use him to spy on all kinds of things. You can set him as a guard over Brita. You can send him searching for Cerna. Curse it, boy, you can use Faust to keep an eye open for strange mobs of people who might be Taken, and possibly avoid ambushes."

"I'm not very good at that kind of thing."

"I know. That's why I'm giving you this opportunity. You need to get better, fast."

"I don't want to. Can't we just let him rest?"

"No, we can't. Faust was restless in life, and death suits him no better. We need to give him something to do before his spirit gets out on its own, and you need the help. Plus, I need to demonstrate that my apprentice is serious about his path as a necromancer, people in the cabal are starting to wonder about your commitment. I've thought about this a lot. I'm not just throwing this on you. I know you don't like to disturb the dead for minor reasons. The thing is, Faust is only sort-of-dead. He still needs some care and feeding from time to time. Otherwise, I will need to send him through the final black door."

"And why don't you?"

She shook her head. "You don't know him. Trust me. He needs the time to get some of the stains from his past deeds off of him."

Miller tried to marshal another argument against the idea. Aileen was having none of it.

"No. You are going to summon him tonight. You are going to tie him with your willpower and give him a task. You need the help, and I need an apprentice necromancer. We have been avoiding this issue for a long time. It's obvious you don't like the darker parts of the craft. I think it's time to step up. We've got some political issues to take on and I can't be distracted by this."

"Political issues?"

"Hermagon and his cabal are making noises that you are unfit to be a White Hand."

Miller's eyebrows shot up in surprise. Hermagon was unusually senior to be making cases against apprentices like that. Normally masters just wait to see if an apprentice dies during training. That seemed to be their only real test they applied to their applicants. Hermagon always had political motives though. He felt goosebumps spring up across his body. Hermagon might want to remove him from this world just to harm Easter's position in the cabal.

"What? What did I do?"

"Nothing. That's the problem. Sadly, given that argument, I can see why they are making headway in the order with that line of reasoning."

"But that's ridiculous."

"Ridiculous? Get used to it. This is an order of necromancers, not nannies. Take out the focus and get to work. We need a spirit helper before morning."

###

"Isn't there some sort of ley line calculation we should be doing?"

Aileen shook her head. "Don't bother. Someone picked out a great piece of land when they built the Gardens. It's got flows tangled all through it. I once spent an entire season trying to map it. We won't have a problem."

Miller didn't back away from his concerns.

"Bringing a spirit through needs power."

"Don't you think I know that?"

"If I don't get it exactly right, the spirit may need to pull flows from the caster. That means me." He couldn't hide the fear in his voice.

"Have a little faith. I've brought Faust through so many times he might as well be the spirit of a greased pig."

"You have. I haven't."

"Well, it's about time then. You are my apprentice, right?"

He seemed doubtful for a moment. "I guess."

"I'm a necromancer, right?"

There it was. She put it right out there. There was no denying it, no matter how Miller tried to avoid the truth.

"Yes."

"So stop grumbling and start casting."

Aileen pointed at the small black bag. It sat atop an ivory table, alone except for a single tall candle next to it. The candle sat on a heavy brass base. Hot wax dripped down its length to pool below. In the dim light, it looked like spilled blood.

"What if he doesn't agree?"

"What if just close your mouth and do what you need to do?"

She had a hint of glee in her voice as she watched Miller squirm. They both knew that he wasn't the best at this kind of casting. He was too careful, too deliberative. Snatching a soul back across the void, past the final black door, required speed, commitment, and more than a little finesse. It didn't require over-thinking.

"Are you enjoying this?"

She smiled back.

"Oddly, yes. You've been doing such a good job of avoiding all necromancy spells over the years, it's amusing to see you in such consternation."

"Thanks." He said dryly.

"Any time."

Miller exhaled, admitting defeat. He reached over to open the bag, spilling its contents onto the table. A small finger-length knife and a nearly empty clay bottle of ink rolled out. He kept shaking the bag gently. Three buttons poured out onto the table's surface. Carvings of bear claws stood out against their dark wooden surfaces. Finally, a single piece of folded paper fell out, finishing the parade of items.

"Is this it?" Aileen asked, seeing his concern.

Miller reached out to pick up the paper, hesitating just before he touched it. Spirit flows rumbled near it, crossing between the worlds of life and death.

Aileen nodded, "Yes. That's it. That's what he anchored himself to."

"It feels cold."

"That's just the spirit link. They are supposed to be cold. If they are hot, you've got a problem."

Miller shook his head, trying to clear the fears away.

"That isn't what I meant. I think there is some residual soul attached as well."

"Sure. That piece of paper was his warrant from the house of questions. Faust got his authorization to be a torturer directly from the temple. It was important to him somehow. The things he did there would attach to anyone's soul."

"I don't remember him being that religious."

"He wasn't. But he did want to be a good person. In the end, his wants didn't really matter though. He thought he was serving Phyllicitus, but in the end, he had only been serving the Eisenvard. When Phyllicitus returned she banished Faust."

"How did the temple have a house of questions anyway?

That doesn't even make sense."

"No, that was part of the problem with Faust. When Faust came to the temple, Phyllicitus had been gone for almost a century. Somehow the temple had bungled into a few wars they were poised to lose. Their solution was to bring in the Eisenvard. The Eisenvard influenced the priests to put survival at a higher priority than their vows to Phyllicitus's teachings. That's when everything went wrong."

"It went wrong because the priests survived the war?"

"In essence, yes."

Miller looked back, confused. He tried to avoid gazing at the paper. He could feel the cold of the spirit link. Soon he would need to pull on that link and guide Faust back. He didn't want to, but there it was, the life of an apprentice.

"You'll have to explain that to me someday. If the priests were all killed, and the temple burned, why bother having a religion, or a goddess anyway?"

"That's what the Eisenvard argued. I can't blame the priests for choosing to survive. If it happened again, I would suggest simply abandoning the temple instead. It would have been easier, and better for Phyllicitus."

"Really? Why?"

"Because Phyllicitus would have been preserved. I'm speaking of her inner light, her reason for being. She would have returned much earlier and much stronger. Abandoning her teachings and peaceful philosophy caused a great deal of harm to her. I think it is one of the reasons she couldn't get back."

"You are saying that gods get their powers from their believers?"

"No, not at all. A human god gets their power from, well, the universe. In essence, the god is the power, which is the god. It's all tangled together. The priests were part of her when they chose to ally with the Eisenvard and fight. That choice essentially caused part of Phyllicitus to fight against her own peaceful nature. Thus, the damage."

Miller reached a little closer to the paper. The cold grew less sharp as he narrowed the distance. He stopped a finger's breath away.

Aileen nodded approvingly. "You're being careful."

"I don't want to shock him when I pull him out."

"He's dead. Will he care?"

"I have no idea. I would like to avoid surprising him though. I owe him that much for what he did for me between the worlds."

Faust had rescued him from between the worlds, acted as a guide, and kept him company when he was lost. Miller wasn't going to repay that with rudeness.

"Do you remember your channels for crossing?"

"Yes. I remember the lessons. It's been a few years though. I'm going to do this very slow and careful."

"If you aren't quick enough, the spirit tail may be cut. That will bind Faust beyond the door forever."

"I think he would be fine with that."

Aileen peered back suspiciously.

"Or is it you that would be fine with that?"

"Either way. I'm the one casting, so I get to decide how it goes."

Aileen's eyes opened wide as she realized what Miller had meant. He had not been joking. In that one statement, Miller had claimed ownership of the spell and banned Aileen from interfering. She was his master and could wipe that claim aside with impunity. She didn't.

Miller began the crafting as he started to hum, moving will through his mind channels, then out to his voice. Its pitch began low and slowly rose. The magic of his channel moved against the spirit link, causing it to tremble like a taut string.

He began to gently pull on the spirit link. It resisted at first, but he slowed again and restarted. His magic infused voice rippled along the link, sounding a high pitch counter note to Miller's own voice. Ten heartbeats later he pulled again. The spirit link moved freely.

He counted as he pulled. Each breath marked a step that

Faust had moved back toward the world. A soul arrived one hundred and sixty-two steps later.

The soul looked like a misshapen blob of darkness. It had neither form nor substance. Guiding the soul across the table, he moved it atop a weak ley line.

"That isn't going to be enough," Aileen said, whispering her advice.

Miller ignored her. He bent over and began to whisper to Faust's soul. He told stories of their travels. He updated Faust about Brita, and how she had become so beautiful.

An hour passed. Each minute the soul grew in size, but only a little.

Aileen glanced down, then stood.

"I'll be back." She said as she left the room.

Miller nodded and kept talking to the spirit. Miller had seen many spirit summonings. They had all been quick, and violent. He didn't want to be that kind of mage. In this place, at this time, so near Phyllicius herself, there was no need. He tried to use his necromancy training to keep a line open beyond the world, then to utilize Phyllicitus 's presence in the city to ease the passage.

It wasn't any magic he had ever learned. It just felt right.

He could feel Faust growing closer. Then he heard a faint voice.

"Did she need to use the jakes?" The voice said.

A smile cracked Miller's face. That may have been what Aileen needed to do after all.

"No idea. I'm not going to ask."

Within thirty heartbeats, Faust had re-entered the world. His spirit form was stable and looked exactly as he had in life except he was partially transparent. A familiar smirk looked down at Miller, half full of laughter, and half of the sadness.

Miller repeated the command binding. Its words were taught to every apprentice in the Order since its inception. A command binding tied a soul to service, it acted to ensure the obedience of any who might return from beyond the final door, it anchored them in the world of the living.

Miller spoke the words with kindness, welcoming an old friend. "I command you into this world. Obey. Serve. Sense. Hunt."

He was surprised when he felt a tear fall upon his cheek. The only thing that was left of Faust was this soul and a pile of rotted meat at the bottom of a grave. At one point in time, Faust had been his companion, mayhap even a friend in his own way.

The spirit of Faust reached out to him with a ghostly arm. His blond hair was a mess, as it had always been in life. The spirit touched Miller, and he felt the slight tingle ring as a note in his own soul.

Faust spoke.

"Thanks."

Miller nodded. A smile broke out on his face. He had been so nervous, terrified even, of cutting Faust off, losing him beyond the final door.

A voice emerged from behind him, "Well done. That may have been the most touching necromantic spell I have ever seen in my life."

Miller turned quickly. Aileen stood there, staring wide-eyed. Tears of sadness and joy mixed on her face as well. She spoke words, but they seemed to be words that belonged in her heart rather than in the open world.

"That was perfect. You just brought a soul back from the dead with no terror, no pain, no damage. I've always dreamed of being able to do that. It's why I left the temple and joined the order."

She sank to her knees and began to weep, a smile on her face.

Three old friends gathered together. Their spirits touched each other in welcome, even with only two bodies between them. Miller joined Aileen on the floor, touching the spirit of Faust, exploring, trying to find problems or rips in his self. There was none. A few minutes later, Aileen touched Miller to check his own soul, then smiled. Miller took her by the hand, then held Faust as well.

They were together again. But unlike every time before, it was perfect.

The apartment door opened. Phyllicitus took a step out and looked down at them. She offered a smile, then nodded her approval to Miller. Happily, she retreated back into her chambers.

"What was that about?" Faust asked.

Aileen replied. "Joy. She's always been drawn to it."

Miller let out a breath in relief.

"Joy."

DEMONSTRATION

Chamise walked through the white marble entryway. Golden vases stood atop dark walnut display stands on either side of the room. Grey marble slabs, veined with blue, covered the floor. Everything was spotless, including the doorman named Sheeks, who stood in front of her with one eyebrow raised.

"You are here for what?" Sheeks asked.

He stood three hands taller than her. His size towered over her, not only in height but in girth. The gray hair rising chaotically from his head testified to how long he had been on this world. Thin scars rippled across his neck and hands, coating bulging muscles and calloused hands. His body showed signs of hard work. He wore a white and yellow coat over a pristine white tunic. Black pants that ended mid-calf completed his ensemble, giving him a foreign look.

She felt a little out of place in her simple dress. It was clean and serviceable but worn from travel. An overly broad belt that she had found in the Eisenvard storerooms tied the look together. She appeared like a girl who tried to dress like a boy but failed. She didn't care. She liked her belt because all of her weapon sheaths fit it.

"I'm here to work with Apprentice Miller. This is supposed to be arranged already." She looked from side to side. "I gather you have some sort of library?"

She didn't know it was possible for Sheeks's eyebrows to raise even further.

"Oh, indeed," he replied, "It's not something that is commonly requested though. As a matter of fact, I've never even heard of an apprentice being allowed in that room."

Chamise didn't want this doorman to know too much. Miller was going to teach magic, and that could put him at risk if the wrong White Hand master heard of it. She knew that she and Miller would be investigating Takers tonight. Chamise didn't want the slightest word of their true activities to be public.

Chamise replied back, her voice became cutting, full of authority. "I'm sorry. Are you the lord here? Are your decisions law in this house?"

Sheeks shook his head side-to-side, scowling. "This is The Garden. We don't have a lord. This place is governed by the sponsors who pay a lot of gold for the privilege. The day to day activities of the Garden are orchestrated by the heads of rooms. I am the head of the library, so unless you have a group of sponsors to tell me otherwise, I am essentially a lord for your purposes, at least here, in the library."

Chamise smiled back at him. An entrenched servant was one thing she understood. "How about Goddess Phyllicitus? Is that a good enough sponsor?"

The unimpressed look on his face spoke volumes. Chamise suddenly became unsure of her footing. "That's one. Do you have another twenty or so?"

She felt anger begin to rear its ugly head. It was almost impossible to find new sources of magical knowledge in this world and now one was a short walk away from her. She wasn't going to let a librarian stop her. She stepped closer to him, her scowl growing deeper.

Then Sheeks abruptly broke out into laughter. "You look so

serious! Relax! I'm not stopping you. I'm just having a little fun."

"Fun?"

"Fun. It's something you need a little more of, if you don't mind me saying. I'm just keeping you busy until Apprentice Miller comes down. He is upstairs with another appointment. I'll bring both of you to the Oracle Pit once he gets here."

The name 'Oracle Pit' sparked interest in Chamise. It seemed to promise secrets and magic.

Before she could respond, Miller walked into the room. His eyes were bloodshot with fatigue. He had awoken early this morning.

Miller waved at her. "Good morning."

She smiled back at him. Excitement began to grow as Sheeks motioned them to follow along. Today would be a magical day, literally.

"You look tired."

"I've been up late moving Brita."

"Brita?" Chamise asked, trying to remember if that was that the possessed person he had spoken about earlier.

"You brought her here last night? Just the two of you?"

"No, I brought her here this morning. I started moving her things last night."

Chamise frowned in suspicion.

"I thought she was at the New Pony. That isn't very far."

"It isn't. I had to wait for the other masters to leave."

She didn't understand. There was no understanding these White Hands, she thought to herself, they didn't make any sense.

Miller continued, "Why are you so curious about the simplest things? It wasn't magic. We didn't need a parade of masters and spell crafters to move Brita the sixteen blocks between the New Pony and here. All we had to do was to wait for the city to go to sleep. Then we put her in a coach, locked the doors, and drove her here. It was pretty easy."

"Can I ask a sensitive question?" She didn't pause for an

answer, "are you two, you know, close?"

"Don't worry about romance if that's what you mean. I knew her a few years ago. She got taken though."

Miller couldn't find the words to describe Brita's fate. He simply shook his head sadly.

Chamise felt relieved. She wondered at the feeling. She should never feel better that someone had been taken. She had to admit that a little jealousy had found its way into her heart. She nodded her head in acknowledgment. "Bringing her directly over here was a good idea. It was simple. I like it."

Miller looked at her quizzically. He didn't understand where these questions were coming from. "We've got some work to do."

He turned to Sheeks. "We're ready. Please lead on."

Sheeks offered a slight bow, then turned to lead them away. walking down a wooden paneled corridor, they passed carvings of leaves and trees that stood against man-sized reliefs of painted nature scenes. At the end of the hall, Sheeks opened a door, revealing a narrow staircase. He motioned them forward. He led them down a single set of stairs then exited. They arrived in a library. Walls of bookshelves occupied a long room with a high ceiling. Dozens of candles burned atop man-sized candle holders. Two long tables occupied the center of the eighty-foot long room. Sheeks continued leading them onward toward another door. He used a brass key to open the door. Leaving the door, he walked into the other room.

"Welcome to the Oracle Pit." A shallow pit took up most of the new room. It stretched along its center. Thirty feet long and fifteen feet wide, it lay surrounded by long wooden benches that faced inward. The center of the room dropped away an arm's length to another kind of floor. Chamise had never seen its like. Swirls and designs filled the lower floor, a mass of chaos and order, all intermixed. It took her breath away.

"What is this? Some kind of theater?"

She paused to take the shapes and patterns. Her heart fluttered as if the room had just spoken to her. She felt it was trying to tell her something, but she couldn't understand what it was saying. She became so engrossed with the pattern she didn't notice Brita sitting alone on a bench at the opposite side of the room.

"It has that effect on people," Brita said to Chamise. "I've been staring at it all morning. It feels like it's trying to tell me something. If it wasn't for these little constraints, I think I would climb down there and roll in it." She held up her hands, showing the silver manacles and slight chain that bound her to the bench she sat upon.

They weren't thick enough to stop anyone from breaking them.

Chamise looked at the silver bindings closely. She could feel power moving through them. Then she glanced at the floor pattern. No power, no flows, no magic. "Can you feel the pattern too? Even with your…" She paused, unsure how to phrase it, "being taken and all."

Brita offered a wry smile. "Yes, even with my little challenges. Actually, when I came into this room, my friends became quieter." She motioned at her head. "I'm more than happy to stay here all day, just for the peace of it."

Miller was surprised. "Really? The Takers have quieted?"

"If they are experiencing what I am, there is no wonder. I've been here an hour, and I'm thinking clearer than I have in months."

"Have you tried to initiate contact with the Takers?"

"Why would I do that? I finally have a little peace and quiet. I can feel them, they haven't left. They are just quiet."

"Don't you find that interesting though?" Miller asked, intent on following up on this.

"It would be interesting if you could figure out how to get them to go away."

Brita took a moment to consider his words before continuing, "Did you hear me? I just spoke about them. They didn't interfere."

Chamise looked back at Miller. "What is this thing?" She

asked, pointing to the floor below.

"It's an ancient form of magic, different from what we use today. It was common back before the gods of man came into the world. Back then, priests of the First Gods could fashion things of power using their own techniques. From what Mistress Aileen tells me, there was once a high priest of Phyllicitus named Stevenson who had an interest in this art. He amassed a collection of books and studied how to craft this. He and his followers were successful at making three of these types of things."

"What happened with them?"

"Not much. They succeeded at three and failed at twenty-four. The last failure was so catastrophic that Stevenson swore it off. He said it was too dangerous."

Chamise had to ask. "Do you have the books?"

"Sadly, no. They are on site though. I think Mistress Aileen has them set aside under the Garden's protection."

"I know this sounds entirely too simple and obvious, but if we could use these patterns to quiet the Takers, could we also not use this art to kill them?"

Miller shook his head. "We have no idea how that could be done."

"We could at least build a big house then put enough of these patterns down so that the taken people could have a life."

"I don't think we have enough knowledge to make decisions like that, at least right now."

"What? Are you going to wait until you have every detail in place before you try?"

"No, but I'll wait until I have enough details to understand the risk. Remember when I said that using these patterns has been tried in the past? One mistake removed an entire city from the map. Let's not bungle this."

She nodded her head, the excitement starting to fade.

"An entire city?" Chamise asked, her voice growing softer.

"Five thousand people, gone. One of Stevenson's followers thought that a new pattern would bring food and health to a small city. She was wrong. Even today, all that remains is dead earth and a hole with a pattern at the bottom of it. So, let's stick to the magic lessons today, shall we?" Miller offered a smile in apology.

Sheeks spoke up. "On that note, I'll be going. If you need anything, I'll be in the library, just outside that door." He offered a shallow bow, turned, and walked away, leaving the three of them alone.

Miller sucked in some air, preparing to start his planned lesson. Gazing over at Brita, he had an idea.

"I know you've been eagerly awaiting some crafting lessons. There are a few other skills you will need in order to succeed. You might not immediately grasp why they are important but trust me, they are."

"Skills. Got it." Chamise spoke up in agreement. Her eyes focused on him as if they were ready to drink in every piece of information he could offer.

Miller began walking toward Brita sitting at the end of the room. "And given these are skills instead of spells, I'd like you to try to follow along as well."

She motioned to her forehead out of habit. She still didn't want to refer to the Friends. "Is that wise?"

"I don't know. I was thinking about it last night. Perhaps one of the problems is that the victims of these Takers simply don't have the skills to fight them off. I don't think my lessons will be harmful to you or anyone else if that is what you are worried about."

"These are necromancer skills?" Brita asked a hint of fear causing her voice to tremble.

"No. It is more of a combination of old caster practices, religious meditation, and clear-headed thinking. Our order has been on this earth for three thousand years, in one form or another. We use a lot of very old techniques in our art."

Brita nodded.

Chamise spoke up. Her voice was eager, driven. "Let's get started then. The day isn't getting any longer."

"Right. Here we go," Miller began, "First off, there are these things we call The Disciplines. They are taught to apprentices early in their training. Essentially, the masters use these skills to help speed up learning, and sometimes, to remove apprentices who can't learn easily."

"Remove?" Chamise asked.

"Typically, those early apprentices will be traded to other masters who don't demand as much learning. Some masters have a less deliberative approach to their art."

Chamise shook her head in confusion. "Less deliberative?"

"You know, like when the Free Mages learn magic, they simply learn the spell. The memorize and repeat. Some White Hand masters continue to teach this to their apprentices. Most have moved on from that approach though."

Miller shook his head, thinking about some of the worse fates of apprentices he had known. The most unfortunate of them were traded away to Master Hermagon's cabal. They were never seen again.

"In any case, that kind of thing doesn't apply to either of you. We are going to concentrate on The Discipline of Vision. It's actually fairly easy at first, but it gets more difficult the longer you practice it. Let me show you."

Miller reached into his pocket and removed an apple. It was bright red, with a single leaf jutting from a mangled stem. He bent down and placed it on a bench where both Chamise and Brita could see it clearly.

"What I want you to do is look at the apple. Remember every detail about it. And later, after I take it out of your sight, you will describe it to me in detail."

"A memory test?" Chamise asked.

"In a way. It's a memory test, and a test of how much detail you may recall. This will be even more challenging since there are two of you."

Brita bent her head indicating confusion.

"When one person recites what they remember, it may cause another person to incorporate that into their memories, essentially filling in a perceived gap. The truth is that all of our minds are susceptible to inventing things on its own. The imagination will supply details that don't exist just so the world makes more sense to us. It's a human thing. You can't get around it without a lot of training. That is what The Vision discipline is all about, recognizing when the mind supplies details that are not there, or when it removes details when they are there."

"Why would the mind remove details."

Miller lowered his voice. "There are things in this world that the mind is not prepared to see, or to admit to."

Brita nodded. "Horrors."

A moment of quiet descended on the room. Another moment passed, and another.

Finally, Miller spoke up, cutting through the silence. "Just look at the apple for an hour. No talking with each other, no looking at anything else but the apple. Then we'll take a break and get something to eat. Then we'll talk about what we remember about the apple."

"Then what?" Chamise asked.

"Then we switch to pears."

Miller stepped away from the apple, walking to the other side of the room. He gazed down at the pattern, immediately feeling its pull. Reaching down to his large belt pouch, he opened it and pulled out a small book. Aileen had given it to him after his last visit. It was filled with short notes and scribbled drawings left over from years ago when she tried to study the patterns. She had done a lot of the background reading and tied several observations and even some theories. There was precious little that helped him now.

To pass the time while Chamise and Brita went about their task, he began to use The Vision discipline as well. Staring down at the pattern, he tried to commit it to memory. He stared at the notebook, finding that easier to process and recall. It was odd how the pattern could be so clear one moment. The details would flee from his memories within seconds of looking away, leaving only broad outlines of the high-level features. By the next day, he knew he would be unable to remember much more than the vaguest description of it.

Why? Why did it flee from the mind so quickly?

The pattern wasn't magic. There was a disturbing lack of magical flows around it as if it acted to calm the world it touched.

Or did it drink the world around it? The thought intrigued him. Could this pattern be a flow, but not only within this world? He membered his short trip between-the-worlds. There were patterns there as well. The entire concept of magical flows was just a model of a magical system that no one had ever proven existed. The entire art of spellcasting depended on people with natural abilities being able to use this model and manipulate the flows of magic. Could these carved patterns be doing the same thing? Just flowing between different worlds?

He shook his head at the complexity of it. But was it complex? If a pattern controlled the flow of magic, would that not indicate that people with magical talents were somehow related to these patterns? If so, how would that even work?

He continued to stare down at the floor, losing track of time as he thought through the ramifications of his idea. It seemed elegant in its simplicity. While it felt right, he had no information to test it with.

"Can we eat now?" Brita asked.

Miller looked up.

"Yes," Chamise added. "I've been staring at this apple so long I'm starting to want to eat it."

"Sorry. I lost track of time. After you gain some more skill with the discipline, that sort of thing will happen to you too."

"Not sure I want that skill." Brita

"Neither was I. You'll get used to it. Let's go eat."

OUT IN THE OPEN

Three men sat around a broad table. Morning sunlight shone down upon their tired faces. The oldest of them looked over at his companions with drooping eyes.

"That was a night, ay?"

"It was surely that." His first companion muttered back to the old man, holding his head above the table through a combination of sheer will and an arm propped up against an adjacent wall. The other companion didn't answer. His face lay peacefully asleep on the table.

"Maybe that last round was a little too much for you two. You both need to learn to handle your liquor."

His companion managed a nod. He was still conscious somehow.

All three of them were in grave danger and didn't know it.

Master December, necromancer, wizard, and murderer, sat two tables from them. He had dried his hair and managed to remove most of the river water. The stink hadn't fully left him. All kinds of disgusting thing filled the sewers tonight, vomit, feces, dead rats, and a few piles of debris that defied description.

It didn't matter though. The three men were tired, drunk, and defenseless. They had life energy available for the plucking. It wasn't a question of whether December would suck their lives away, it was just a question as to how much he could leave them with, if any.

December could feel Phyllicitus's presence in Home's Hearth. He felt her influence everywhere he walked in the city. If she discovered that he was here she could easily destroy him, as weak as he was. He knew that he needed to get strong quickly. If Easter and the rest of the masters were in Home's Hearth, then he suspected that the priests were looking for necromancy. As trivial as the priest's talents were, there were many of them. Whatever he did, it needed to be subtle and quick.

He didn't feel like being subtle. There has been enough subtlety for his taste, thank you. He had been living off the remnants of animal souls for days. Those souls were not very stable in death. The magic could dissipate any moment, leaving him empty of power.

He gave a single dry laugh. If Phyllicitus had a problem with him, he might as well get it over with. There would be a reckoning in any case.

Holding up two fingers, he signaled the innkeeper to come over. Within moments, a graying man wearing a stained apron walked over to him, a smile on his face and a mug of small beer in his hand. With only three other customers this early in the morning, he looked glad to have the business.

"We'll be boiling some eggs soon. Interested?" The innkeeper was always trying to make a sale.

Master December nodded back to him. "Sure. Go ahead and boil three for me. I'll take one for lunch." For a moment, December regretted what was about to happen. It lasted long enough for the innkeeper to turn his back. When he did, December reached out and touched him at a bare elbow.

The old innkeeper stumbled, catching himself by reaching

out to an empty table. He tried to suck air into his lungs while he held his chest tightly with his right hand, as if trying to force his lungs to move. Two heartbeats later he collapsed on the floor.

The three drunken men turned in their chairs, alarm registering on two of their faces. The third looked up from the table with bleary eyes.

December stood up and shouted, feigning surprise.

"Help! Someone, Help him!"

The old man stood up and stumbled toward him, leaving his two friends behind. The night's drinking hadn't fully worn off yet. "What happened?" The old man said.

Smiling back, December motioned to the innkeeper on the floor. "This happened."

December reached out and touched him as well. Within seconds the old man joined the innkeeper on the floor gasping for air. They squirmed in pain, grabbing their chests in an attempt to put air into their lungs.

He could feel the soul energy leaving the two bodies. December cast his flows outward, trying to harvest as much soul energy as he could. He didn't like to waste souls. They were, after all, precious.

There was more to harvest tonight. He walked over to the other two drunken companions. It was easy to open his flows and drink from the two fools. Even sober they would be defenseless. Now, full of liquor, they were simply bags of blood and soul energy. December didn't even need to sever their heart channels to do it. He drank from their souls and the two men felt every second of it. They quickly joined their friend on the floor. Four people now lay on the floor, gasping. He drank them in. Their life power was his.

Then the kitchen door opened. A woman sprang out of the kitchen, knife in hand.

She screamed at December. "What are you doing?"

Leaping forward, she swung the heavy kitchen knife at his face. She never even got close. Her feet disobeyed her, stumbling left and right chaotically across the room. The woman began to scream in fear. Her cries were loud screeching things. December smiled. Terror was normally an aphrodisiac to him.

But tonight, it wasn't.

For a moment, he looked across the room at the screaming woman, at the prone bodies on the floor.

"What's the point?" December muttered. Disgusted with his own weakness, he released the heart bindings and stopped his flows. He had collected plenty of soul energy and had no need for more.

He didn't need to kill them. At least, that's what he told himself.

December walked out of the inn trying to understand what had just happened. Was it Phyllicitus that made him merciful? Was it her power? Or did he just reach the point where he just didn't care anymore?

Thinking for a few blocks, he came to the conclusion that it was probably both. Either way, he had a task to do, and some revenge to seek out.

But he was having a hard time caring. Either way, there were things to do, and a young Free Mage to see.

Shadows surrounded Faust as he waited. The shadows didn't obscure him. Instead they mixed with the dusk and the hazy outline of the spirit's form to completely hide him from sight, even from those with a talent to see those from beyond the final door. His body lay rotting in a grave weeks to the northwest, but his soul, the thing that made him who he was, was free in the world and it had a mission.

Faust didn't mind being given these kinds of tasks. He could almost admit that he enjoyed things that reminded him of being alive. He felt comfortable with this kind of work. Collecting knowledge, sneaking through dark streets, and hiding from sight were all skills of his trade. He thought he would miss being alive, but he didn't. The half-life of an untethered soul suited him. That thought should have frightened him. He knew what doom awaited him beyond the final door. It didn't make Faust afraid though. It simply gave him a sense of purpose. That's all Faust ever really wanted anyway, a purpose.

He watched drunken revelers parading through the street, confident in their safety, full of life. The streets were safe. The beer was excellent. What could go wrong?

Shadows kept him company has he continued his watch, gazing out of the narrow alley to the street beyond. New Pony Inn stood across the street. He could feel magic emanating from the building. It threatened to both repel him away, and to pull him in at the same time. The building wanted to welcome him, perhaps devour him.

For a moment he considered going into the New Pony, if only to satisfy his curiosity. The sense of magic in the air remained a novel feeling. He could never sense it when he was alive. Somehow, now that he had passed from the realm of the living, magic became simpler to perceive, to notice in everyday things.

He wondered what would happen if he did go inside. Before he made up his mind, the door opened. A young man with long red hair walked out of the inn. The man turned to look around, searching for other people out late, before setting out down the street.

The stink of dark magic came from the red-haired man. He was obviously one of the White Hand. Carefully, as the apprentice necromancer might be talented enough to notice him, Faust fell in behind. Darting from shadow to shadow, he followed.

Franz moved purposefully down the street, moving past open doors and revelers until he came to the main market square. The streets stood deserted this late at night. Stars offered a small touch of dim light to the streets, adding their glows to the lamps hung at each street corner.

Franz stopped to gaze about him. Waiting until he was sure the streets were deserted. He turned and walked away from the deserted market, then turned left onto a deserted side street. Faust could hear words that the apprentice spoke, words of power.

Curious, Faust came closer. This new young apprentice had just become interesting to him. For a moment he wished he had the talent of magic, if only to know the spell this apprentice had just cast.

Then he thought again. No. He was better off as he was, a ghost. At least he was useful this way. Before, during his life, had had been a monster.

☐

OATHBOUND

A crowd of forty Eisenvard awaited Chamise's return. She smiled as she walked into their midst. Then her smile faltered. The men, the Eisenvard, looked at her with hate on their faces. Each one walked away from her as she passed through their midst. She knew only half of them. She wondered where the other half had come from.

"What's going on?"

Schaller walked up to her. The crowd parted around him until there were only two of them within arm's reach. The crowd had retreated ten paces. It looked like a dueling circle without steel. There were weapons though, she could tell. Hate and fear could always be weapons.

The entrance of the keep towered above them. Torchlight cut through the darkness, sending shadows in every direction away from its grand opening. Chamise didn't like the feel of this, not one bit. In the torch-lit night, the entrance looked like something had crawled up from below and opened its giant maw to swallow her.

"Where have you been?" Schaller asked.

She bit back a sharp retort, looking across them empty ground between them. He wore a heavy tabbard, its white cloth emblazoned with the old Eisenvard emblem. She could hear armor rustling from beneath the folds of his clothing. The old emblem had been banned in the city by the goddess herself. She thought that He must have a point to make if he dared wear that symbol openly. The symbol always brought thoughts of her mother with it, and not the good ones.

Now the symbol stood before her, proud and traitorous.

Chamise narrowed her eyes. Rage began to creep into her voice. Some things would never change.

"You know where I've been. Where have you been? And what is all this?" She waved at the men surrounding her.

"I do know where you've been. You've been at the lust gardens with your necromancer boy. What little deeds have you been doing tonight?" His voice was tainted with malice.

"What are your playing at, Schaller? Do you want to go one on one with me?" She marched closer to him until her face was just below his chin. "I'll plant my boot so far up your arse you won't be able to use the privy for a month."

"Don't act all high and mighty with me. You've been laying with a necromancer. You've stained your soul as well as ours. You're a fool to return here."

Quick as lightning, she struck out. Her fist instantly slammed upward, smashing into Schaller's jaw. His head rocked upwards and back, he swayed, then his entire body collapsed onto the lawn.

"You dare accuse me of what?" She screamed her defiance in his face as he tried to shake off the force of her blow. All he could mutter was "the way, the codex, the rules." His words didn't connect in a sensible way. He was trying to find justification, just like the Eisenvard had done when they had burned her mother.

Her last bit of restraint snapped.

"The rules? The codex? What do you know about such

things? You don't know a thrice-cursed thing. The Eisenvard has been making up rules for no good reason for so long, you've all forgotten what the original purpose was. That's why Phyllicitus turned her back on you. It isn't because she was wrong. It's because you're broken."

The crowd of Eisenvard glowered at her. She saw short red hair and a pointed goatee, then she stabbed her index finger at the man.

"Reegan!" She stepped away from Schaller, allowing him to crawl back to his feet. Marching toward the man who played Center at every Nets game she had ever won, she grabbed him by the collar and pulled him forward. He seemed unsure, unwilling to commit to a larger conflict.

She continued to pull him. "You try to follow the ancient ways! The ancient ways left this world long ago." She shouted at both Schaller and the crowd as they moved across the open circle, moving back into the crowd on the opposite side. The crowd split before her. They didn't walk far away, only breaking far enough for her to walk through.

She continued to pull Reegan forward. He tried to pull back. She screamed and forced him onward. She pulled him up the gray stone stairs into the main entrance. The crowd of Eisenvard followed close behind. In their hearts, they stood balanced between curiosity and rage.

She entered the Eisenvard keep. Pulling Reegan along, she turned the corner into the hall. The mass of Eisenvard followed behind.

"Look at these!" She commanded, gesturing at the stone commandments that decorated the long hallway. Reegan pulled back against her, but she moved forward and swept his leg out from under him. He spilled on the entryway floor. Schaller staggered into the entrance as she moved her hand about, pointing ad the different credos carved into the wall.

She spun, facing the crowd. They stopped as one. She had produced her mace. It was held menacingly in her hands.

She screamed at the crowd. "Do you want to follow the

ancient ways? Do you want to reclaim what it means to be Eisenvard?" She pointed words carved into a stone tile. "This tells us to guard the roads and protect the travelers! Have you done that lately? It was written three hundred years ago!"

She took ten more steps and pointed at another tile. This one was darker, featured a crack through its center that testified to its age. "Do you see this one? We don't even know how old it is. It tells us to gift food to abandoned children. Have you done that lately?"

Schaller walked to the front of the crowd. "We know every one of these. They are engraved on our heart. What is your point."

She took ten more steps down the hallway and used her mace to point to all of the remaining tiles. "My point? Do you see all of the rest of these tiles? They were all made less than two hundred years ago. They were made when the order was exiled from the north. These tiles, these rules, are filled with anger and hate against those that exiled them. Do you actually believe that the witches of the north were influential enough to expel an army? No. The Jarls and the warriors of the north had grown angry with us. That is how we were exiled. It wasn't magic, it was stupidity. That's the reason we were pushed out of the north. That's the reason we were pushed away from Phyllicitus. If we had continued with our original ways instead of adding all of this nonsense to our credo, we would still be there today."

Schaller spit his words back at her. "So your solution is to lie with the necromancers?"

"No. My solution is to fight against the Takers, and damn your corrupted ways. If I cared about your ancient wisdom, I would have done this!"

She lifted her mace and smashed it down into the wall. Light-brown stone exploded into the hallway, sending stone chips into the crowd of Eisenvard. Dust coated her as the ruins of the tile fell to the floor, shattering into two dozen pieces. She screamed the Eisenvard battle cry and began to destroy the tiles on either side. Chamise didn't care what ancient words had been scrawled on the tile's surface, or what historical figure the author was. She began destroying everything that was less than three centuries old, everything she could reach.

Her mace smashed into another tile, breaking it from the wall if five pieces, each shattering as it struck the stone floor. She felt more alive and more free with every shattered tile. Another tile exploded nearby. She looked over and saw Reegan next to her. He nodded over and smiled.

"We've been off course for a long time now. I've felt it in my heart." Reegan said, "It's time to go back to the old ways and reclaim who we should be. Enough of all this. For too long, we have been adrift in the wilderness. Phyllicitus didn't take our cause, we surrendered it long ago. I want it back."

Others in the crowd nodded. They reached for daggers, for tools, for anything heavy and metal they could find. Eisenvard began to slowly walk into the hallway. They searched the walls for the newer rules, then pulled them off, tossing them aside like so much waste.

"What are you doing?"

Schaller yelled at them. Chamise turned from the wall to stare over at him. "We're doing what should have been done a century ago. We are cleansing ourselves. We are reclaiming who we are."

"Who we are? How do you know that? You aren't old enough to know who you are, let alone us."

She gestured at the thirty Eisenvard warriors who were busily removing tiles from the wall. "I know it because I can see it right in front of me. You need to make a decision, Schaller. Are you willing to reclaim what the Eisenvard were before or do you want to keep the stains of the last three centuries burned into you forever? No matter what you decide, the rest of us have made our decision."

Schaller looked around him. There were only four other men standing with him. He looked at those men and didn't like what he saw. These were the cruelest of the remaining Eisenvard, the most black-hearted souls among them. He shook he head, not liking the company he found himself in.

Chamise turned away and resumed her demolition of the wall. After a minute of hesitation, Schaller walked into the hallway, and with a heavy heart, began to tear out the tiles.

###

"I'm telling you, something with Franz is off. He and Darjeeling are up to something." Faust said.

"Up to something? Like what?"

Aileen leaned forward in her chair. She lifted a glass decanter of wine from the table and poured the bright rose-colored liquid into her dark green glass. The small room was crowded with the three of them. Miller looked on from across the table. He missed the luxury of the Garden, but this place was more private.

Faust replied, his spirit whispering from the beyond. Only those with magical talents could ever hear them, and only those well trained in the ways of the dead would understand the words. They echoed from the beyond, from the near realm of death. "I didn't get close enough to find out. Franz has some necromancer sight. If I get close, he will see me. Darjeeling? No, I'm not even going to try that one."

Aileen finished the pour. She grasped her wine glass and gulped a large serving of wine, not taking time to enjoy the drink as she usually did. Then she refilled it. She scowled across the table.

"Let's say you are right." Miller began, wondering if here were too eager to find something wrong with Franz. Miller knew that he could easily offer a biased judgment if he didn't gather all the information he could.

"I am," Faust replied.

Miller nodded, conceding the point. "You're right. They're up to something. What are we supposed to do about it? It might be something in our interest. It might be something completely unrelated to our goals. We need more information before we make any accusations."

Aileen nodded. Her voice didn't sound convinced as she described how Easter supported Darjeeling. "I've got it on the highest authority that Darjeeling isn't acting against us."

"Darjeeling is insane. I don't trust anything he does." Faust replied. "I'm dead and I won't even trust him. How confident are you?"

"Not very," Aileen replied as she poured her third glass of wine.

"Did you know…" she began, pausing for dramatic effect, "that when you become a master it becomes more difficult to get drunk? I'm not sure why. Easter says it's because that part of you that loved such things is dying."

Miller raised an eyebrow at that. "Becoming a master kills joy?"

"That's what all the evidence says."

"What does that have to do with Franz and Darjeeling?"

"Not much. It just means that these powers can change us, and not for the better."

They paused for a moment, letting the words soak in.

"Again, what do we do about it? Especially when we don't even know what it is." Miller said, emphasizing the word 'it' as if the word had a greater meaning.

"I think its time to bring in some help. I know the areas in town that Franz visits most often. Can we get some street people to go through there, then report if they see Franz or Darjeeling doing something?"

Aileen shook her head. "Not if Darjeeling is around. He'll pick up on that in no time. We should just assume that he reads everyone's mind continuously."

"Not everyone," Miller said. He was getting a bad feeling about his next idea. "The Eisenvard have disciplines. If you give them some potions to improve their capabilities, they could probably do it."

"Probably?" Aileen asked.

"Probably. This might be a bad idea, but it's all I have right now."

Aileen nodded. "That makes the decision easier. If we only have one idea, we go with that one." She gestured to Miller. "Reach out to your Eisenvard friend and see if she can recruit a few more to help us. Faust, can you give Miller the locations and times where we can expect Franz?"

"Sure. But what do we do if one of them gets detected? Darjeeling might not be able to read their minds if we give them potions of discipline, but he might notice that he can't read their minds." Miller asked.

Faust replied with a chuckle. "I don't think we need to worry about that. Given Darjeeling's past, I think he will probably just kill the Eisenvard then pull information from their risen spirits."

Miller waved his hands back and forth, hoping to push the idea away. "We can't do that. These are people we are talking about."

Aileen responded curtly. She had little love for the Eisenvard as a whole, and no concern for them individually. "No, these are Eisenvard. Set it up. If you don't want to feel guilty then just blame it all on me, even though it was your idea. Trust me, if you give them a cause, they will be standing in line for the honor of dying for it."

RETURN

In shadows, the necromancer navigated the streets intent on his dark task. He approached the open gates of the Eisenvard compound, intent on his prey. As he came closer, he opened a casting channel sending power into himself, heightening his alertness, making his perceptions sharper.

She as definitely here. He could smell her in the wind. He also felt a tingle of channeled forces. She was a Free Mage. She could be preparing for him, lying in wait.

He smiled. Master December liked the idea of a competent adversary. He hadn't expected any resistance from her. Her spell crafting was basic and unfocused. Her passions controlled her every move, making her easy to anticipate.

The spells being crafted within these gates were new. They felt undisciplined and imperfect, but effective. There was a pull from the magic that sent mental passions inward toward a goal, no, to a vision. Master December thought it felt familiar. It felt like someone was manipulating minds or influencing people with raw magic. He nodded as he recognized the flows that passed around him. Only a strong casting would reach this far.

Pushing every other thought out of his awareness, he concentrated on the flows. He wanted to see her skills in action. So far, the flows were ragged, inefficient, and somewhat wasteful of power. But if she improved, they could become focused, sharp, and beautiful.

He shook his head, sadly contemplating her fate. She would never live to conquer the art of mind control. Chamise would have been talented, perhaps even enough to recruit as an apprentice. She was too old now for that now, too embedded in her ways.

Plus, she was Eisenvard, and she had stabbed him. Her fate was sealed at this point.

But it had been a well-executed betrayal. December had to admit that, even if only to himself. If he had met her earlier, then he could have done something with her. It was really too bad, he reflected, now it was time to kill her.

December stepped forward to walk through the doorway. Wrapping shadows around himself along the way, he blended into the night and became harder and harder to see. He could see the courtyard perfectly. Men were lined up in front of the building. They formed a chain. Each man in the chain passed back chunks of shattered stone. December wondered why they chose to do construction this late at night.

Then he stepped into the courtyard.

A bell rang to the side of him. It rang out clearly in the night. It was a subtle thing, loud enough to be noticed, but barely. December turned to look where the sound came from. A brass bell the size of his thumb hung on a small cord. It hung tied to the branches of a ragged green bush that had gone wild.

Something else about the bell caused his hackles to rise. He could feel it, magic and nervous energy combined. The energy flirted with some kind of channel that he didn't recognize.

It only took a moment before he realized what that channel did. More bell chimes sounded from around the wall's perimeter. The channel had been sent from this small bell and been heard by the others. They responded with their own chimes. The small sounds grew in number and volume.

The line of men noticed the sounds and began looking around. The system of small bells sounded an alert, and the Eisenvard began to investigate.

He could feel another channeling touch his skin. It came from all directions, from the bells themselves. He felt his shroud of darkness dissipate, exposing his presence to the Eisenvard. They were not happy to see him.

The bells had sounded the alarm, and now their enchantments acted to defend the compound.

Someone in the past few centuries had prepared. They had set up a little trap using small magics that were both minor and hard to find. Now he faced a growing crowd of Eisenvard across the courtyard. Three of the Eisenvard began walking toward him wearing scowls on their faces.

He could reach out from here and pinch their lives away, cutting their souls from their bodies. He thought about channeling simple magic to separating mind from their hearts, thus ending their pitiful little lives.

Then he thought better of it. A better move would be to retreat from the confrontation. He could return later if it were necessary. There wasn't any need for a fight over a stupid dagger. He wanted his blade back, and the Free Mage had it in her possession or at least knew where it was.

Then Master December recognized what was going on. He was falling under the sway of Phyllicitus. Her magic permeated the entire town of Home's Hearth. It softened rage, quieted anger, and dulled the knife of hate. It was mind control. More subtle than his magical channeling, but similar in many ways.

The Eisenvard continued to walk closer. They were thirty steps away from him. The easy path would be to retreat through the gates then blend into the darkened streets.

Mind control. He had used magic channels to control the thoughts of others before. Such spells were harsh. They battered down the victim's sense of identity and substituted their own will. Phyllicitus's control was different. It felt soft. It urged kindness. December didn't like mind control to be used on him. He wasn't a victim.

In a heartbeat, he reached into his own emotions, calming them, then cutting them off from his logical mind. The mastery of disciplines allowed him to separate his thinking from his feeling. Within three heartbeats he was disconnected from any feelings at all. He still felt the call of Phyllicitus. It urged him to retreat, to avoid conflict. He no longer cared. He would not be controlled.

It was time for a demonstration. He would not be toyed with, goddess or no goddess.

Snapping his fingers, December released a channel of power. It whipped out, disconnected from his will and control, then cut through the three Eisenvard men. The one closest to December blinked, then collapsed onto the grass. Another grabbed his chest in pain and went to his knees struggling to breathe. The third rocked back as the lash of magic went through his chest. He did not fall. His eyes went wide with shock.

A battle cry rang out from the doorway leading to the Eisenvard keep. Twelve men streamed out from the door, sprinting toward December. Only three held weapons, but their rage alone was enough to kill. December saw the smaller form of Chamise step out of the doorway as well, turning to the side in an effort to avoid being trampled by those behind her.

He had a moment to decide what to do. Should he cut down Chamise? She had begun channeling some sort of nature crafting. He wasn't worried. He was more worried about the armed Eisenvard reaching him.

Things would get interesting if they laid hands on him. December had died more than a dozen times before. He did not worry about his own death. Another death would delay the recovery of his dagger though. December didn't want his instrument to be even farther out of reach when he returned from beyond the final door.

Suddenly the grass beneath his feet began to grow. He

watched as the entire field grew a hands-breadth, then two. The stalks of grass moved like a million grass tentacles. Each long blade of green reached out toward him, trying to grasp, to hold, to take.

Snapping his fingers, December channeled fire. A rolling wave of flame sprung out from the ground where he stood, washing over the courtyard and transforming the living sea of grass into so much ash. Whatever Chamise had planned burned away into smoke.

Chamise wasn't finished with her surprises though. The wave of flame passed over, and harmlessly through the charging Eisenvard. Her protective channeling held against the fire, diffused across the courtyard as it was.

The Eisenvard reached him. A broad man, bald and muscular, stabbed at December with a long broad-bladed knife. December snapped his hand down, touching, turning aside the knife. He channeled his flows, hooking the attacker's souls into his own life channel. He snapped it away, breaking the men's connections with their souls. The man fell, spent like empty husks.

A metal rod struck December's skull. He could not see if it was a fireplace poker or a blacksmithing rod. The blow would have crushed any other man's skull. Enchantments activated to preserve his skull, though the force of the blow spun December into the air. The third Eisenvard, a tall ruddy-faced warrior, reached out to grab his leg and hold him in place.

December screamed and released the spell he had prepared hours ago. It was one of the more difficult spells that he had learned, and it was fantastic for escaping situations like this. Streams of magic poured from his body, grabbing the physicality of what made him real. It took what anchored December in the physical world and moved it across the line between life and death, bypassing the final door for only a few minutes. It would be long enough to escape.

He called out in the other realms, commanding his dagger to respond, to announce its location. There was only silence.

Chamise didn't have it. It wasn't here.

Chamise wasn't reaching for any daggers. She was struggling to figure out how to defend against an enemy that reality could not touch. Nothing she had studied as a Free Mage had prepared her for this. Eisenvard fell upon him, uselessly stabbing and striking, only to see their weapons pass through him as if he were made of smoke.

He could only stay this way for a few short minutes. Even that would cost him greatly, draining magic and emptying his flows.

The dagger was not here. There was no longer any point to this battle. He ceased to be amused. December turned toward the wall that surrounded the courtyard. He walked directly toward its brick surface, then through it. He kept walking into the darkness of Home's Hearth leaving the Eisenvard behind.

It had been surprisingly easy to escape that melee. December pondered on what it meant to battle in a city controlled by Phyllicitus. Her power would make it easier to survive such encounters even if it made it more difficult to start them.

Just because someone could survive did not mean they could present a threat. December began to think about how he could strike his enemies down yet leave them alive.

He planned how he would leave Chamise in pain and madness.

Master December moved through Home's Hearth, passing through houses, tree trunks, and any other object that stood in his way. He enjoyed the feeling of being, yet not being at the same time. In this state, he was as close to being dead as he could get without passing through the final door. This feeling of being separate from the world and apart from its denizens gave him comfort.

He had an opportunity to think as he passed through the midnight surrounding Home's Hearth. Chamise didn't carry his knife with her, nor did he feel its presence within the Eisenvard camp. Someone had it. Such items did not stay lost for long. He had laid many dark sorceries upon that shining steel blade over the decades. If he didn't find it soon, it would most likely find him.

Something tingled ahead of him, at the edge of his perception. He didn't see it, but he felt a discontinuity in the world. It was a gap where life should be but wasn't. Something like him, dead, or partially dead, lurked beneath a covered porch. The porch stood in front of a leather worker's shop, dark and deserted, lit only by the half moon and the embers of a dying city torch.

December began to move toward the leather worker's shop, slowing his approach. He opened channels to find the mysterious presence. A few moments later, he had it. It was some kind of ghost. The ghost lurked, yet seemed to follow his every move, edging forward when December threatened to move farther away. He thought it was odd that such a spirit would travel the streets of Home's Hearth with the goddess in residence. In any case, it was no matter. He opened his soul channel and sent tendrils of power toward the ghost. He would seek out the ghost's soul connection to the beyond and snap it like a twig. Powerful ghosts could be terrifying creatures to most foes, but not to necromancers.

"Are you Master December?" The ghost asked. Its voice traveled to him through the realm of death giving it a harsh gravely tone. December was surprised to be named directly. He relaxed his channels but did not release them.

"Who wants to know?"

"My name is Faust. I normally work with Mistress Aileen. I'm not a threat."

"Oh, that is for sure." December wondered how this dead thing ever thought it could be a threat to someone like him. "What do you want then? I've only got a moment." Indeed, the power that sent him into the near-death realm would soon fade, leaving him alone in the middle of Home's Hearth. He would need to recoup some power before he could continue with this conversation, especially if this spirit had been sent by Aileen as it claimed. He considered snatching this wayward soul and embedding it into some kind of item for analysis later. If it spoke the truth, this was one of Aileen's toys. She might get cross if he broke it.

He didn't really care if she became cross, but allies had become harder to find over the years. December realized that it was best to preserve the few he had.

"I'd like to talk to you about this Eisenvard woman, Chamise," Faust said.

"You've got my attention. Eisenvard don't normally send ghosts as representatives." December wondered what dear little Chamise had been dabbling in. She had magical skills, but he didn't smell any necromancy on her last time they had met. She seemed to be more resourceful than he had assumed.

"Chamise didn't send me. Miller did."

"Miller should keep out of this. It's not is business and its way beyond his talent level. If he keeps interjecting himself into other people's business, he's going to get hurt."

"Oh yes, on that I heartily agree. I don't think he is cut out for this necromancer life. He would be far happier as a simple crafter."

"So would I. I didn't get that choice," December said with a hint of anger in his voice.

"Sadly, neither will he."

"Get on with it. What does Aileen's boy want of me?"

"He told me to pass this message to you. Miller understands that Chamise betrayed you at the tower. You share in the blame because you didn't tell her what you were doing. You left an Eisenvard to figure it out by themselves. There is a typical pattern to their behaviors when they don't have enough information."

"Yes. They just start killing things until they can figure it all out. But I thought that Chamise was a Free Mage now."

"Free Mage now. Yes. Eisenvard from birth though. One

doesn't just forget that."

December nodded, agreeing with the obvious statement. "I guess not. It's understandable that she stabbed me in the back. Truthfully, I admire how she did it. It was quick and mostly painless, without a lot of screaming and bleeding out. It's a shame that I'm going to kill her anyway."

"That's just it. Miller asks that you don't. He would like you to forgive her this once as a favor to him."

"Seriously? It would be easier to just kill both of them."

"Then you would have to deal with Mistress Aileen's displeasure."

"So? Soon enough I'll be exiled. Once the conclave meets I'll be banished beyond the world edge. I expect I'll be gone for at least a century. Aileen can't stop it. Easter can't stop it. Hermagon has been getting this ready for three hundred years. I have no fear of repercussions from either Miller or Aileen."

Faust continued. "As a gesture of friendship and goodwill, Miller has gained possession of your dagger. He holds it for you on his person."

December's voice grew angry. "He dares to hold my blade hostage?"

"No. He will give it back to you without condition when you meet. He simply wants to talk to you about some internal politics."

"He wants to beg for Chamise's life?"

"No. He trusts that you will see the Chamise issue differently once you are reunited with your blade."

Faust stepped out from the porch, exposing himself to December's channels and sorceries. There had been little use in hiding in the first place.

Faust continued on. "He is afraid that Master Darjeeling might be acting against Aileen and Easter in secret. He seeks your assistance with this matter."

"Betrayal? From Darjeeling? I've got to hear about this. Speak quickly ghost of Faust. I have little time."

Faust began by describing the New Pony Inn, and how

Darjeeling and his apprentice Franz had been behaving. He talked about the alliance with the leftover Eisenvard, and how Darjeeling seemed bent on disrupting it. As he began to describe what was happening in the Gardens, and how Franz had been keeping tabs on Miller December felt his power begin to fade, and he released the channels that allowed him to communicate with the dead. He took a minute to rest. A few moments later December was whole, alive, and exceptionally hungry. December could feel the spirit of Faust still there, but he lacked strength. He could no longer speak with the ghost. He shrugged and began to walk through the dark streets in search of   an   inn.

PATTERN OF LIFE

The pattern lay upon the floor. It's meaning escaped Miller. He stared at it, concentrating, trying to recall every lesson on spell crafting and channeling he had ever learned. None of it was meaningful. The pattern defied logic, magical abstraction, and intuition. It was something separate, something different. It might as well be from another world. Perhaps it was.

He shook his head, thinking about his problem. His knowledge of magic had been taught to him by White Hand masters. They laid a foundation of disciplines, followed by the study of channels. Other methods of casting magic existed besides channels. He had never found one that he could not understand, and sometimes use, until now.

The pattern seemed to stare back at him, taunting him. It hid its secrets, unwilling to divulge the smallest hint.

The books Mistress Aileen provided helped little. They were mostly full of thought experiments. None gave the smallest hint on how to create these patterns. He didn't even know what meaning of the pattern was, let alone how to make them. Books from Stevenson and his students lay opened and scattered across wooden benches across the room. Each held a page that might be a hint, a clue into the pattern's mystery. None of it made sense.

Magic crafting fascinated Miller, it always had. He relished discovering and mastering new ways of using the forces of the universe. He had learned five methods of casting magic. Some methods were better at enchanting. Some were better at controlling the forces of the physical world. A rigorous theoretical basis supported all of these methods. Such approaches relied on understanding the universe and magic to theorize a magical system and discover how it connects to the world.

Until now.

The pattern defied his ability to master its secrets. It wasn't because crafting the pattern was difficult. There were no rules to it. It was as if the crafter of this pattern, supposedly Stevenson or one of his students, had invented the entire thing out of whole cloth without any underlying system of magic. It seemed to come from intuition more than discipline.

He could feel the power emanating from the pattern though. The tone of it felt different than what he had found before. The pattern was awash in magic. He was sure of that. He wanted to pry open its secrets, to read it and understand it. He wanted to drink from it like a fountain, yet it denied him.

A door opened across the room. Echoes sounded, breaking his thoughts away from the pattern. Miller didn't remember how long he had been here working and studying. Time seemed to slip away when he was in this room.

He snatched up an empty journal and a quill, ignoring the newcomer and trying to preserve a stray thought for later. He scratched onto the thick pages. 'Does time move differently in patterns? If so, why?'

"Here you are. I've been looking for you."

He looked up to see Chamise. She was standing in front of him tapping her foot impatiently, staring at him with a hint of anger.

"You will never guess who came to see me tonight," She began.

Miller glanced up from his leather-bound journal. "Really? Who?"

His eyes started to return to the journal but stopped as her faced transformed into a grimace. He stopped his scribbling and gave his full attention to her. Taking his best guess, he tried to remain calm.

"Master December?"

She nodded. "He appeared to be quite out of sorts."

Miller glanced about the room, looking for clues that could indicate a necromancer hidden by some kind of crafting.

"I talked to the staff here. They tell me that this place has been protected from magic and necromancers for a long time. They told me not to worry."

Miller wondered if he sounded as terrified as he felt. December returning to Home's Hearth did not bode well for either of them.

"I've seen Mistress Aileen here several times, so don't let your guard down. I guess that this place should be protected from Free Mages as well, at least as far as the crafting practice goes. If I were you, I would be more worried."

Her voice began to shake, only slightly, but Miller could hear it. necromancers returning from the grave intent on revenge could frighten anyone, even Chamise.

Miller continued. "What did he have to say?"

"It wasn't so much a conversation. It was more of a small battle."

"Anyone hurt?"

"Just one. Nobody you know."

"Was it bad?"

She nodded. "Yes. It was bad." She took a moment before continuing, "He's coming after me as well." Chamise took a deep breath. "What do I do?"

"You stay here and stay out of sight. I've got someone

working this issue as we speak. I should hear back from him soon. That will give us our next step."

"Us?" Chamise asked, surprised by the word. She felt a glimmer of hope. She had always assumed that Miller would leave her to December's not-so-tender mercies. Siding with her in any small way would become difficult for him, especially when facing his own masters.

"Yes, I said us. It's always been you and me, right?"

She offered a smile. "Lately it has."

"Good enough. I need all the allies I can get. Plus, you're growing on me. I think I'm getting to like you." The smile he offered was full of mirth, yet his eyes remained worried.

"Seriously?" She asked, surprise in her voice. "You picked right now to discuss your feelings?"

Miller smiled back. "There's nothing like impending doom to focus the mind."

She didn't respond. Miller changed the subject.

"I'm going to meet up with my friend and figure out what December is up to. You stay here where it's safe."

"Not going to happen. I need to hear all of the details. I want to ask questions."

"Please don't do this. You are not going to be comfortable with the situation. My friend is kind of different."

"Different?"

Her impatient foot tapping began again. Miller looked at her closely. Her nerves were taut. She seemed ready for battle the way her hand rubbed against her mace shaft repeatedly.

Miller shrugged, realizing that there would be no getting around this issue.

"My friend is sort of dead." He began, hoping she would back down from her plan.

Chamise took a moment to make sure she could remain calm. Her voice began to grow louder. "Dead? How can you be sort of dead?"

"There are plenty of ways to be dead. My friend Faust has been idling between here and the final black door for three years now. Once in a while he likes to help out here the the world of the living. I think he gets bored."

"Between? Like a ghost? Are you insane?"

Miller thought about the different kinds of undead, how they came to roam on the earth, and what their motivations could be. Ghosts typically sought vengeance for a betrayal in life. He didn't think Chamise was interested in the minute details of the afterlife. Faust was clearly not a ghost. He had no betrayal to avenge. Faust believed in causes. Those kinds of spirits could morph into true horrors, into things that killed for a cause long gone. If not managed, Faust could go that route, he could become a revenant.

He shuddered at the thought of an immortal spirit that could kill by touch, and with exquisite knowledge of torture.

"Sure. Let's call him a ghost. It seems to work well enough. In any case, I sent him to talk to December and make a trade."

"Trade? What are you trading? The souls of virgins?"

Miller spit out a quick chuckle. "Virgins? December? Not very likely. No, I'm going to give him his death-knife back, and he is going to take you off of his list."

"List? There's a list? What list?"

"Yes. He keeps a few lists of people he wants to kill. I think he keeps multiple lists to keep track of how much pain he wants to inflict. December can be evil like that."

"After hearing that, I definitely want to talk to this ghost of yours. After all, what's the worst that can happen?"

Miller led Chamise away from the Gardens. He was sad to leave his work at the pattern. He didn't have any idea what to do next, but he wasn't going to beat the pattern running after December. He moved through the dark streets. The sun would rise in an hour. He wanted to find Faust quickly before the light made it more difficult for Faust's spirit to communicate. It was easier to talk to spirits in the darkness.

Why? Miller didn't know. He placed that question aside for later.

Now he moved between buildings. Chamise walked at his side. She held the mace at waist level, ready for action. In an instant, she could crush someone's skull, break their arms, or bash their chest. His spell crafting might be able to slow December down for a moment or two, maybe long enough for Chamise's weapon to come in useful.

The long thin knife at his side might be a danger as well. He wouldn't put it past December to enchant the cursed thing. It could come alive at any moment.

That was another reason Miller thought it would be best to simply give it back. The knife would not make December any more dangerous but keeping it from December might make him angrier.

They passed through the empty market. Stalls lay empty, no longer filled with wares or merchants. Instead, darkness and a hint of fog claimed it. The market was the focal point of the town, where living people moved every day. Miller could see remnants of their life energies when he gazed through his spirit channels. Spirit energy filled the market even though it had been deserted for hours. There was enough here for Miller's purpose. He held up his hand and stopped in the center of the market.

Stopping beside him, Chamise looked up quizzically, looking for a clue as to what comes next. Miller reached to his belt and released the small bag. He quickly untied the laces and opened it. The bag was made of soft brown leather. Rough hand-stitched seams made it look like someone botched trying to make a coin pouch. It was larger than his hand but not by much. Miller opened his empty palm and carefully began to pour.

"What is that?" Chamise began.

"Keep your voice down," Miller whispered, "Let's not get noticed. I'll explain later."

Sand had begun to pour from the bag as he tipped it to the side. It moved oddly, much slower than sand should. As the sand touched his bare hand, the granules began to glow, disrupting the darkness with their intensity. When his hand became nearly full, he stopped pouring and held the bag out to Chamise.

She looked at him with fear in her eyes, not daring to touch whatever was in the bag. She had started to fear the arts of necromancers a while ago. Now she decided fear was a good thing.

"Don't be afraid. Just hold this so it doesn't spill."

"What if it gets on me?"

Miller looked down at the glowing sand in his bare palm. "Oh, I don't know. Maybe go wash it off?"

"It isn't poison or cursed?"

"Maybe just a little. Toughen up and hold the darn bag so it doesn't spill. This stuff is valuable."

She grimaced as she reached out, carefully grabbing the bag by the top.

Miller bent over and began pouring the sand from his hand onto the ground. Whispered chants filled the night air. Chamise could barely hear the words. She could feel the flow of power though the air and across her skin.

Miller began drawing on the earth with the sand. An outline of a man pushed up from the earth as if a body lay just beneath the surface. Waves of power came from the shape as the sand surrounded it. Within thirty seconds Miller had drawn a complicated design on the ground, occult geographical symbols weaved a net around the body shape.

"I need to summon my friend. Since you are here, I'll need to give him a form that you can see. Don't worry, it might look a little dark-magicy, but Faust has already come into the world. I'm just going to pull him a bit closer to us.

Chamise recognized the symbols. She had seen them in books but never dared use them herself. Runes to pull spirits. Triangles to open gateways to death, to the final black door. A circle to protect them from those forces. A final circle to instantly cut off the other world if needed. Miller wasn't taking any chances.

He reached out and took the bag from her hands, retying it and returned it to his belt. Finally, he knelt down and placed his face near the freshly drawn glyph. He spoke a single name.

"Faust."

The white powder began to sparkle, the sound of breaking sticks, or perhaps bones, emerged as the sand erupted in violence. It crackled and glittered for six heartbeats, filling with turbulent waves. Slowly the motion came to a stop. The glow retreated giving way to the night.

"I'm here." A voice emerged from the place where the shape had been.

Faust began to slowly fade into the world, standing in the center of Miller's glowing pattern. One moment they were alone in the market square. The next, a semi-transparent image of a man stood with them. Faust had been a large muscular man in life. A light brown beard jutted out from his chin a hands length. It wasn't well kept, looking like it had gone wild.

But this was Faust's image in death. It was how he looked the moment he had passed from life's embrace. Now the man who at one point was the hidden dagger of the temple and the dark instrument of the Eisenvard stood before Miller and Chamise appearing like he had just run through a bramble forest.

"Did you find him?" Miller asked, skipping right to the point.

"Sure." Faust grinned back. "You never like to catch up on old times, do you?"

"And? December?" Miller continued, ignoring his attempts at small talk.

Faust replied, "And what? I told him you had the knife. He seemed a little angry about it. When I told him that you just wanted to give it back, he seemed a little surprised."

Miller urged him to continue, "Then?"

Faust had a knack of predicting what people would do. He had proven to be unusually good at predicting what evil people would do on more than one occasion.

"Then he cast some kind of spell. I have no idea what it was. I told him where to find you so he could get his knife back. That's about it."

Chamise looked back with suspicion. "Did you get a chance to see his face? His body language? Anything look, well, off?"

"Sure. He's always acting creepy, like he's about to murder a puppy at any moment. Nothing new there."

Miller began opening his spirit-vision. He checked Faust's spirit. Something was different.

"A spell ay? Have you felt any differently since meeting Master December?" Miller asked.

"Oh sure. I've got something going on, I just don't know what. It's probably some kind of tracking spell," Faust said.

"You guessed right. I'm sure he followed you here," Miller said.

Chamise gasped. "You led him here? Are you insane?"

Faust moved toward her. She took a step back before remembering that there wasn't much her mace could do against the already-dead, especially those who had shed their physical body.

"Yeah, I didn't worry. I assumed this was the intention." Faust said.

Miller nodded. "Yes. I doubted Master December would ever follow anyone else's plans but his own."

"Your plan was to just let him know where we are? Are you insane?" Chamise said, her mace ready in both hands. Her nostrils flared.

A voice came from the darkness. It sounded like something had crawled from the grave. "Insanity is the mark of a capable necromancer. Or so I've been told."

A shadow detached itself from the wall of a wool trader's shop. It drifted closer. Miller didn't need to see the face to know who it was. Master December came into view.

"I'm here for my knife."

"I know." Miller reached to his side and pulled the knife from his belt, still in its sheath. "It's right here."

"What? No talking? No begging for the life of your poor friend?"

Miller shook his head sadly. "What's the point? You've got your knife. If you want to kill Chamise, or even me, there isn't much I can do to stop you."

"There isn't anything you could do to stop me."

The mace in Chamise's right hand began to rise. She was getting ready to move on December. Miller decided to interrupt.

"That's why we are having this talk instead of slinging magical fire all over the town. I'm hoping that I can talk you into setting aside your anger. Yes, Chamise murdered you when you weren't watching. That's what you get for not telling her the plan. What was she supposed to do, p-atiently wait for you to see her? Seriously?"

"How about this. She could have done anything that didn't involve betraying then murdering me."

"You look fine. You didn't share your plan and got your ego bruised. Who's the White Hand master here? It isn't Chamise. Since you didn't tell her what was going on, it's all on you. You are the master, not her."

"I am the master, you have better not forget it. Soon enough it will be your turn, I'm sure."

"It's going to be hard getting a master's ring if you kill me."

"Nah, I'll just drag your cold lifeless body in front of Aileen. I'm sure that she will sacrifice almost all of her spirit to bring your ungrateful soul back to this world."

Miller couldn't argue. That sounded like the exact thing she would do. "You're probably right about that. You can take a priestess from the temple, but you can't take the temple from a priestess."

December stopped walking toward him. Now he stood ten paces away. "You don't know much about Aileen. There isn't much of the temple left in there. It never did fit her very well."

"I'll have to disagree."

"Who cares what you agree with? You don't know anything about Aileen. You only know what she wants you to know.

Aileen picks and chooses which side of her personality to show to whom. If I were you, I would pay better attention."

Miller didn't like where this conversation was going. The last thing he needed was to allow December to plant doubts to Aileen's loyalty. Of course, that begged the question - how loyal was December to Aileen?

Miller held out the knife to Master December. Even in the darkness, his coal-black shadow seemed to stretch toward it. A jolt of fear passed up his spine. He had no idea what he was toying with. He had only one thought, one hope. December hadn't killed them yet. At the very least, he must be interested in where all this was going.

"I wanted to talk to you about something," Miller said.

December snatched the knife from his hand. It was quick. The knife was in December's hands before Miller could have even tried to pull it away.

"Now we get to the point of all this." December offered a resigned sigh. "Alright. I paid the price of admission so I might as well see the show."

Chamise squirmed nervously, uncomfortable in her role as a potential murder victim. Miller offered her a smile before he began his pitch.

"I want to talk to you about Darjeeling."

"Really? What do we have to talk about?"

"I think he's involved in something. I think he's playing games with the situation here. The Takers are near, and he is missing more than usual. He's got his apprentices acting strangely."

"So? Strange is normal in the White Hand. If Darjeeling decided to take up carpentry and devote time to meeting pretty women, then I'd be worried."

Miller smiled back at December. The vision of the fat wrinkly husk of a necromancer trying to charm women at the beer halls seemed ludicrous. What woman in her right mind would want to be near that? He glanced over to Chamise, looking for encouragement.

"Don't look at me," Chamise said. "I'm not averse to dallying with a necromancer, I draw the line at 100 years old though. Just too old for my taste."

December's cold look was the only reply she received from that remark. Even Miller kept quiet. There was no telling if her age jibe offended December. He had killed for less, many times.

Miller cleared his throat to banish the silence. "About Darjeeling then. He's got Franz running errands around town. That's pretty normal. But Franz is up to more than that. He seems to have gotten pretty comfortable with a local alchemist and his daughter. I've observed him with the daughter at least three times."

"Oh, so you're saying that Franz is vulnerable to the female persuasion?" December's eyebrows were raised, highlighting the irony of Miller's charges.

"No. I'm saying that something else is going on. Franz is very careful to avoid being followed when he visits there. Sometimes a temple priest visits there as well. And on two occasions, the alchemist has had meetings in obscure locations that just look suspicious. Normally I would just count that as typical weirdness, but with the Takers on the move I don't think we can risk much."

"What do you want me to do? Kill this apprentice? I always thought that you frowned on that sort of thing."

"Dear no. I need you to get a feel for what Master Darjeeling is up to. I won't be able to see past any of his magic. I'm not powerful enough. But you could without much difficulty, I imagine."

"You do know that Darjeeling proved his loyalty a long time ago. He is a master as well. Masters can't be taken."

"I don't know if that's true."

"What? A master can be taken?" Chamise blurted out. Surprise filled her voice. A taken White Hand master would be a terrifying force.

"Not by channels that we know of. I'm discovering that there is more to the Taker's power than channels. I've been investigating pattern magic at the Gardens. I think that ties into the place between the worlds. Magic doesn't work the same there. Takers come from between the worlds. That means that we can't assume anything."

"Sure. How do you test that?" December questioned, sounding interested.

"I have a prisoner, a woman who was taken a few months ago. I've placed her in a pattern room. Guess what? The Takers have gone quiet. She isn't cured, but she seems improved. My guess is that as soon as I take her out of the pattern room, the Takers will assert their power and she will be lost again. I suspect they use pattern forces as their way of channeling magic, whatever that means as far as patterns go."

"Your theory sounds far-fetched to me. If Takers use pattern magic, why don't they cast power the way we can?"

"I don't think pattern magic works that way. As near as I can figure, the patterns are based on something more solid."

"Solid? Explain."

Miller took a breath before he launched into his latest theory of magic. It didn't sound very plausible, but after weeks of observing Brita and the chaos in her mind, it was the only theory he had.

"I think the pattern is based on something fixed in reality. That contrasts with the idea of channels and flows. The White Hand understand magic by imagining forces in motion. I think the pattern reflects forces that are stationary in the world. In essence, it gets its power from some kind of identity. If an identity is changed then the reality of the world changes along with it. Takers have some kind of power that allows them access to our world from another. They have to use a force that is reachable across whatever realm they start from to our world."

"You're losing me," Chamise interjected.

"Shhh." December cut her off. "Let him go on."

Miller struggled with finding a better description, but it just slipped away. "We don't have any stories or histories of magic like this. I traveled between the worlds and saw what lay there. The forces we channel are missing between the worlds. A different kind of power lies at the root of all the worlds though, something they all share in common."

"Here's a question then. If I'm hung outside the edge of the world as a punishment, would this newly discovered force exist there too?" December asked.

"I don't see why not. If this identity magic weren't there, could anything exist at all? Some force needs to be at the root of reality itself. This has the feel of something that would support both the existence of patterns and the existence of magic as we know it."

Sounds like you are talking about some kind of root, a root of all magic. Are you saying that what we know as magic is merely a reflection of this other force?"

"Not entirely. I suspect that our concept of magic is built from this identity power. It could be the building blocks of everything though."

December looked down at his knife. A break had started to form in the clouds, allowing starlight to shine down on its silver blade. The barking of a faraway dog interrupted the silence.

"How are you going to verify this theory?"

Miller was surprised. December hadn't even tried to argue any of the points. He seemed genuinely interested. He allowed himself the luxury of smiling in relief. "Step one is to talk you into not killing my friend here."

Chamise offered a shrug. She knew that her life wasn't in her own hands. She might as well let this play out. If Miller was right, she might be involved with one of the most amazing discoveries in the history of magic. She wasn't going to do anything to jeopardize that.

"You stabbed me in the back." December spit out coldly.

"You stabbed my friend in the front." Chamise countered. She knew better than to cower. December would kill her just for the point of it.

"There's one more thing. It's about Franz and his new friends."

"Oh? There's more."

"Yeah. I think the woman, the alchemist's daughter. I think she is involved with Cerna's disappearance.

18

OLD FRIENDS

Trudging through the puddles, Miller moved toward his goal, the New Pony Inn. Rain started falling an hour ago. It wasn't torrential. He felt miserable walking through the cold downpour. The rain had been enough to break up his meeting with Master December at least. After December's body returned to the world, he seemed no more eager to stand in the cold spray as Miller did. December wasn't the sort you went out for after-meeting drinks with either. He had made his case. December hadn't killed Chamise. Overall, it was a good night.

Chamise wasn't happy with it though. She acted like a sword hung over her head, as if she expected December to leap from the shadows at any moment. Miller wanted to comfort her and tell her it was all finished. She was right to worry though. December could be unpredictable at times. He could lash out when his mood went sour, with little consideration for the consequences.

Now December was looking into Darjeeling and his apprentice. Chamise wasn't the immediate target anymore, at least for now.

He saw the New Pony Inn a few blocks down the street. Two lanterns hung outside the entrance doorway, giving a hint of light as they struggled against the black of night. It would be dawn in a few hours. For now, clouds covered the sky blotting out all starlight. Quiet ruled the streets.

Fatigue settled down on him like a heavy blanket. It had been too long since he had last slept well. Tonight would be no different. He was beginning to regret setting up camp at the New Pony. Every trip back and forth to the Gardens would be an opportunity for the Takers to strike. He didn't like that idea, but he couldn't think of a way around it in his sleep deprived state.

Eventually, he arrived at the door to the New Pony. Legs screamed their complaints as he walked up the stairs. A newly painted white glyph stood out against the door. It wasn't painted skillfully, at least not with an artist's skill. He looked at it carefully, noting the turn of arcs and the dimensionality of the triangular anchors. It was a warding enchantment. This door wasn't going to open for anyone who wasn't allowed in here.

Glyphs like these could kill people. A caster typically embedded items from either targeted victims, or from those who were allowed to pass safely. Miller hoped that whoever cast this glyph had included him on the list of people not to kill. There was only one way to know.

As a precaution, he opened up his channels, all of them. Bending over, he laid his hand on the bare wood of the steps, connecting his powers with the dead wood below. He sent out tendrils of force to explore the wood, searching for remnants and spillover from the door glyph. He couldn't nullify it as it stood, but at least he could get a hint of its design. He felt remnants of the glyph, echos of a caster painting it. The casting felt rushed, imprecise.

It might be a trap, or it might not. If some form of a curse was waiting for him, then at least he would sense it coming. The glyph was only haphazardly connected to the door. The casting felt raw and a bit hasty. Miller smiled as he sent a few more tendrils into the floor, pushing forces toward the glyph. It barely responded, only drinking in a touch of his essence channel. He pushed the door open.

Nothing happened. He breathed out in relief. The curse would not target him, at least for now. He stood up and walked in, shutting the door and silently as he made his way toward the stairs the room he slept in.

"Where have you been?"

Brita's voice came out of the dark room's interior. It sounded soft, perhaps sad.

Miller took a moment before he responded. He wanted his wits sharp whenever he spoke with her.

"I've been out dealing with some order business. I had to talk with someone."

"Someone? Chamise?"

Miller held his open hand out and whispered a few words of power. His magic leaped to attention as the words passed his lips. The discipline of revitalization gave him energy, at least for the short term. Most times he did not need this discipline but tonight he did. He was tired, bone tired. But there was no room error when dealing with Brita and the Takers within her.

With his magic strong, at least temporarily, he released quick elemental channeling of light. He held his hand out and a light began to grow from his palm. It rose up a finger's length and glowed brighter. He saw Brita kneeling by the edge of the circle.

"How long have you been there?" Miller asked.

"All night," Brita responded, her voice meek as if she were trying to hide in the shadows.

"All night? Why?"

"I was waiting for you."

Miller wanted to turn away and retreat upstairs, toward sleep and momentary sanity. Her face would not allow it. She stared at him with wide eyes, almost feverish in desperation. Shrugging, he walked across the hall and came up to the edge of the circle. He sat down a mere arm's length from her. It might have been a thousand miles though. The circle and its narrow border of magical forces kept them away from each other, the thin edge more barrier than an ocean.

"What's wrong?" Miller could see the distress in her eyes. Something felt different now. Something had happened. "Who put the glyph up?"

"One of the boys came by." Brita always called the other apprentices 'the boys'. "Lord Easter had him paint the door."

"Lord Easter? He's a master, not a lord."

"Oh, you lot don't call him that, but he's a lord. He says jump and the lot of you ask how high."

Miller nodded. The Order had no concept of Lords or nobility. Their roots stretched back three thousand years, back to the time of trade guilds, far-traveling merchants, and the First Gods. The world had matured since then. Cities formed and grew. Kingdoms had been born, risen, and fallen many times.

A stray thought entered his mind. The order accumulated knowledge over thousands of years, yet they lost the secret of the patterns. It didn't make sense.

Brita continued. "Something happened today. It scared me. I was so afraid I called out and Lord Easter heard me. He called for his boys right away and had the door painted. Not sure why, but I felt a little better. It's good that someone is paying attention to me."

Miller nodded, taking the slight as it was intended. He hadn't done a good job seeing to her.

"What happened?"

"I felt them, the Takers." She gestured weakly toward the circle boundaries. "I could feel them through the circle. They were close."

A chill ran down Miller's spine.

"Inside the city?" Miller asked.

"It stands to reason, I couldn't tell." Brita's hands shook.

"They must have been very close."

"That's what Master Easter said. He said they must have touched the walls of the building."

"Yeah. That could do it." Miller grimaced as he quickly ran through calculations. Touching the side of the inn would not trigger the protective circle but the Takers weren't using magic as he understood it.

But that meant the Takers were close, very close.

"And no one will tell me where Cerna is. Where did he go? Easter doesn't know. Franz won't tell me anything. He was supposed to be the guard. What happened to him?"

Miller shook his head. He didn't know either.

She pointed across the room at a pile of gear. A tear started to fall from the corner of her right eye. Her voice softened. "He left his helmet."

Miller nodded back. Cerna had been on his mind but he didn't have the time to search for him. Threats seemed to be around every corner, even though they lay in the middle of Phyllicitus's city, a city of peace.

"I want to help. I want to find him. I just don't know how." Miller said, trying to comfort her.

"You're a wizard. Figure it out."

"I'm just an apprentice."

"I thought you just said that your order doesn't have titles. You have no lords. That means that there is no difference between a master and an apprentice other than skill and the willingness to do something."

Thoughts of the dark ring flowed into his mind. A flash of vision, the ring was waiting for him between the worlds. He had denied it. It was terror and insanity wrapped up in a metal band, and if he took it up, the ring would tie itself to his soul.

"There's more to it than that."

"No. There isn't." She replied, adamant in her belief.

A feeling of loneliness fell upon Miller. He wanted to help Cerna. Seeking any kind of inspiration, he stood and walked over toward Cerna's helmet. It stood alone on top of a waist-high pile of supplies.

"Some wizards can use personal things to track others across wide distances."

"Easter told me that. He says Cerna is too far away."

"Is he dead?"

"Easter says he isn't. I figured that he would know how to do that."

"Yeah. He would." Miller stopped to visualize the map of the area. He thought about how far Cerna could travel within the last few days. Even if he took a fast ship, Cerna should still be close enough to find with spellcraft.

"If Easter can't find him, that means that Cerna isn't far away. He is hidden, with magic."

Miller picked up the helmet. It was rounded on the top. Rivets poked through, scraping across his bare skin. This helmet was used for battle, not for decoration. He held it close to his stomach as he began to pace. Eventually, he ended up walking along the edge of the protective circle. Brita stood and stared at him, not interrupting. Miller thought about the forces of magic. He looked down at the circle, a piece of spellcraft built from channels and anchored with glyphs.

The White Hand did not have a monopoly on magic. Free Mages used memorized rituals. Shamans from Dog's Run used carved runes. Even spell dancers from the Cursed Desert had the ability to create a protective barrier. Miller thought about those methods. He wondered how he could use magic to detect something meant to deflect magic. It didn't seem to make any sense. It would be like trying to make water wet with more water. Such a thing would just make more water. It was circular.

The thought struck him like a hammer. It wasn't circular. It was an identity problem. Magic channel circles could block the flows. It rendered them invisible to magical scrying and impenetrable flows. Miller gazed at the helmet. It was solid in his hands. He knew that Cerna would be somewhere, if alive, and be just as solid. The issue wasn't that he couldn't find Cerna. It was that there were forces that could hide him.

Miller had tried using his channels to find Cerna three times. Each time resulted in nothing. It was as if Cerna had stepped out of this world. Perhaps he could use necromancy to call

Cerna's spirit. But that would involve opening a way to beyond the final door, and many things could answer his call. No, Miller decided, he would let Easter make that decision.

He gazed down at the circle's edge. Two chalk loops surrounded Brita, their power re-enforced by glyphs drawn between them. The glyphs were held the two circles apart with a maelstrom of forces. Anyone strong enough to break a circle would unleash those forces and the curses that rode within them.

Glyphs were different that magical flows. They anchored magic, changed its course, stored it. A cold tingle ran across his back. The image of the pattern drawn in the library came to his mind. Then images of the place between the worlds.

Miller wondered. Could it all be connected?

He glanced down at Cerna's helmet, then at the circle, then at Brita. Her eyes were wide as if she could feel Miller's excitement.

"You thought of something."

"Something crazy. I need to go somewhere and try some crafting."

Biting her lip, she turned away. She stood and began to walk slowly back to the center of the circle as if she had been dismissed.

"I want you to come with me," Miller said.

She gasped. "What do you need me to do?"

"I just need you to be you."

Cerna hung from chains. The cold iron, oiled recently and kept immaculate, supported him from a hook on the top of the cage. Chains wrapped him completely like a shroud of iron. The cage was large enough to hold a single man, but not large enough for that man to be comfortable. If Cerna could stretch his arms out in any direction he would not be able to touch the cage wall. If he swung his weight enough to get some motion, then his feet would knock against the cage walls.

His feet were chained together. The iron wrapped him from his feet to his neck. A single chain connected that hook to the small of his back. Cerna wanted to struggle, wanted to get free. Now he was so full of whatever garbage they were feeding him he could barely concentrate. He had been here days. His beard now thick and black with sprinkles of gray testified to his years.

He heard the door open downstairs. The steady pace of footsteps moved up the stairs, slow and sure in their approach. The door opened and a woman entered.

Hazel walked into the room. Her dark brown hair was tied into a ponytail. She carried a wooden serving tray with a silver teapot on it. Two wooden cups of poor quality stood next to it.

"Shhhhit." Cerna mumbled out. He struggled to say a single word. The drugs interfered with his speech as well as his thoughts.

"Good mornin' to you too. Tis a bright and cheery day, ay?"

"Bite'n beery."

She smiled up at him. Cerna would normally tower over her. The additional hand-span of height he gained from being hung from the chain made him even taller. Hazel didn't seem to care.

She walked over to a small table and set the tray down. Picking up the silver teapot, she slowly poured two cups. A rich aroma of plants and mint filled the room. Chains rattled as Cerna struggled against them. Once he drank that tea he would be unable to do even that. At least the pain would go away, he thought. He had been hanging for days. The tea killed pains in his shoulders and arms. If he ever escaped, he doubted he could even pick himself up from the ground let alone break out of this cage.

Easter had told him that his task would be the most dangerous one of all. He hadn't been kidding. Cerna thought again about how Easter had used his magic to save his young daughter's life. He owed Easter, and he would never betray that debt. He didn't regret agreeing to come with Easter, he only regretting how long it was taking these bastards to kill him.

Once they cut his throat Easter would know exactly where he was, then Easter would come for both the alchemist and his lovely daughter.

Hazel stood and walked over to the cage door. Its heavy iron door was fastened shut with another chain and a different lock. She pulled at a white cord wrapped around her waist, fetching a key the size of her palm from its end. She placed the key in the lock and turned. It opened quietly and easily.

"Mrph. Giton widdit."

"Soon enough, soon enough," She said, unconcerned with whatever gibberish he uttered.

Easter nodded, "Nor should there be a risk of one. Long ago the order decided that it would be unfair to the child if their father, or mother, gained their ring and lost the ability to love them. As I said, we have our own ways, and we have them for a reason."

Miller came back to join them. He led Brita by the hand and placed her near the pile of chalk.

"Are we ready?" Miller asked. "We can't keep Brita out all night."

Chamise asked, "Are you going to build the glyph?"

"No," Miller answered. "You are. I'm going to set up the channels. Use the discipline I just showed you. You'll do fine."

Chamise breathed out in exhaustion. Easter offered an encouraging nod before he stood and walked to the other side of the room.

"Should I start?" she asked.

"Yes, now is a good time."

Chamise stared at the rune book Miller had given her earlier, memorizing the glyph she was tasked to draw. Moments passed as she committed every detail to memory. She reached out to scoop a handful of chalk dust, then started to draw.

"You're going too quickly," Miller cautioned. "Try to go slow, then go slower. The goal isn't speed, its accuracy. Slow wins the race."

Nodding, Chamise slowed her drawing. Each finger's length

of powder had previously required only a heartbeat to pour onto the floor, now it needed ten. She ran out of chalk dust, then went back for more. Sixteen times she refilled her palm with dust until she finally connected the glyph into a cohesive whole.

"Perfect," Miller said as he released his channels. Chamise felt the hair on the back of her arms spring up. Her shoulder length hair began to dance wildly.

"What's going on?" Chamise asked.

"Don't worry, that's normal. You got the glyph right, but not perfect. There's some leakage. Leakage won't matter for what we are doing today. You'll get better with practice."

They stood in silence as Miller channeled more and more of his power into the glyph.

Brita began to sing a childhood song, filled with nonsense words about colors that would chase farm animals. Her voice filled the room with joy as if she could sense her coming freedom. Chamise, for some reason she didn't understand, felt a hint of jealousy. She knew that her own voice would never be so clear, so happy.

"Chamise, you're up," Miller said as he stepped away. She saw him sway before he sat on the ground, then he began reciting yet another discipline to recover his channeled energy. Chamise stepped up and opened her channels. For a second, she didn't know what to do. She wanted to aim the magic, to command it into being. The glyph merely pulled it away from her. It felt like someone had poured warm water over her skin, and it flowed from her into a windstorm. Soon enough she began to feel tired, disoriented, then confused. She wasn't sure what this spell would accomplish.

She felt Miller's hand on her shoulder. "That's enough, my turn," he said as he gently pulled her back away from the glyph. She sat on the ground for a moment, recovering her wits. Miller walked to the place she had stood before, copying what she had just done. Chamise didn't have a firm grasp on the spell, so she trusted in Miller's example, copying the discipline he had just shown her.

Energy came flowing back into her channels. Five minutes later, she felt like she had just risen from bed, fresh for the new day. She stood and approached Miller, tapping his shoulder as he had done to her.

No conversation was necessary. Miller nodded, then stepped back and to the side, allowing her access to the glyph. They repeated that dance six times, each of them gaining power, then giving that same power to the glyph.

Brita stopped singing. Chamise looked over to see her shaking as if she stood naked in the deep winter cold.

"Miller, is that what you expected?" Chamise asked.

"No. I think we're out of time. I'm going to release the spell before Brita gets worse. Ready?"

Before she could ask Miller what she should be ready for, the glyph erupted. The chalk dust began to light up as it rose into the air, becoming a series of clouds that surrounded Brita. Tears began to fall from her eyes.

"It hurts!" she called out, pain evident in her voice.

Miller's face transformed. Chamise stared as fear came into his eyes. She knew that Miller was going to end the spell.

"Just a little longer!" Chamise called out. "The Takers might be controlling her, making her pretend."

Brita collapsed onto the floor. She writhed back and forth until finally settling into the fetal position. She screamed, sounding as if someone were pulling her eyeballs from her skull.

Miller couldn't withstand her cries. He ended the spell. The glow faded as the chalk dust settled back to the ground.

Easter walked forward to see the results. He looked down at Brita for a few moments, then turned to Miller.

"I think the Takers are still with her," Easter said.

"I know," Miller replied sadly.

Easter walked to Brita's side and held a hand down to her. She took it and pulled herself up.

"I'll bring her back. We will try another method after she's fully recovered," Easter said.

Miller and Chamise watched as they left the room. Her heart continued to beat fast, angry that Brita's salvation had never come. If they would have saved her, they could have saved every one of the Taken.

She shook her head in sadness, looking over to Miller.

A single tear had fallen from his eye, creating a streak across his dust-covered cheek.

"Do you have another spell?" Chamise asked.

"Not yet," Miller said, shaking his head sadly. "We just need a little more time."

Chamise nodded. "Why don't I believe we have it?"

PATIENT TEACHER

A light rain fell upon Home's Hearth, coating the town with a gray haze and a wet sheen. Miller sat on a stone pedestal. Each of the legs stood carved into the likeness of rearing lions. He loved the peace of the Gardens. In the soft rain, it seemed even more calm than usual. Even the sounds from the city seemed farther away.

Footsteps disturbed his tranquility. He looked up to see a tall man walking down the trail, his long tail of well-kept hair trailing down across his shoulders. The man moved at a slow, tranquil pace. He wore the uniform of a servant yet looked as if he commanded the world. Chamise followed in his wake. The servant led her down the stone pathway toward Miller. A broad smile covered Chamise's face. Miller thought that he saw a slight skip as she stepped behind the servant as if she could barely contain her eagerness for the day to begin.

Chamise didn't wait for the servant. She sped up, moving around him, rushing to stand in front of Miller and blocking his view of the stone fountain.

"It's time!" She said, barely containing a scream. Her eyes went wide in excitement.

Miller offered a smile back. He looked up at her. Her shoulder length hair had been meticulously brushed. She wore a woolen knee-length dress with thin hosiery beneath, perfect for a day of manual labor. Whatever she thought she was going to be doing, she had clearly decided to be ready for hard work.

"You look good," Miller said, gazing at her strong, muscular form. He thought about attempting to flirt with her but gave up. She simply overpowered his imagination. As always, his eyes were drawn to hers. He drowned in their depths, like a blue sea to infinity. Every time he looked into them, he felt lost. Today was no different.

Chamise laughed. "Hardly. I look like I'm a house servant. Got any chimneys that need cleaning?"

"Not really. I've got a few chores though." Miller said. He stood up, then reached out to take Chamise by the hand. "Ready?"

"I was born ready." She replied.

Miller nodded to the servant, dismissing him, then began to walk toward the house. He didn't let go of Chamise's hand. He pulled her along behind him. His mood began to improve as he fed off her joy. Happiness created more happiness, Miller noted. Perhaps Aileen's philosophy of strength didn't agree with Phyllicitus, but Phyllicitus had a point. She was a goddess after all.

They moved into the great hall, moved past the tables stacked with fruits and meats. A dozen people sat, talking and eating their morning meal. Chamise reached out and grabbed a yellow pear as they moved through, chewing quickly as they arrived at the stairs.

"Didn't have breakfast yet?" Miller asked, watching Chamise jam food into her mouth.

Her response sounded garbled as she tried to speak past the chewed pear in her mouth, "Forgot. Don't want to eat while working."

She continued chewing as they descended. Miller turned left, leading Chamise to the left, passing through a hall, and arriving at a basin of water sitting atop a side table carved from walnut. A lion's head had been carved into its surface then filled with silver. The silver shone against the light. Ten candles line the walls of the hallway giving light to all that entered.

"What?" Chamise asked, unsure what the purpose of the dish was.

"Wash your hands. We are going to be working with materials today. Trust me, you don't want sticky fingers."

She nodded, then dipped her hands into the basin, rubbing them free of the sticky fruit juice. She wiped her hands dry on the cloth that hung next to the basin.

She looked down at the basin. Fruit juice, dust, road dirt, and the remains that had recently lived beneath her fingernails floated in the pool of water.

She shrugged, "They have a cleaning staff. I'm sure the Garden will survive."

Miller turned and walked away, "Come on, I'm giving up on your civility lessons for today."

She laughed as she followed behind, nearly skipping with excitement.

Miller led Chamise through a maze of passageways. Eventually, they began to seem familiar to her. They arrived in the library. Rows of bookshelves mixed with man-high candelabras to fill the space. Arches stretched overhead, formed by skilled brick artisans more than a century ago. They walked past the pattern room walking ten more steps to arrive at a black unadorned door.

"This used to be a study room. They moved the table out to give us space to work." Miller said as he opened the door.

Brita stood in the room. She stared at them as they entered. Master Easter leaned against the left wall, a bored look on his face.

"That took a while," Easter said.

Miller gestured at Chamise, "Someone needed to grab

breakfast."

Easter nodded, "Smart. It's going to be a long day."

"Faah!" Chamise grunted in frustration. White powdery chalk dust coated her hands. The circular design featured a new odd curve that she hadn't intended.

"That was better," Miller said, patiently observing her third failure. Chamise clearly did not have a native talent for art. "Clean it up and go again."

Looking up at Miller, Chamise exhaled in frustration. Instead of standing, she simply leaned back and sat on the floor, her legs sore from the hours of uncomfortable squatting and crawling she continued to endure.

"Remind me why we are doing all this, again." She said.

"We need a magic circle to constrain our channel energy. It will let us slowly add to the total core and heighten the power of our end spell. Essentially, we are going to channel as much spell power as we can into the circle over a few hours, then we will drain in all at once in a single spell. The order does this all the time. It lets two crafters gain the power of four and reduces the complexity of casting since only two people need to synchronize their crafting."

"But this method assumes that everyone is an artist. I'm not."

Miller walked next to Chamise and sat next to her. Her eyes drooped with fatigue. "This isn't working." She muttered, almost to herself.

"It's going to work. I guarantee it." Miller said.

"No, it isn't. I can't even draw a circle with stupid chalk dust. How is this going to work."

"You are going to beat this because I'm going to teach you the trick."

Scowling, Chamise narrowed her eyes and looked over at him. "Trick?"

"Well, it is not really a trick. What you need is a technique improvement. We call them disciplines."

Chamise rolled her eyes. "You've been talking about disciplines for more than a week. Disciplines aren't magic, they're just tricks. Magic is about getting the art perfect, not in fooling yourself that the spell is easier than it actually is."

"And that's why the White Hand is a powerful organization of wizards, and the Free Mages hide in some broken down house in Ingalls."

Turning aside, Chamise turned her attention back to the scattered chalk dust. Miller reached out and placed his hand over hers.

She froze. Seconds passed before she asked, "What are you doing?"

"Trying to reassure you. I want to teach you a discipline, and I need you to trust me. It's going to be a hard journey, but I think you will thank me in the end."

Chamise looked back to his face. Their eyes met.

"Can you trust me? Even if just for a few moments?" Miller asked.

Chamise kept her hand still as he held it, unsure where he was heading with this new tack. "Alright," she replied.

"Good," Miller pulled her hand upwards, toward him. "Turn and face me."

Rotating on the cold surface, she turned her entire body to face him. Miller reached into his pouch and produced a silver coin. Holding it up, Miller placed it directly in front of her face.

"Do you see the coin?"

"Of course I see the coin, idiot." She said.

Miller gently squeezed her hand again. "You are not in danger. You have no need for fear."

"I'm not afraid."

"Yes, you are. Why are you afraid of learning disciplines."

"You call it discipline. Everyone else calls it necromancy. I wanted to learn about magic, not how to raise the dead."

"Disciplines have nothing to do with necromancy."

"Then why don't other mages know of disciplines."

"They know, they just don't care. Necromancy is about cutting through the boundaries between worlds, moving souls back and forth, and creating magical channels that can simulate life. Disciplines are about understanding yourself. Most mages simply want power, they want to change the world. The White Hand learned long ago that its harder to change the world if you can't change yourself."

Dropping her head in surrender, she said, "All right, let's do the coin thing."

"What do you see?" Miller asked again as he held up the coin.

"A coin."

"What else?" Miller asked, leading her with a question.

Chamise began to look around the room. Miller forced the coin closer to her face. "No, keep to the coin, ignore everything else."

"It's silver."

"More," Miller demanded.

Chamise looked for a mere second before she responded, "It's silver with the shape of the temple stamped on it."

"How big is the shape."

"The size of my thumb," Chamise replied, a hint of aggravation in her voice.

Miller closed his palm, then dropped it to his side.

He continued, "Now, empty your mind of all thoughts. Bring back the image of the coin in your mind. Try to visualize it, to remember details."

Chamise dutifully closed her eyes. After three seconds, she said. "I've got it. Now what."

"You don't have it."

"Yes, I do."

"Describe what you see in your mind's eye."

"I see a silver coin with a temple shape stamped on it."

"You just repeated what you told me earlier. It's not the same. How deep is the shape in the metal?"

"I don't know, like a fingernail's width."

Miller frowned. "Are you making things up?"

"No, well, yes, but the coin is only so thick, it can't be very deep."

Miller replied, "True, but it doesn't matter. I'm trying to teach you to visualize the coin, answering questions is meaningless if you can't see it clearly. Open your eyes. Let's do it again."

Miller held up the coin and allowed her to look. This time she concentrated harder. He closed his hand again and asked a series of questions.

Chamise answered the questions she expected easily, but the unexpected questions eluded her. Miller asked questions that demanded detailed answers. Was the temple straight or slightly curved? How many score marks did she see on the edge of the coin? Was the coin perfectly straight? The questions went on and on. Miller repeatedly showed her to coin, hid it from her, then asked more difficult questions.

Two hours passed. Easter, who had left the room some time ago, returned with a tray of food.

"Let's take a break," Miller said.

Chamise gratefully concurred. Easter walked to their side, then bent down and set the tray on the floor.

Miller looked up at Easter quizzically. "Enjoy," Easter said as he motioned them toward the food.

"I've never had a master bring food to me before, I'm not sure what to do?" Miller said, smiling.

Easter looked back at Miller and said, "I've never seen an apprentice teach so well. Consider this a reward. Good job."

Miller reached out and picked up a small loaf of bread. Ripping a piece off, he chewed a few moments before offering Chamise the remaining loaf.

"I'll get my own bread if you don't mind," Chamise said.

"Fine," Miller said, "but keep it in mind that White Hand masters routinely poison their students, just to weed out the stupid ones."

Chamise abruptly halted reaching for the bread. Miller set the half-ripped loaf in her hand. She shrugged and began to eat.

"What can I say?" Easter began, "If you are going to be a necromancer, someone is bound to poison you. It is better for everyone if you know what to do when it happens."

"Are you serious? Why don't you simply craft an illusion of the taste and effects of poison? Then use the illusion on your apprentices. It seems a little, well, less stupid." Chamise pointed out.

"We could do that. Or we could just poison them and let them learn firsthand. We've been around a while. Our way seems to make the lessons stick a little longer," Easter said.

"I'm going to check on Brita," Miller said, shaking his head as he plucked up a hunk of cheese. He stood and walked to the other side of the room, heading for Brita.

Chamise watched him go before she turned to Easter.

"Good job? Really? Poison your own students? You people are insane." She said, unsure if she was about to be poisoned.

Eater replied patiently, "Yes, we do tend to end up that way in the end. If you don't understand the reasons, then I suggest that you don't judge us until you do."

Chamise finished her bread, then shrugged, reaching to snatch a piece of dried meat from the tray.

"If you're going to poison me, I'm already dead anyway. I might as well not die hungry." She took a bite of the meat.

Easter chuckled. "Don't worry. We save those kinds of lessons for our own apprentices. You are Miller's student today, not mine. Poisoning you would be up to him."

She scowled. "I'm not his apprentice. He's just giving me a few pointers."

"Is that what we are calling it nowadays? Forgive me, but I was under the impression that you two were becoming close."

"No, he isn't interested in me. I wonder some days if he is interested in anyone."

Easter pointed at Brita, "He seems interested in Brita. Actually, that wasn't fair. Miller has always tried to guard all of the people he considers a friend, even when those people would act against him."

"I believe it," Chamise said, "He's going to make the worst necromancer ever. He doesn't have the right attitude."

Nodding in agreement, Easter said, "Yes, we worry about him. His first master was Mistress Sword, she was particularly hard on him. There are days that I'm amazed he hasn't simply killed himself."

"Killed himself?" Chamise asked, concern in her voice, "What happened?"

"Let's just say that Sword has the idea that apprentices need to be toughened up. For example," Easter said, gesturing at the chalk still decorating the floor, "when Miller failed at making a glyph, she would cut off a finger and make him do it again. After all the fingers were gone, she used her craft to regrow the fingers, then training resumed. She taught him for four years."

Chamise couldn't help but put a hand in front of her mouth as it hung wide open in shock.

"And you approve of that kind of training?" She hissed, unsure if this lesson was going to end with a knife in Easter's lung.

"No, I think it's stupid. Her cabal has a different philosophy than mine. I've been trying to convince her to switch to our cabal for years. Hopefully, Aileen will succeed where I fail."

"What does Aileen have to do with that?"

"Oh, you didn't know? Aileen took Sword for a lover. I think she still has some of her old ways in her. That will fade in time."

Chamise almost jumped at Easter with her question, "Wait a minute. You necromancers take lovers?"

"Sure, but rarely. Usually, we lose interest in the flesh a few years after gaining our ring. I guess being so close to death somehow lessens our connection to life. We can't have children, we can't love with all our heart, or at least most of us can't." Easter paused to look at her face a moment before continuing, "I see you are confused though. Masters can take on lovers. Apprentices are forbidden the joys of the flesh. Their task is to learn the craft, not to make babies. After all, what would an apprentice do with a wife and a child?"

"There doesn't have to be a child," Chamise muttered, understanding what Easter was alluding to.

Easter nodded, "Nor should there be a risk of one. Long ago the order decided that it would be unfair to the child if their father, or mother, gained their ring and lost the ability to love them. As I said, we have our own ways, and we have them for a reason."

Miller came back to join them. He led Brita by the hand and place her near the pile of chalk.

"Are we ready?" Miller asked as he prepared for another trek through the streets of Home's Hearth, "We can't keep Brita out all night."

Chamise asked, "Are you going to build the glyph?"

"No," Miller answered, "you are. I'm going to set up the channels. Use the discipline I just showed you. You'll do fine."

Chamise breathed out in exhaustion. Easter offered an encouraging nod before he stood and walked to the other side of the room.

"Should I start?" She asked.

"Yes, now is a good time."

Chamise stared at the rune book Miller had given her earlier, memorizing the glyph she was tasked to draw. Moments passed as she committed every detail to memory. She reached out to scoop a handful of chalk dust, then started to draw.

"You're going too quickly," Miller cautioned, "try to go slow, then go slower. The goal isn't speed, its accuracy. Slow wins the race."

Nodding, Chamise slowed her drawing. Each finger's length of powder had previously required only a heartbeat to pour onto the floor, now it needed ten. She ran out of chalk dust, then went back for more. Sixteen times she refilled her palm with dust until she finally connected the glyph into a cohesive whole.

"Great," Miller said as he released his channels. Chamise felt the hair on the back of her arms spring up. Her shoulder length hair began to dance wildly.

"What's going on?" Chamise asked.

"Don't worry, that's normal. You got the glyph cast, but it isn't perfect. There's some leakage. Leakage won't matter for what we are doing today. You'll get better with practice."

They stood in silence as Miller channeled more and more of his power into the glyph.

Brita began to sing a childhood song, filled with nonsense words about colors that would chase farm animals. Her voice filled the room with joy as if she could sense her coming freedom. Chamise, for some reason she didn't understand, felt a kind of jealousy. She knew that her own voice would never be so clear, so happy.

"Chamise, you're up," Miller said as he stepped away. She saw him sway before he sat on the ground, then he began reciting yet another discipline to recover his channeled energy. Chamise stepped up and opened her channels. For a second, she didn't know what to do. She wanted to aim the magic, to command it into being. The glyph merely pulled it away from her. It felt like someone had poured warm water over her skin, and it flowed from her into a windstorm. Soon enough she began to feel tired, disoriented, then confused. She wasn't sure what this spell would accomplish.

She felt Miller's hand on her shoulder. "That's enough, my turn." He said as he gently pulled her back away from the glyph. She sat on the ground for a moment, recovering her wits. Miller walked to the place she had stood before, copying what she had just done. Chamise didn't have a firm grasp on the spell, so she trusted in Miller's example, copying the discipline he had just shown her.

Energy came flowing back into her channels. Five minutes later, she felt like she had just risen from bed, fresh for the new day. She stood and approached Miller, tapping his shoulder as he had done to her.

No conversation was necessary. Miller nodded, then stepped

back and to the side, allowing her to access the glyph. They repeated that dance six times, each of them gaining power, then giving that same power to the glyph.

Brita stopped singing. Chamise looked over to see her shaking as if she stood naked in the deep winter cold.

"Miller, is that what you expected?" Chamise asked.

"No. I think we're out of time. I'm going to release the spell before Brita gets worse. Ready?"

Before she could ask Miller what she should be ready for, the glyph erupted. The chalk-dust began to light up as it rose into the air, becoming a series of clouds that surrounded Brita. Tears began to fall from her eyes.

"It hurts!" She called out; pain evident in her voice.

Miller's face transformed. Chamise stared as fear came into his eyes. She knew that Miller was going to end the spell.

"Just a little longer!" Chamise called out, "The Takers might be controlling her, making her pretend."

Brita collapsed on the floor. She writhed back and forth until finally settling into the fetal position. She screamed, sounding as if someone were pulling her eyeballs from her skull.

Miller couldn't withstand her cries. He ended the spell. The glow faded as the chalk dust settled back to the ground.

Easter walked forward to see the results. He looked down at Brita for a few moments, then turned to Miller.

"I think the Takers are still with her," Easter said.

"I know," Miller replied sadly.

Easter walked to Brita's side and held a hand down to her. She took it and pulled herself up.

"I'll bring her back. We will try another method after she's fully recovered." Easter said.

Miller and Chamise watched as they left the room. Her heart continued to beat fast, angry that Brita's salvation had never come. If they would have saved her, they could have saved every one of the Taken.

She shook her head in sadness, looking over to Miller.

A single tear had fallen from his eye, creating a streak across his dust-covered cheek.

"Do you have another spell?" Chamise asked.

"Not yet," Miller said, shaking his head sadly. "We just need a little more time."

Chamise nodded. "Why don't I believe we have it?"

DECEMBER'S WRATH

Master December, murderer, liar, and necromancer stood in the street looking at the alchemy shop. Alchemists used to be highly in demand before Phyllicitus had returned. When the priesthood were the only healers, they were constantly overtaxed with the sick and injured. The priesthood gained more power and more energy to aid the unfortunate now that Phyllicitus had returned. In extreme cases, Goddess Phyllicitus healed the sick and injured herself, using her own power and her own hands. Alchemists filled the role of useful trinket vendors nowadays. Their knowledge and skill focused on supplying the temple with raw ingredients. Commoners could not afford the more expensive mixtures and the temple didn't need them.

Miller gave him directions to this place. It was six blocks east of the city market, close enough to be busy during the day and far enough to be empty at night. The two-story brick building that served as the alchemist's home and storefront stood in good repair. Fresh white paint shone along the trim-work.

Wooden entry stairs bore small paintings of the seal of alchemy, the First God of their craft. A wooden sign in the shape of a cauldron hung from above the door. Slatted shutters stood closed against the night.

December narrowed his eyes as he glanced about. He knew that alchemists could be tricky enemies. They tended to be smart. People who dealt in poisons for a living generally were, or they didn't last long enough to matter. This alchemist appeared to be prospering, but no more than his neighbors. His home was clean and presentable. Behind the brick house, a lonely alchemy tower stood out against the morning.

Towns like these with a history of alchemists commonly possessed towers like this. When particularly noxious or dangerous materials were being brewed, alchemists would do so above the street level, and only when the wind was reliably strong. Such courtesies kept the local townsfolk from getting ill and ejecting the offending alchemist from the town.

Less than an hour remained before the sun would fully rise. December expected the townsfolk to rise from their slumbers soon after that. He stared at the door, wondering what he would find in there, and who he would see coming along to chat with the alchemist if he but waited. He knew staying close and watching would give him what he needed. December had fought with Eisenvard, negotiated with an annoying apprentice, and got his only set of clothing wet through and through, all in one day. He didn't feel patient at the moment.

Standing still and quiet, he tried to sense magical flows that originated from the alchemist's store. He didn't feel anything powerful but that didn't mean things weren't hidden. Alchemists had their own crafting lore, different than the White Hand. They could produce magical potions that did similar things to what White Hand could provide. Many ways of gathering and using magical force existed in the world. Some performed better than others, but none were perfect.

A shoulder-high iron fence surrounded the yard, protecting both the shop and the tower from unwanted intruders. An iron lock held a barred gate closed.

He cursed. "To the final door with it." He opened up his illusion channel, pulling the glamour of perceptions into being around him. Darkness pooled around his feet, pouring over his body like an oily coating. Within seconds he was a shadow in the morning light, a spot that was just a little harder to see. He began to walk.

Keeping his pace careful and measured, he walked alongside the alchemy shop, past an empty flower wagon, past a black-walled inn, and around a corner. He turned left into the first alley, then walked along a loosely packed gravel road. He eventually came to the rear of the shop where another gate barred his entry. The alchemy tower jutted into the sky four stories high. A back gate stood at ground level, closed against him.

He couldn't feel any magical channels here, but a locked gate in Home's Hearth raised his hackles. December didn't trust the way that Phyllicitus's power would soften his instincts, reducing the violence of his natural responses. Her power infected everyone in the town. He doubted that her power had any effect on the enemy between the worlds. If anything, it weakened the people here in the city. They could see an enemy in their midst and take no notice of them. Peace in the name of peace spelled disaster in the deadly war the human race found itself in, even when they didn't understand who they were fighting.

December glanced toward the alchemist's shop. The door of the shop stood closed. He could see dim light through a rear window. Someone had woken already. Quiet ruled the night. He heard no sound coming from the tower, nor did he feel any magic flows either. He didn't trust it. He expected an alchemist's tower to have some power, even if only residual. He felt nothing. Either nothing was there, or it was hidden exceptionally well.

Phyllicitus's power strove to promote the best in humanity, all while blunting the worst of it. December thought it a sad attempt at mind control at best. He looked at the gate with suspicion, feeling resistance to his desire. Something wanted to dull his will to go through the gate, to see what was up in the tower. All of his instincts were crying out in alarm. This situation felt wrong, dangerous. December spit onto the ground.

"Enough games." He said to the empty night.

He spoke a word of ruin. As he uttered the syllables, a blacker than black spirit swam from his lips. It flew to the gate slowly, moving back and forth, twisting as a snake would. When it reached the lock, the smoke wrapped around the iron. Rust formed on the lock. It aged, degraded, and within ten heartbeats, disintegrated.

December pushed the outer gate open and strode into the yard. He walked directly to the tower entrance.

Reaching out with his hand, he laid his palm against the door. He opened a channel to death, to the power that allowed all people to pass between worlds one final time. The power immediately sucked in all of the life-force from the wooden door.

Many things were made of the once-living. Trees, plants, and even insects had all been alive at some point in time before someone re-purposed their corpses. They kept a residual slice of life energy after they died. Within moments the door transformed from a hard barrier into a brittle wooden screen of ancient rotted timber. It morphed outward, splitting. Cracks emerged, then gaps broke into its surface. December pushed against the door and it shattered into a dozen pieces, falling to the ground. He glanced down at the remaining dust and rot. In the end, he thought, everything left the world like that.

Channels began to flow through the open door. They caught December's attention. Something was happening upstairs. Flows danced about the tower unfocused and abandoned. He stepped through the door, realizing fully that he was entering a trap.

A set of stairs lay directly before him. A table, three chairs, and someone's leftover dinner stood abandoned on the lower floor. Another door stood atop the stairs. This one looked thick enough to withstand a siege. Three iron bands re-enforced it, giving it strength.

December grinned. He felt elated, like a wolf on the prowl. Let them have their traps, he would take their lives, he thought to himself.

If anyone was looking for a magician, they would find one now. December grinned. Temple priestesses would be waking up early this morning.

He pointed his arm toward the door. A ball of magic shot forward, transforming into an electrical maelstrom. Energy flowed out of December's channels and exploded as the ball struck. The door shattered, exploding inward in seven pieces. Iron bands shot randomly across the room. One flew by his head passing arm's length away from his skull.

Smiling with pleasure, Master December sprinted up the stairs. A room filled with crates and six stacked barrels met him. A single lantern hung from a peg on the wall illuminating an open doorway. More stairs led upward toward the top of the tower. December continued his sprint up the stairs.

As soon as he stepped forward a set eight runes appeared on the walls. Dark brown smoke began to fill the stairway. He smelled the lethal poison and recognized it. The foul smell would kill anyone within a single breath. Master December didn't care. He had prepared for the worst sort of encounter today against another master, Darjeeling. Earlier enchantments and crafting had made poisons into the least of his worries.

Loud noises came from above. December pulled energy toward his physical channels, increasing his speed, his strength, and his reaction time. He turned a corner to find a hall, a door, and more stairs. He sprinted around the final corner hoping to reach the final set of stairs before whoever was waiting above could react.

It didn't happen.

December ran around the corner onto the final set of stairs. Hazel stood on the landing above, a barrel resting beneath her foot. A small burning rag stuck from the end of the barrel. She kicked the barrel down at him. There wasn't room to leap or to dodge. It didn't even hit him. Instead, the barrel smashed into the wall next to him. Flaming liquid splashed about, covering the entire hallway.

The liquid caught fire. A wall of fire reached up and burned from floor of the landing to the ceiling. Hazel screamed with joy as she watched the master necromancer engulfed in the terrible alchemical fire.

"You lose! You bastards! You lose!" She cried, terrible joy in her voice.

The flames gave off searing heat. Hazel's face began to hurt as she approached, slinging profanities and taunts into the wall of flame targeting the unseen necromancer.

Then her breath caught in her throat. A man's form walked out from the fire and began to climb the stairs. It was entirely alight with an alchemical blaze. A burning knife was held in his right hand.

"You." She hissed.

The burning knife stabbed into her heart. Hazel reached down to pull her own knife, trusting the Takers to give her power. She had the will, but her muscles refused to obey her command.

She could smell burning meat. The Takers in her blood screamed at her, but she could not obey. The knife had ended her ability to fight. Flame burned inside her heart, and enchantments from the knife crawled through her soul rendering it docile. The fight deserted her.

"It isn't fair." She cried out in disbelief. A small line of blood dripped down her chin.

"It never is." December agreed.

Master December picked her up by the neck with one arm. Grabbing his knife handle, he slung her off of the blade. Hazel's dead body rolled across the across the stair, flopping down into the inferno leaving a trail of blood behind.

Turning, he opened his fire channels and quelled the flame. It took five heartbeats for the inferno to dissipate, then December moved up the final set of stairs.

Hazel had left the door open above. He looked through to see an iron cage hanging in the center of the top floor room. Chains tied it to stout rafters above. The ceiling of this room jutted upward, expanding into the pointed roof. Cerna looked out from the cage. Dried blood and some grey mess stuck to his chest. Bruises and puncture wounds decorated his arms as if someone had been stabbing him repeatedly through the bars. His face looked like someone had beaten it with a club, his nose disjointed, his eyes bruised.

Cerna tried to say something but his effort was futile. December simply didn't care what he had to say. Cerna had no teeth remaining in his mouth, and that garbled his words. The necromancer master thought it was more important to wipe the blood from his dagger and ensuring none of Hazel's blood touched his own skin. He briefly thought about stabbing Cerna with the blade to see how long it took to become infected, all in the name of discovery. Miller would probably like to know that information as well, but he was too weak to get it himself.

But Cerna was Easter's man. That meant that there was surely an unseen trap. There weren't many forces in the world that December would back away from. He backed away from any confrontation with Easter where surprise could be on his side.

He turned to walk out of the room. Cerna grunted and rattled his chains. Cerna's pain and distress didn't matter to December. He thought about the tower. If the tower burned to the ground, then his headaches would be finished. If the tower survived, then Cerna was Easter's problem. He was done here.

He moved back toward the stairs. Bending down, he pulled Hazel's dead body up by her hair, then he used his long thin knife to cut it. Two hand-spans of Hazel's hair left with Master

December. Cerna stayed behind.

☐

TEST

Miller woke in the late morning. He lay sprawled on the floor fully clothed from the previous night. Brita lay on the floor beside him separated by the boundaries of the magic circle. Her light skin and dark lips made her look like she was from a painting, an artist's imagination.

Pushing himself from the floor, he walked to his small pile of belongings and began going through them. His journal stood open from last night. Notes that he barely remembered were hastily scribbled across the margins. Small pictures of clouds and arrows decorated the center of the page.

"What was I thinking last night?" he said to no one in particular. Brita opened her tired eyes and looked over at him.

"You said a lot of things last night. Do you remember it?"

"Not really. I was very tired. I'm sure it will come back to me."

She smiled back as she whispered, "I hope so."

They had finished their work in depths of night, searching for some path forward, some way to pull the Takers out of her.

179

Miller picked up the journal and walked over to his table. The quill and ink were still there. He inspected the quill to ensure there was no leftover ink at its tip. It was clean. Finally, he opened the jar of ink, turned a page in the journal, and began writing. As he wrote, more of last night came back to him.

The Takers can find Brita even through the magic circle. Do they use magic? Brita says they don't.

The illustrations of clouds and arrows. He remembered how Brita had described how the Takers could communicate with only emotion. They could also directly take over her thoughts and force ideas into her. They never had conversations though, they communicated with pure emotion. Brita had described it as a cloud of desires, of ultimate wants.

Miller wondered at how they communicated. Are Takers even capable of speech? Is this only a human concept? He pondered.

They had stayed up the entire night. Brita had described more of her experiences than ever. It had been the human touch that opened her up. A little company in her prison, the prison that he had placed her in.

Miller looked up to see Brita looking intently at the stairs. He heard footsteps from above. One of the others was awake. Franz came down to the main floor carrying a bucket. A disgusting smell followed behind him closely.

He scowled at Miller. "Decided to live down here? Can't you figure out how a simple set of stairs works?"

"Sorry. I was up late last night doing important things. How is your apprenticeship going?" Miller smirked as he pointed at the bucket of morning waste.

"Better than yours." Franz looked at the open journal. "Found anything new?"

Franz walked over to gaze at Miller's intricate drawings. What had begun as rough line sketches had transformed into art. Shading gave the clouds depth. Each cloud had been labeled with ornate lettering. Even the lines that connected them possessed labels testifying to Miller's assumptions.

Miller wanted to understand how to communicate without words, what kind of person this worked best with, and who might be prime candidates for this kind of thing. He suspected that the Takers might be targeting specific people due to their affinities to their communication talents.

"What's this?" Franz pointed at the center of a drawing. A crude depiction of a man and woman standing together took up the center of the page. They were surrounded by a dozen other small sketches. Words were scrawled beneath the couple, Alchemists.

"I'm not sure yet. There were a father and daughter that had showed an interest in Cerna. It could be a coincidence. It might not." Miller replied.

Miller placed his hand on his chin, momentarily adrift in though. "Have you heard any new information? How can the Taken even function within Home's Hearth?"

Franz shook his head, grimacing. "The Taken used to be easy to find. That made Home's Hearth a great place to defend against them. Now it's a lot harder. Even the temple is blind."

Franz looked up the stairs. "I had better check on Master Darjeeling. He should be waking up soon. I'm sure he will have tasks for me."

Before Miller could respond, Franz turned and walked quickly up the stairs. Miller hadn't heard any movement above. That didn't mean that Franz was wrong. Miller closed the book and returned to speak with Brita.

"What is his problem? Do you work for him or something?" Brita asked.

"Franz? No. He's just difficult by nature. He always has been. Plus, he is Darjeeling's apprentice. That will ruin a person's manners in any case. I just like to be careful around him."

Brita smiled coyly as if she was part of some hidden secret. "Don't like him?"

"Like him? This is an order of necromancers. Nobody likes each other. They don't recruit for likability."

"So you don't like Mistress Aileen? I thought you were kind of soft on her."

Miller paused to remember some of his fonder dreams. He had imagined leaving with Aileen, fleeing from the order and running away from the chaos. Aileen had claimed to dislike the White Hand as much as he did. Now that he had gained a little distance from her, Miler saw that it was more complicated than that. Aileen truly believed in the cause of the White Hand. She might not agree with how it was being done, but she certainly agreed that it needed to be done.

Plus, Mistress Sword was around to comfort her. Aileen hadn't been at the New Pony for days. She might still at the Garden with Phyllicitus, or perhaps she had moved on by now.

"I like you, a lot," Brita said. "If you get the Takers out of me, I will be ever so grateful." She stood there staring at him. Her gaze seized his attention causing his heart to race. It was a sultry look that promised love, lust, and endless pleasures. The magic of human connection crossed the circle barrier as if it wasn't even there.

Miller stepped forward toward the barrier. Brita took a step forward as well. They were separated by less than an arm's reach, yet they might as well have been an ocean away.

"You can save me, can't you?"

She licked her lips, hungry for his touch.

She unbuttoned a single button from her nightgown, showing a hint of skin from her ample bosom.

Footsteps pounded down the stairs. Franz appeared wearing his coat and carrying a short sword at his side. It seemed odd for a necromancer to walk the streets of Home's Hearth with any weapon, let alone one as common as that.

"What's happening? Is there a problem?"

"Bugger off Miller. I told you that Master Darjeeling would have some work for me."

"What kind of work do you need a short sword for," Miller asked, trying to pry just a little information from him.

Franz stopped and looked over at both of them. "Pray that

you don't find out."

He spun, stomped over to the door, swung it open, then marched out to the street.

Miller didn't like the look of that. Even Brita looked surprised. "What do you think that was about?"

He looked across at his journal then up at the stairs. Franz had seen something in there, and he reported it to Darjeeling. The sword didn't make much sense, even as an apprentice, there wasn't much in Home's Hearth that Franz could not kill.

"Franz might be going to the alchemists."

"Why would he bring a sword?"

"Maybe he thinks he can help find Cerna?"

"With a sword?" Brita looked unconvinced.

"The sword is new, isn't it? I haven't seen it before." Miller asked.

Miller bent down, attempting to return to his journal. After a few moments of gazing at it, he looked back at Brita.

"I have no idea what to do next. I'm hitting a wall."

Brita smiled. "I have a few ideas. Why don't you come into my circle and I will show you?" Her eyes danced with coquettish mischief.

Miller smiled back. "Is your plan to flirt your way out of here?"

"Out of here? No. This place isn't so bad. I'd rather be stuck with you and your crusty necromancers than be out on the street at the Taker's mercy. I would like to go out alone though, just to go to the market or maybe have a little privacy. Unless you can get your magic circle to move with me, then I'm stuck here if I want to be by myself. As boring as it is here, at least it's safer than outside.

"The circle won't move. There are other ways though. I could craft something that might last a day or two if you needed to get out alone."

"You can craft a mobile circle?" She asked, amazed.

"No. It would be more like a ring that you would wear."

"It would block the Takers?"

Miller shook his head sadly. "Only for a while. Any concerted effort would still get through."

"They got through earlier. I felt them outside. Even this circle isn't safe."

"I agree. We need to make more progress. We just aren't making much headway here."

"Is there a better place?"

"I think every place in Home's Hearth will be about the same."

"Is that because of the temple?"

"More because of Phyllicitus. She has some way of tampering with emotions. Some castings require aggressive emotions. Her power unintentionally softens many of the magic spells."

"Even in the Gardens? That place we went, the one with the patterns on the floor, that place felt different somehow."

Miller nodded in agreement. "I felt that as well. I think that place dates back to the days when Phyllicitus had just come into her power. Mistress Aileen told me that her first head priest, a man by the name of Stevenson, carved that pattern. There hasn't been much progress in understanding those patterns since."

"Why is that?"

"I don't know. I don't even know what they do, let alone how they work."

"It isn't just magic? Things don't work the same everywhere?"

Miller shook his head. "If only that were the case. My life would be much easier if there was only one way to craft. No, instead there are at least a dozen ways. I'm sure there are more."

"Really?"

"Yes. Crafting magic is a lot like crafting wood. There are dozens of ways to carve, join, glue, or cut wood. Any of which will result in the same types of things. I can make a chair with only an ax and a box of nails if I'm desperate and I'm willing to tolerate a lot of slivers."

"What makes that pattern so different? Why bother putting it there?"

"I wish I knew." Miller thought back to his time between the worlds, where forces obeyed different laws and his castings had been useless at best. "As far as I can guess, the pattern channels some other type of force that we don't have access to."

"What forces? Who has access to them?"

"I have no idea. Nobody that I know of. That's the difficult part of all of this. The Takers seem to use a completely different set of rules than us. It's like they're from a different world."

Brita continued her questioning, curious even if ignorant. "So again, if the forces don't exist, and nobody can get at them, why build the pattern in the library?"

"I'm not sure. Maybe they put it there to advertise it? Were they trying to attract attention?"

"Necromancy is dark stuff. Would they really want to do it in public? Also, why is the pattern in the Gardens so dangerous? If it is, then why is it still here?"

Miller shook his head as he tried to chase the chain of unanswerable questions away. "Those are the big questions. I have some theories, but I need to test them."

Her eyebrows shot up. "Oh, that sounds exciting."

"You won't like my tests."

She grew quiet. "Are you going to test them on me?"

"More like I'd like to test them with you. I just need to think of a way to do it safely. It involves the Takers."

She wrapped her arms around herself, plainly terrified. "What are the tests?" She asked in a soft voice.

Miller walked over to an abandoned chair and dragged it over until it was next to the edge of the circle. Brita stayed where she was. Sitting on the chair, he began to speak slowly as he stared at her face as if he didn't want to miss any of Brita's reactions.

"The order has never been able to stop the Takers from coming into our lands. Many of our masters have searched for their nests and their entry points into these lands. We have never found where they come from. I think I know."

She didn't respond. She waited on his words like she was waiting for him to speak her doom. In a way, she was.

"There is a place that is not a place. We call it the place-between-the-worlds."

"Worlds?" The word was unfamiliar to her. The idea of a single all-encompassing world is familiar to philosophers and the learned. Peasants and bar wenches might not ever encounter it. That word seemed to be occurring more and more often now that wizards surrounded her.

"A world is everything. It is the air, the land, the sea. This other place is different. Instead of a vast endless land, it is a series of cracks that we can traverse. Many of the magical forces we take for granted here just don't work there. It's a different kind of place."

"Traverse? To where?"

"We have no idea. There have been explorations in the past. None of them were successful. I think the Takers are coming from some other place where the magic works differently. That explains why they never use crafting against us, it's alien to them."

Brita's eyes widened. She had never considered the Takers using magic. It terrified her. "Thank the goddess that they haven't."

"The goddess doesn't have anything to do with it. Her powers are built here in our world. They have nothing to do with the Takers."

"But don't Gods have different powers as well?"

"Not really. Only the First Gods use magical forces differently. Even then, it could be just a more primal method of using the same forces. First Gods are embodiments of forces present in the world. The Takers are completely different."

"What is your test all about then?"

"I'd like to see if I can get them to react to magic found only between-the-worlds. If I can get them to react with similar forces it would tell me a lot about them."

"What does that have to do with me?"

"You are going to be the bait."

"What? Bait? Are you going to dangle me into this place-between-the-worlds and see how badly I get eaten?"

Miller frowned. "You see the problem clearly. I'd prefer it if you   didn't   get   eaten."

PATTERNS WITHIN PATTERNS

Mistress Aileen walked through the halls. She felt at peace after spending five days in the Gardens. The visit with Phyllicitus had been exactly what she needed. The emotional stresses, outrages, and depression caused by all of the dire decisions she needed to make added up to a heavy load.

Phyllicitus was great for finding inner peace and love. She was terrible at preventing the destruction of humanity by the Takers though. Aileen thought about what was coming, the new Takers and the decisions that needed to be made.

Hermagon was cooking up his own god to fight these things. She shook her head in despair at the thought. A necromancer god would probably be worse than just letting the Takers win.

She frowned, unsure where that thought had come from. Out of an abundance of caution, she stopped walking and opened her channels, seeking the presence of enchantments, or worse. She thought about what December had told her the day after gaining her ring. "It isn't paranoia if they really are out to get you."

Sadly, she knew exactly what he was talking about now. She had no idea back then, three short years ago.

Not finding any crafting cast upon her, or any indication of Takers, she continued through the hall into the banquet room. Bowls stood on five the eight round tables. Three people sat in a group at one of the tables discussing their previous night. The other tables stood empty, making the room seem cavernous and lonely. She recognized one of them as a city Alderman's son. She thought the other might be a priestess.

Aileen walked up to the first table. It stood abandoned, without diners yet overflowing with food. Eight empty chairs stood around it. Three heaping piles of fresh fruit lay piled high atop silver platters. A stack of wooden serving plates stood neatly beside them. She selected an apple then a crimson blood-orange. She had no idea how the Garden had managed to ship the blood-orange here and it still preserve its freshness.

Picking up a wooden plate, she set the fruit on it then walked to an empty table. Before Aileen had taken three bites into the apple, which was tasty even if a hint under-ripe for her liking, the priestess stood from her seat at the other table and shyly approached her. The priestess appeared young. Aileen estimated that she had only recently gained her full womanhood. The priestess wrung her hands in front of her, fidgeting like a shy adolescent.

Aileen normally hated it when her breakfast was interrupted, but somehow, she was happy to have company right here, right now. She felt safe here.

The priestess bowed respectfully. "Sister Aileen", she paused to gather her thoughts, "I see you are alone this morning. Would it be bothersome if we joined you?"

The idea brought a smile to Aileen's face. "Please do." The title of Sister hadn't shocked her. She had been outside of the temple for years, but somehow it had never been far from her heart. After a moment's thought, Aileen remembered the priestesses name, Deborah. It should have changed since she finished her initiation though. All priestess took new names when the entered service.

"Deborah?" Aileen tried to be polite, giving her an opportunity to use her new priestess name.

"It's Sister Unity now."

Aileen nodded, showing approval of her new name. A stray thought occurred to her. Goddess Phyllicitus gave every one of her accepted servants a new name. When a White Hand achieved their ring, they were given a new name as well. White Hand names usually signified something unique about their history or personality. In the long lives of White Hand masters, they were asked to change their name at least every three hundred years, if not more frequently.

Names had no magical power that Aileen knew of. But there was a common thread here. She made a mental note to speak with Miller about it. He always showed interested in these sorts of odd details.

The priestess sat at Aileen's right with the Alderman's son next to her. Aileen remembered the young man's name, Jacon. She had known his father years ago. Looking at Jacon, she remembered how his father had died, ripped apart by December's garden party of the dead three years ago in Ingalls. The memory didn't fill her with sadness as it would be expected, instead, it gave her hope in the world that such a wound could heal.

"Jacon." Aileen nodded. Jacon smiled, delighted that Aileen had remembered him.

The third member of their group sat at the opposite side of the table, farthest from Aileen. He was older than the other two, nearing forty summers of age. His dark short hair was cut in the way of the city dwellers, fashionable and neatly trimmed. He looked about the room with suspicion. Scars on his hands and arms, as well as his wild long hair, showed him as an outsider.

"This is Nikolson." Jacon supplied, "He has newly arrived in town. We thought that you would want to meet. He is from Jarlsland, just arrived in Home's Hearth yesterday."

"Jarlsland? I know a few people up there. It's rare to see a northerner here," Aileen gestured at an empty chair. "Please join me."

Nikolson didn't move closer. He scowled, glancing into the corners the room, then at her. "Yes, you are well known in Jarlsland still, Mistress Aileen."

"Oh my, are you that famous?" Sister Unity asked, unaware of her dark and bloody history with Jarlsland.

"Famous? More like infamous," Nikolson said.

Aileen looked across the table, directly into Nikolson's eyes. "Your point?"

"My point is that I came all the way here to speak to you. I've got some news you will want to hear."

"Let's have it then." Aileen didn't like how this conversation was getting started. Sister Unity stared back at her wide eyes. She hadn't known that Nikolson had used her to get in contact with Aileen.

Aileen nodded. The tactic made sense. The Gardens would not have allowed a foreigner like Nikolson to come without a member. That meant either Jacon or Sister Unity must have achieved some form of status over the past three years.

"Two months ago, I sailed on a longboat to a village called Cherats just west of Dog's Run, " Nikolson began, "We were hauling iron bars and cotton, hoping to trade for salt and red wine. When we arrived, the town was empty of people. We visited there three times before, and the town was healthy then. It had more than five hundred people living there, now it was empty. The crops still laid in the fields. The livestock wandered the streets unkept. The people had disappeared."

A cold feeling began to creep up her spine. She had been in that area before on conclave business. It lay only twenty leagues from where Hermagon's cabal met in their secret caves.

Nikolson paused, a hint of anger showing in his eyes.

"There's more, isn't there?" Aileen asked.

"Yes. The animals had changed. We saw a cow that grew an extra head. It wasn't a cow head though. It was some sort of bird. We found a dog with only three legs. A snake grew from where one of his legs used to be."

"What did you do?" Aileen asked, worried that some of her worst fears may have come true. She had always thought that Hermagon's plans for creating a god were sheer madness. Last time she traveled near that place, only a year before, she had found evidence of oddities in the local area. It hadn't been anything so strong as Nikolson described. She wondered how much time she had until Hermagon's god would be released into the world.

Nikolson continued, surprised at the question. "Do? That place was cursed, what was I to do? I rounded up the crew. We pushed off and sailed straight for Leeds across the bay. From there I spent almost every coin I had on a fast horse and rode straight to Home's Hearth. I went to the temple and talked to this Sister Fidelity woman. She didn't give me much confidence that this was being treated seriously. Then I went to the market and started talking to folks. I heard you were here at The Garden."

"You heard?"

"Yes, I heard. You're sort of well-known in this town."

"I'm not sure what I can do about it either. I know a few people though, and I can send someone over to find out what happened to the townsfolk."

"As I said, it looked like they all just walked out of town."

Aileen thought about what the other masters were capable of. Darjeeling could certainly charm an entire town to do his bidding. A cold feeling began to swell in her gut. She wasn't sure they needed to worry about the townsfolk anymore. They were probably dead.

She signaled a servant to bring her something to drink, then started to feel a hint of anger at herself. She had been ignoring Hermagon's efforts, trying to convince the conclave to end it. The conclave was narrowly split on the issue but with the new emergence of the Takers, more of the masters were willing to try extreme measures. The felt under threat and threatened people make bad decisions.

Cozying up with Phyllicitus had made it all worse. She had been captivated with peacefulness and love. Aileen had lost track of not only the Takers but from the machinations of the other masters. She shook her head, disappointed in herself.

Jacon spoke up. "Aileen, are you alright?"

Before she could answer, a servant returned with a steaming cup of tea. As he set it in front of Aileen, he bent to whisper in her ear.

"A message boy just arrived. He says that your apprentice requests your presence at the New Pony Inn. Apparently, he needs your help getting someone moved."

She stood up, grabbing her remaining apple for later. She quickly drank her remaining tea and grimaced in pain as the tea burned her throat. If Miller was thinking about moving their Brita through town again, then Aileen wanted to be there. Every time they took Brita out, it invited the Takers to make an attempt on her.

Aileen wondered why the Garden's hadn't let Brita stay there. It would have been far better for everyone to keep Brita close, and safe within the Gardens. That is, unless the Gardens weren't as safe as she assumed they were. The though gave her pause.

When the servant turned to leave Aileen jutted her index finger at the man. "Is that boy still here?"

"Yes, Sister Aileen." The messenger replied.

"Give him a silver ducat from my account," Aileen instructed.

The servant turned to leave. Sister Unity stared up at Aileen intently. Jacob had started to rise as well. Only Nikolson remained in place. She had the feeling they would follow her out, and they would try to help. That just might get all of them killed.

"One more thing." She called to the servant as he walked off.

The servant stopped and turned.

She thought about the Temple, the White Hand, and the strange patterns of culture that joined them. They had named her Mistress Shield, but it had never fit right. The Takers were coming, and she had spent way too much of her time in service to her soul. She needed to commit to the fight all the way.

The name Mistress Shield brought a slight smile to her face, then a wince of sadness passed over her. Someone in the conclave had decided to award her the name Mistress Shield when she gained her Master's ring. All masters were given a new name to begin their new lives with. Every few hundred years, masters were encouraged to choose new names as well. The White Hand believed that changing your name would change your identity, and thus make it more difficult for enemies to send curses, or Takers.

Aileen thought the name 'Mistress Shield' seemed name entirely too coincidental. She guessed that Easter was behind it somehow as if he was trying to set up everything he would need to draw her together with Mistress Sword. Two women masters in the Order of the White Hand would naturally be drawn to each other, and given the names, they would almost be driven toward each other. She didn't know what Easter's purpose was and she didn't like playing the game on his terms.

Easter's plan had worked in the end. With names so close, there was no way they could stay apart. Somehow fondness overcame enmity, and they became lovers, and sometimes friends as well. She pondered on the power of names, and how her inner view of herself could change her fate, and she didn't like how easily Easter had used it to his advantage. True, he had avoided an inter-order conflict. At the time, Hermagon's cabal was ready to enter into outright combat with Easter's cabal. Mistress Sword had been Hermagon's greatest, and least sane killer. Now she was closer to Aileen than she had ever been to Hermagon.

She had to admit, Easter had maneuvered everything perfectly so far. She didn't like it. She didn't like being a toy in his games. She wanted her own fate, and she wanted to claim her own name.

In a heartbeat, she knew what her name should have been.

She thought about her years at the temple, serving in far Jarlsland. She had wielded the power of the elements to free the north from the Eisenvard curse. Now she needed to do the same. The world didn't need a shield, it needs a cleansing.

"My name isn't Sister Aileen anymore. My name is Mistress Storm of the White Hand. I suggest that you use it."

The door to the New Pony opened. Aileen found Miller in conversation with Easter. Brita stood in the center of the protective circle. She had dressed for travel and now looked impatient for the journey to begin. Easter looked over at Aileen and held up his hand to stop Miller from speaking. She walked into the room, scowling.

"Where are you moving Brita?"

Miller tried to respond but Easter hadn't put down his palm.

Easter spoke slowly as he gazed sharply at Aileen, "You changed your name."

Aileen wasn't surprised that he knew. She just didn't know how.

Miller tried to say something but the look on Easter's face told him that talking would be a very bad idea right now. After a moment of silence, Easter reached over and patted Miller's shoulder reassuringly. He stood, then walked up to the woman who was once known as Aileen. He started to walk around her, staring at her every detail. He circled her and looked at her from head to toe. Aileen tried to speak but he held up his index finger to stop her. The gesture was more polite than the one he had just given Miller.

"You are different," Miller said, noticing a change in her. This new Aileen felt different. The magical flows that he had grown to know so well over the years had shifted slightly.

Easter continued pacing, looking at her every detail. "Was it Phyllicitus?" He asked, clearly not expecting an answer. Aileen narrowed her eyes, annoyed by this little game. Easter walked up close to her, holding out his hand. His black master's ring drew everyone's attention, two black tears stood out from its plain band. It was something not of this world, yet it was also Easter.

Aileen held out her own ring. It was thinner, more feminine. Black roses were tied together with black thorns. Then encircled her finger, protecting it, feeding off of it.

Easter held out his hand to touch hers, bringing their rings into contact. "Apprentice, meet your new mistress. Mistress Storm."

Miller stood there for a moment, unaware of why this was important. Lots of masters have adopted new names over the years. He always thought it was expected. Then the thought hit him. He stood there flabbergasted. The White Hand was an ancient organization with ancient rituals. Most of those rituals had been developed for a reason. Necromancers could be oddly pragmatic. Easter had reached out with his ring to touch hers. It wasn't a name change he was talking about. Aileen had changed her identity.

Visions of the pattern came to mind. The patterns were magic based on the very fact that it existed. Channels were not necessary or even encouraged. There was no sense interpreting the pattern, it simply was. The Gods achieved their powers through 'becoming enlightened'. The Takers used powers based only on their ability to affect people with their magic from between-the-worlds. Miller saw a vision of all magical systems connected to one simple truth.

"I am. You are."

Mistress Storm looked back at him. "What?"

Miller didn't know how to explain it. He saw all the connections in his mind. Magic connected to self-connected to the world connected to... something? Other worlds? There were no words to describe it sufficiently. No one had created a vocabulary to describe such a thing.

But it was the core truth of everything. It would be impossible to describe through any other means than a similar epiphany.

"Do you see it?" Easter asked Miller, concern showing on his face.

"I see it," Miller responded.

Easter followed it with a question. It sounded more like an accusation. "Then why don't you have a ring?"

MORE TESTS

Miller grew silent after Easter's comment. He didn't want to admit it to Easter, but the comment had raised his hackles. Miller knew five people who had gained their Master's ring, just in the past three years. His magical skills far surpassed every one of those new masters when they gained their rings. Miller knew that if he wanted the ring and the power that went with it, it was his for the taking. He didn't want it though. The price seemed too high.

So he went back to planning the next stage of his investigations into the Takers, into Brita. There were too many White Hand Masters around and he was finding it difficult to get anything done. Just at this small planning session, he had Master Easter and Aileen with her new name of 'Mistress Storm'. Every minute that went by seemed to cause more chaos and confusion.

"We need to move Brita again tomorrow. I'd like to do it just after breakfast." Miller began. He liked the idea of having a day to prepare.

"You want to move her to the Gardens in the middle of the day?" Easter asked.

Miller nodded. "I think we have to. The Takers are starting to make their moves. If we let them set the schedule, then we will be spending a lot of time defending her. We need to grab the initiative before they do."

"Makes sense, but it will be risky. If only a dozen Takers joined together, they could just rush your group and overwhelm you right here in Home's Hearth." Easter said.

Mistress Storm nodded in agreement. "Let's not give them a chance to hit us then."

Easter nodded along with Storm. "Agreed. We will need more people. We need to keep the crowd away from Brita when we move her through town. I'll send Darjeeling a message and see if I can get some help."

Miller held out his arms, motioning him to stop. The last thing he needed was to involve Darjeeling in anything, at least until he had heard from December. "I've got some people I can use for this."

Easter narrowed his eyes, unconvinced. "Who?"

"I think I can get Chamise to help. She knows where the Gardens are, and she's got the Eisenvard."

Easter's voice deepened with suspicion, "Eisenvard you mean."

"Yes, I guess I do. We could use the help right now."

Mistress Storm cut them all off. "The time for debate is over. Forget Darjeeling. Send for Chamise. If she brings help so much the better. If not, then we go anyway."

Miller thought about that tactic. Moving quickly could catch the Takers off guard. It would put Brita at risk. It would also be easy for Taken to approach in the street, and perhaps influence, if not murder her in transit.

"Give me an hour," Miller said.

"You have thirty minutes," Easter said. "After that Darjeeling may be back here and we go anyway."

Miller didn't know what to say. Mistress Storm urged him on.

"Don't just stand there, go!" She pointed at the door.

Miller turned and sprinted from the hall. He thought he had time to run to the Eisenvard keep and spend ten minutes to convince Chamise to come along. He didn't know how long it would take the Eisenvard to get organized and come along as well. He ran harder.

Every pace he took brought him closer to danger, yet farther from the things he needed to know. The only tool he had that could yield information about the Takers was Brita. He felt surrounded by enemies within the walls of the New Pony, as well as by Takers on the streets.

And now Aileen had changed her name. His leather-soled shoes tapped lightly across cobblestone as he thought about that event. The White Hand always changed their names when they became Masters. They were encouraged to change them again every few hundred years. Now Aileen, or Storm, or whoever she was now had changed her name yet again, and within just a few years of gaining her ring. He didn't understand why she would do such a thing.

A cart backed out of a side street, almost hitting him. He planted his right foot and bolted to the side and came to a stop, narrowly missing the trundling heavily-laden cargo hauler as it creaked unsteadily into the road.

A tall man with a stomach that hung past his belt shouted curses at the deaf cart as he scrambled behind it. An untethered draft horse followed behind, curious at what the disturbance was. The tall man ceased his shouts when he saw Miller.

"You, did the cart hit you?"

Miller shook his head, surprised at the man's immediate concern for his welfare. But this was Home's Hearth, he remembered, that sort of thing was normal here now that Phyllicitus had returned.

"You seemed to have lost control of your cart," Miller began, then stopped as he realized how obvious that statement was.

"You would think that, wouldn't you? No, the cart went exactly where it was sent to. The problem is my darn horse has a sick sense of humor. He likes to kick the cart out into the middle of the street."

Miller gazed at the horse. It was a handsome mare, much larger than the riding horses that he was used to. It stood in the street gazing left, then right, swishing its tail as if it hadn't a care in the world.

"The horse? Why would a horse like kicking carts in the middle of the road?" Miller asked, thinking his own horse.

Miller smiled at the humor.

The tall man frowned back, unamused. "What can I say? This horse is just like that. There isn't any reason for it, it just is. It's his nature."

Miler started to reply, then a thought struck him. There was no complicated reason that the horse was kicking carts into the street, it just did it. Then a torrent of thoughts began to flash through his mind. He thought about the place between the worlds, and how magic was different there. It just was and there was no reason for it. But that difference resulted in a very different place than the world that surrounded him now. Then he thought about the patterns he had found, nested old powers leftover from the time of the First Gods. Those patterns had no mechanics, no semantics, no syntax. The patterns merely existed and that seemed to be enough to move reality without magical channels, willpower, or disciplines.

A jolt of excitement hit him as he understood why the White Hand Masters changed their names. They could be trying to stand apart from the world and become something disconnected from it. Disconnecting would be an ideal way to protect themselves from those who would use patterns against them, but what would the cost be? What happens to a person when they are disconnected from their family, from their friends, from those that love them?

The jolt of excitement began to transform into fear. Miller had seen prisoners driven mad by years of captivity. Every year or two he saw White Hand Masters take another small step toward madness. He thought about Aileen and suddenly he knew why she had to change her name again.

Aileen might not a firm plan in her mind, but she might have the intuition to see that something was wrong. She might not want the name the White Hand Masters had given her, not because she disliked the name, but because she felt disconnected from the world she had so loved to be part of just a few short years before.

The carter began speaking to Miller as he guided the draft horse around the cart, then began to connect the harness to the cart. Miller didn't respond. He had become lost in a tirade of thoughts. His mind explored a dozen possibilities but one kept re-emerging.

The Takers didn't use magic, yet they had powers. They could exist between the worlds and exist almost in a ghost-like-state here as well. They didn't use crafting, nor did they use channels. Their power was deep and rooted in who or what they were. A droplet of sweat began to form on his back as Miller thought of the ramifications. The Takers were based on the same power as the patterns were, the same as whatever created the cracks between the worlds.

Miller knew that he had to discover more, had to find a way to use these patterns to defend from the Takers. In his heart, he knew that he was running out of time.

The lawn had been transformed into a mass of construction debris. A pile of stonework lay haphazardly collected near the entrance to the Eisenvard's keep. Miller watched with interest as two men walked out of the keep carrying large fragments of stone shattered stone. He recognized the stone as the same kind of stone that their credo was carved on, the rules they lived by. Now their laws were as shattered as the Eisenvard. Miller thought it was fitting.

Miller recognized one of the men from the nets game that Chamise had played. After the man dropped the block onto the pile, he motioned Miller to come over. The man turned and walked toward the entrance stopping to pick up a wooden cup. He filled it with water from a bucket next to it and began to drink. Then he poured the water over his sweat-soaked head.

Miller recognized him and offered a greeting, "Schaller, Its good to see you well."

Schaller scowled back at him, skipping right to the point. "Here for our girl, are you?"

Miller squinted, confused. He had never heard Chamise referred to as 'our girl' before. Something had changed. "In a way. I was hoping to get a few additional helpers though. Are you free this afternoon?"

"Free? For what? Digging up bodies from the grave? Casting curses at the full moon? Eating babies?"

Miller was unsure how to respond until Schaller's scowl broke into a broad grin. He pointed at Miller and laughed. "You might as well get used to it. You are going to spend a lot of time dealing with that kind of attitude, given your crafting choice."

Miller offered a not-exactly-honest grin back, "The plan is to avoid that kind of thing."

Schaller's eyebrows rose, almost on their own accord. "Do tell." He invited Miller to go on. Miller changed the subject.

"Where is Chamise?" Miller asked, skipping past Schaller's question.

"She'll be along soon. We sent word to her when we saw you turning toward the compound. She should be packing up what she is doing right now. I'm sure she will want to talk with you."

Another man stepped out of the door. He carried a leather sack, bulky with contents. It left a trail of sand behind it.

"Making a lot of changes around here, are you?" Miller asked, trying to pass the time until Chamise arrived.

"No. It's more like we are removing a lot of changes. Sometimes you just need to get back to the basics." Schaller's voice possessed a hint of sadness, of resignation.

Miller nodded, pretending to know what Schaller was talking about. He had no idea.

Chamise finally emerged from the outer door of the Eisenvard Keep. She wore filthy work clothes. Small bits of broken mortar decorated her hair. She saw him looking at her disheveled state and offered a grin in return.

"What's wrong? Never seen a woman who worked on masonry before?" Chamise asked with her voice full of sarcasm.

Miller responded, "Not like you. You bring a whole new style to it." He offered, returning his own grin. He found himself happy to see Chamise. He felt even happier that she didn't call him out for missing their last tutoring session.

"So?" She asked expectantly. Her gaze was hungry, eager for something. Miller knew what she wanted. He couldn't deny her, but first, there was work to do.

"I have a rare opportunity for you," He said, beginning the old line that Mistress Aileen, Storm now, used on him throughout his apprenticeship.

Chamise crossed her arms defensively. Schaller grinned along, feeling like he was on the inside of a joke when he actually wasn't. "This is going to be good." He cracked.

"I need to move Brita to the Garden." Miller began.

"So move her. You've got carriages and all that, right?" She said, thinking of the last time the White Hand had moved through Home's Hearth in mass.

"Darjeeling supplied those. We were hoping to avoid distracting him with this task."

Chamise didn't miss the context. "Don't want the crazy master there to eat Brita, ay?"

She had come uncomfortably close to the truth for Miller's taste. "Something like that. It gets better though. Master Easter thinks that the Taken will make a move and attempt to get Brita back next time we move her. We need to do things differently every time we move her."

Chamise jutted her lower lip out, thinking through the details before she spoke. "That is probably smart. But if you are expecting Takers then you will need more than an escort to clear away pedestrians. You might need some swords if trouble comes."

Miller spread his hands in acknowledgment and bowed. "Thus, I am here."

Chamise shook her head in disagreement, "No way. It's safer for everyone to keep Brita at the New Pony. Draw your own shapes on your own floor."

Miller sighed. He had hoped to avoid this kind of back and forth haggling. He had the winning card though.

"That's too bad. I had asked the masters to include you in our work with Brita. Of course, you would have to learn to power a two-tier channel circle with glyphs though."

She didn't hesitate. "With glyphs? Tied to the circle?" It would be decades before someone offered to teach her such a thing, and she knew it.

"Of course," Miller responded, sure that he had her.

Chamise glanced up as Schaller. He nodded up and down slowly as he thought about the details. "I don't know what a two-tier channel is but getting someone across town unnoticed could work. We should be finished with this work tonight though. How about tomorrow night?" Schaller gestured at the pile of broken stone to underscore his point.

"That's the challenge though. I was hoping to get started in less than an hour."

Miller wasn't disappointed. Less than an hour later, twelve Eisenvard arrived at the New Pony. They had used the time to clean up and change, a lot. The stains and mud-spattering were gone from their clothing. Now, instead of wearing their work clothes and game clothes, they stood in their white Eisenvard tabards layered over chain mail. These men and one woman looked ready for a fight. Swords and maces hung from belts. Five of the Eisenvard carried spears tipped with crossed hafts specially designed to use against mounted cavalry.

He didn't think they would need to fight cavalry in the streets of Home's Hearth, but he hadn't expected to fear Takers attacking in the streets either.

The sun shone from the horizon without a cloud to be seen. Miller felt impatient to get started. Hours had passed since he had originally wanted to move Brita. The Eisenvard had needed time to not only prepare and organize, but to grab a few hours rest before morning. Now the crowds were starting to form in the market and people had begun to awaken to their normal day's work.

Miller walked to Mistress Storm's side, bowing respectfully to both her and Master Easter. Six mastiffs stood about him, surrounding Easter and Mistress Storm as they spoke together quietly. Miller didn't worry about the dogs anymore. The dogs knew how to warn him away when wasn't welcome. It usually involved a bit of growling and showing of teeth. Today they were tolerant of him.

"Masters, are you ready?" Miller began, intentionally using the general term of master. He didn't know how to deal with Aileen's transformation yet, but he was sure that Mistress Storm would tell him later if he crossed some kind of line. She always did, or at least she used to.

That brought an uncomfortable thought. Mistress Aileen was his master, his trainer, his confidant. Who was this new person, Mistress Storm, to him? A simple change in name had ripples and he didn't know where they were headed. The concept of a person's identity, and how that identity tied them to the world, filled his thoughts when Easter began walking back toward the New Pony Inn. Easter walked through the front door and disappeared from sight.

Mistress Storm walked toward Miller, stopping an arm's reach away.

"You know they are going to come for her, don't you?" She said.

Miller looked back at Mistress Storm. "Yes. The Takers are going to come in any case. At least this way we might catch them off balance."

"These are the Takers. They don't get off balance." Mistress Storm replied; her tone harsh enough to cut the air.

Miller frowned, "Thanks for the encouraging words."

He decided to stop talking after that. After a quick bow, he moved to join with Chamise and the rest of the Eisenvard. These were warriors, born and bred to kill spell-crafters. They had wreaked terror across the lands only a few short years ago. Now, three years after their fall, he felt safer with them than with his own order. But his order was composed of necromancers, Miller considered, so that sort of made sense.

"Ready?" He asked Chamise.

She flashed him a smile of encouragement. "Aren't I always?"

Miller replied, "Yes. I just like to ask."

"And I just like to ignore you." Chamise offered in response, mirth dancing in her eyes.

Now it was Miller's turn to smile. As much as Chamise talked about ignoring him, she never had. Most of their early days of knowing each other had little to do with being ignored. She had been his first and only experience with how love might be, only three years ago. Somehow, he would always hold her in his heart tenderly. Sadly, as an apprentice in the Order of the White Hand, any affection toward her would only bring doom. The order was jealous of its apprentices.

Why? Miller had no idea. He could only smile in return. A pang of loneliness jutted into his heart.

"You brought out all the old uniforms?" Miller asked, trying to change the subject.

Chamise nodded, "People take you more seriously when everyone is dressed the same. Don't ask me why, they just do."

He nodded in understanding. "When we arrive, I'd like you to take Brita in with us. I doubt the Garden will give the entire group permission to enter. I'd like you near the front of the line, so we don't get pushed out."

"Worried about the Gardens?" The thought hadn't occurred to Chamise.

Miller continued, "More like worried about showing up with a group of necromancers. Historically they have been forbidden from entry. I guess the Gardens has some kind of protective crafting to protect against necromancers, but I'm not sure."

"What about Aileen?" Chamise brought up.

"Aileen? She's Mistress Storm now. I guess she's special, given her service to the goddess." Miller guessed.

"Isn't she still in the order?" Chamise asked, slightly confused at Mistress Storm's new name.

He thought about the new Mistress Storm for only a moment. "Oh yes. She is definitely in the order. Without a doubt."

The doors of the New Pony opened. Easter walked out carrying a flame-blackened staff. He held it in front of him as if to clear the way. Two enchanted brass caps covered each end of the staff, only a hand-span in length and covered in runes. Miller felt tingles from magical flows. Whatever that staff contained would be impressive. He felt magical flows from thirty steps away.

Then Brita emerged. She paced herself to match Easter's walk staying five steps behind, with the black dogs taking up positions at their side. It seemed like some Noble's procession, Brita being escorted by Easter, and followed up by the adoring crowd of well-wishers. Only, in this case, the Herald was a necromancer, and the adoring well-wishers had been replaced by a pack of hell-hounds. Brita seemed nervous, glancing left and right, looking at the Eisenvard, at the masters, and at the small gathering crowd outside the gates, back to the dogs. The townsfolk could tell something was happening, they just had no idea what it was. They gathered to witness the parade, unsure of what it actually represented.

There was no carriage this time. Instead of riding, they all formed into a line, then they began to walk.

Chamise shouted orders to the Eisenvard. "Take up positions!"

As one, the Eisenvard sprang into action. Four of the men

sprinted to the front of Easter's line. Each carried a spear wrapped in a white cloth. Before Miller could ask what that was about, Chamise walked quickly up to him, tapped him on the shoulder, and pointed at a position behind Easter right of Brita. Mistress Storm raised an eyebrow, nodded, and moved to the left of Brita. Four more Eisenvard walked up behind them. Each of them carried a sword and shield. The coat of arms, a black sword crossed with a black star atop it, stood out on their white shields. The other Eisenvard filled in the sides of the column.

The column of marchers paused. Townsfolk began to glance at them with interest. Miller didn't know what the next move was, but Chamise seemed to have done some planning. He didn't think that was a bad thing, as he doubted Darjeeling had a spy in the ranks of the Eisenvard, at least not yet. Darjeeling had never liked the Eisenvard and he wasn't the forgiving kind.

"Prepare!" Chamise shouted.

The four spearmen unfurled the cloth at the end of their spears. White banners decorated with crossed swords and star emerged into the light. It had been three years since the city had seen such a procession. He remembered back then when the Eisenvard ruled the city before Phyllicitus's return.

The banners of the Eisenvard unfurled into the evening air.

Miller had a thought. While this column would keep unwelcome townsfolk away and be ideal for defending against a Taker raid as well. It might cause some problems with Phyllicitus as well. The goddess had banned the Eisenvard only three years ago. She had allowed these few Eisenvard to stay out of mercy, and only when they had taken some other form of work and sworn off their warlike ways. Now the Eisenvard stood proud in the streets of her city, swords ready, spears in hand.

Chamise began to speak. Her voice loud, clear, and filled with strength. It carried across the yard and echoed off the keep. Her tone filled Miller with confidence and gave him hope that even if the Takers tried to make a move, they would be ready.

"Eisenvard!" She shouted.

The men answered back with affirmative shouts. "Huzzah!"

"Wizards!" Chamise shouted again.

The necromancers answered only with silence.

"Home's Hearth!" She continued to no one in particular. The Eisenvard cheered anyway.

"It has been a long time since we have been called on. The Takers are here in Home's Hearth. They seek to recover the soul of their little lost lamb." She said, pointing at Brita as she cringed slightly away from Chamise.

"Is that going to happen?" Chamise shouted to the crowd.

The voices of the Eisenvard erupted. "No!"

Miller saw Mistress Storm calling out as well. Easter stood with a face of stone, unmoved by the cheers.

Chamise smiled at them. "By the last door, it isn't! You know the Takers! You know what they can do!"

"We know! We are ready!" The Eisenvard answered in unison.

A chill shot up Miller's back. This wasn't some kind of plan that Chamise had arranged. This was an Eisenvard ritual. The words had been learned by all of the Eisenvard decades ago. Miller's worries about a resurgent Eisenvard seemed all too prescient. The Eisenvard were more than a group of people, it was a philosophy that favored might, regardless of right. It favored using violence to solve the 'problem' of rouge magicians, and lawful ones as well.

"Drink your sanity juice then!" Chamise cried, holding up a small glass flask of potion she had dug up from the keep. Miller recognized it as the very potions he had made only three years ago, mental discipline potions that prevented the Takers from seizing the drinker's soul.

The Eisenvard began moving about, removing vials from their pouches and drinking them. The potion would help them fight off the influence of the Takers. Their minds would be defended if any of the Taken's blood touched them. Miller had always thought that somehow the Takers could live in the blood of their victims. There was no way to prove it, but this potion had helped prevent the Eisenvard from being completely Taken before. The fact that they still had it now said a lot about their readiness.

The men finished their potions.

Chamise called out. "Let's go!"

The column began its twenty-minute march to the Gardens.

Miller hoped those potions would be of any use against these new Takers. He doubted it.

.

CERNA'S FATE

Workman Street stood gloomy in the night as Franz turned onto it. Three blocks from the New Pony, and already he was starting to gain some energy for the day's work. Home's Hearth awakened around him. While the bakers have been working for hours, the rest of the town now joined them. The shouts of workmen filled the air as they began their labors. A line of three-story buildings stood side by side at the end of the street with no room between them, forming a barrier between where the necromancers made their nest and the rest of Home's Hearth. He wondered if Easter had picked the New Pony Inn because of that wall of buildings. Those buildings could shield the order of necromancers from the temple's view, or it could shield the temple from theirs.

For a brief moment, Franz wondered how Master Darjeeling ever put up with Easter. With all of his sly tricks and backward maneuvering, Easter should have passed into oblivion long ago. Yet now Easter stood, ready to push back all of Master Darjeeling's carefully laid plans. It wouldn't matter soon enough, he thought. The final test was close at hand. Darjeeling had hinted just a few months ago that this was so. Franz would undergo whatever secret trial the Order had in store for him. He would pass, he had no doubt. Then Master Franz would pick a new name and find a new destiny, one as master instead of servant.

Franz wanted to get to Moon Street where the herbalists, mystics, and alchemists made their homes. A crowd of fifteen people stood where Moon Street crossed with Workman Street a block before the street's end. He watched as a small boy, perhaps no older than six years, pointed to the distance. The crowd talked excitedly.

When he arrived at the corner a sense of foreboding overcame him. More buildings looked down on the street, each painted with bright colors of blue, red, and yellow occupied the sides of the road like sentries. A plume of black smoke stretched in a thin line across the sky pouring, from a tower several blocks ahead like a giant furnace's chimney, or a cremation pit. Three three massive five-story towers stood far in the background, their tops obscured within a stream of windblown smoke. A single work tower stood alone and engulfed in fire. Franz recognized the source of the flame. He had been there before. The alchemist's tower burned against the morning sky. Fire shot into the air, spilling flame and coating the neighboring buildings with burning ash.

He felt dumbstruck. Looking back toward the New Pony Inn, Franz thought about how his report to Darjeeling would go. Darjeeling would ask for details. How did it happen? Was it on purpose? Who could have done it?

Franz swallowed nervously, tasting ash and phlegm. He simply didn't know. He stared at the burning tower thinking, analyzing, trying to reason out what could have happened. It seemed a strange coincidence to him. He had just seen Miller's journal yesterday. Franz smiled inwardly, bemused at Miller's initial lack of caution, and thought about how naive Miller was. Leaving his journal in easy access was an invitation to the other

White Hand members to steal his research and at least take credit for it.

He had begun to notice small changes in Miller's behavior though. Miller had somehow grown suspicious of the alchemist and his daughter. Franz wondered what Miller suspected. Did Miller know something that he didn't? Did Easter?

He took in a deep breath, attempting to calm his racing heart. The masters constantly allied and then fought against each other based on their own interests. He wondered if Easter and Aileen had allied together against Darjeeling. Goosebumps rose from his skin as he thought what that would mean. Worse yet, Master December had passed through the final door more than a month before, he was surely overdue to return.

Miller was at the New Pony this morning. Franz doubted Miller would set fire to a tower in the middle of Home's Hearth, he wasn't strong enough for it, but Aileen was. And Aileen had Mistress Sword in town as well. A vision of being surrounded by dark necromancers, outmaneuvered by Easter, and left to die by his Darjeeling sprung into his mind. Miller could have brought along the Eisenvard as well. The certainly would not hesitate to burn an alchemist's tower to the ground.

One final terrifying thought came to his head. Mistress Aileen could be behind it all. She would be the type to simply burn a building down, roasting all of its occupants alive. As much as she claimed to still follow the ways of the temple, Franz had seen her make truly frightening decisions before. Aileen didn't just decide to do things. She took action as well. Miller was just an apprentice and an unmotivated one at that. He would never do something this extreme. Mistress Aileen was a different matter.

The towering fire grew more dangerous and more beautiful each minute he watched it. When he reported this, Master December would want to know if Aileen was at fault. There were politics among the masters. If she had lit such a fire in Phyllicitus's city there would be repercussions. Master Easter would have to call her to task. Of course, if Easter had ordered the the fire, that would be different.

But being too curious would be dangerous as well. If Aileen had set the fire, then the entire event could be a trap. She could be lying in wait, observing who would come to the alchemist's rescue. Franz needed to know who set the fire, but the alchemist's fate was more problematic. Master Darjeeling had been toying with dangerous forces. Franz wasn't entirely sure about what the alchemist's secret was, but it had to involve the Takers. Somehow Master Darjeeling was pushing the alchemist toward some dark end, and only time would show the full scope of his plan.

Soon, he would have his master's ring in any case. Master Darjeeling had promised him as much. Only last week Darjeeling had told him that his time of trial was approaching. He didn't know what the trial was. He assumed it would be terrible. He half expected to be required to murder some children, re-animate their corpses, then to watch as the children devoured their own parents. That sounded like something that the Order of the White Hand would use as a trial. Franz grinned at the thought.

He began to swear under his breath. Franz wondered if this could be the trial he was promised. If he was too cowardly to check on the alchemist, then the Master's ring might pass him by. The more he thought about it, the more this seemed like the kind of trial that the Order would engineer, one without a clear answer.

The Order seemed to love problems without clear answers, Franz thought.

Franz began to walk down Moon Street toward the inferno. After a few steps, he began to jog. He needed to get there before the fire destroyed all of the evidence along with the alchemist himself. The woman, Hazel, he didn't really care about.

After a minute of running, he noticed a few others running along as well. Volunteers grabbed buckets and ran along to fight the fire. Flaming debris shot up into the sky then fell upon the town. The fire leaped up from a building in the next block, passing from a dry thatch roof to a small home. The fire had begun to spread. Screams filled the night as people confronted the flames, first in fear, then with resolve.

This was Home's Hearth, the seat of Goddess Phyllicitus. He assumed that God-magic would protect the people of this town in a limited way, but not all of them. The power of Phyllicitus gave them bravery and faith, she didn't even need to be here for it to happen.

A young woman sprinted up to him. Her long red ponytails flailed along behind her. She offered a bucket to Franz as she came near. Franz smiled and took the bucket. He couldn't think of a better way to hide than in the middle of a crowd. He continued sprinting along Workman street, every pounding step bringing him nearer to the flaming tower.

The crowd roared with fear. Fire sprang from a room on the top story of the alchemist's tower. Instead of breaking apart, a flaming wall slid down from the side of the building. It exploded into a cloud of sparks as it hit the ground. The tower roof sprung alight, belching smoke out from its center to coat the morning sky. Above, exposed for the world to see, hung a cage. A single man could be seen waving his arms wildly at the crowd through its iron bars. He shouted but the noise of the crowd interfered with Franz's hearing.

Reaching into his physical channels, Franz heightened his ability to hear. At first, the noise of the crowd seemed to deafen him. He quickly moved to narrow his hearing focus at the tower. The man screamed at the crowd. "The Alchemist's Daughter! The Alchemist! They are Taken! Beware!"

Franz recognized the voice. There could be no mistaking the low rough tone of Cerna. Stopping, Franz stared above, manipulating his body channels until his vision improved and he could see within the tower opening. It was Cerna. He was imprisoned in an iron cage. It hung from a burning rafter.

Soon enough the building would collapse. Cerna would fall three stories and then be buried in flaming wood. He would die a horrible slow death as he was broken, burned, then asphyxiated by lack of air.

A vision came to Franz's mind. Easter would feel it when Cerna passed. He would come to the ruin and raise Cerna from the dead. It sounded like Easter would have a lot of secrets to discuss with Cerna, secrets that probably involved his master.

Franz swore, damning Cerna for putting him through this, damning whoever imprisoned Cerna in the tower. If Easter learned of the alchemist before Darjeeling's plan was complete, then Franz knew his time as an apprentice would rapidly reach a terminal conclusion. When it came to dueling, he had absolute confidence in Easter's ability to come out on top whether dueling Darjeeling, or himself. Darjeeling would return from the final black door eventually, but Franz knew that he would not. Darjeeling would discard him like yesterday's waste.

There was nothing else to do. He ran to the side of the street, letting the crowd surge forward in their need to help. Human compassion mixed with a goddess-given need to do right ruled the crowd. The townsfolk bravely sprinted toward the fire. Franz allowed his body channel to close and return his hearing to normal. He reached down and grasped a brown pouch that hung from his belt. He pulled out a metal vial. Breaking the seal, he drank a potion that Darjeeling had taught him to brew. It refilled his spirit. His channels surged and screamed to be released. Franz knew how to use the elemental channels but not expertly, this potion would give him power. He whispered the five words of evocation, opening his fire channel. Standing straight, he stabbed his arm into the air. His forefinger extended pointing directly at the tower. The word of release left his lips.

"Ahigap!"

Magical flows released within Franz. They traveled up his arm as fast as a scream. Leaving his arm, invisible power rippled upward until it struck the metal cage. He pushed his channels into the cage and enveloped Cerna. The power dug into his mind, forcing itself into Cerna's center of will in an effort to control him, to make him a puppet.

Then it touched a small latent spell that had lain in wait, buried deep in Cerna's soul. His magic mixed with hidden spell another flow began to yet another hidden spell. Within a second twenty tiny hidden spells pulled power in from the surrounding world. Before apprentice Franz could puzzle out what that mean, all of the spells exploded at once. The sky erupted into a flaming ball larger than a house. The tower shattered into countless burning pieces. Fist-sized shrapnel shot upward toward the sky, then arced to finally pour down on the crowd below. Small pockets of fire sprung up from a hundred rooftops in every direction. The crowd screamed in terror almost as one.

With confusion on his face, Franz paused to watch the glorious spectacle. Flames continued to shoot into the air as the entire tower became a tornado of flame. The crowd seemed stunned, unable to determine if they should rush forward to save the other buildings or to flee Home's Hearth and leave it in the hands of the goddess. He coughed as he witnessed the power of the goddess spurring the people to help others and urging them not to escape. The smoke grew thicker as new fires began to spread. As he turned to leave, he felt a cold spike traveled up his back. Something was wrong here. Something from beyond the grave was here.

"Too soon for you." He whispered under his breath. Franz knew how these things worked. The dead might be robbed of their lives, but it took more than that to allow them to walk free in the world. It took power. He has assumed that Easter's trap would be the end of it, then he reconsidered.

He opened his spirit channels. Gazing back into the smoke, he saw the cloudy form of a spirit. The spirit stood barely visible to his spirit-sense. Franz looked at the spirit. It used to a muscular man who had a short beard in life. Franz didn't know him and he didn't care who he was, but he did care that the spirit seemed very interested in what he was doing. Most spirits didn't really concern themselves with what the living went about.

He extended a hand forming his fingers into the symbol of

binding. After years of apprenticeship to Master Darjeeling, he didn't need to utter power words or use ley lines to cast spells, he simply pushed with his will to bind the spirit to him. He would devour the spirit much like he devoured his lunch earlier.

It didn't happen. Instead of dissipating into spirit energy the ghost simply walked toward him. It passed through the people in the crowd, an abandoned wagon, and a horse trough like they weren't even there. It stopped five paces from him. The crowd began to surge forward, the hidden power of Phyllicitus urging them to do the right thing, to fight the fire, to save the town. The ghost made no other move than to stand and watch. Opening his spirit channel wider, Franz asked "What are you doing here spirit? Who sent you?"

The spirit cocked what appeared to be his head to the side. The spirit's words were like ice pouring into his mind. "I'm just getting a good look at you, Franz. I want to make sure that I know who I'm dealing with. I'm sure that I will be asked who burned up the tower when I get back."

His hair shot up. This wasn't a stray spirit. It had been sent here. It could have been following him for days. One of the Master's had been watching him. Was it Aileen? No. He had been so careful. Easter? Easter would have confronted him.

He shouted back to the spirit through his channel. "Who sent you?" Franz began the true binding to compel truth from the spirit, but it simply laughed at him.

"You are not ready for this Franz. Don't worry, I'm sure that we will get to talk about this event at length once the other masters are finished with you."

The ghost began to move down the street. It moved unhurried but made quick time as it passed through barriers and townsfolk with ease. Franz sprinted after it even though he had no idea what he would do when he caught the thing. Whatever master had raised the spirit was strong enough to defend it, even at a distance. And something else the spirit had said bothered him, that he would talk with him about this later. It gave him pause, then Franz stopped running.

He knew who the ghost was. It was Aileen's old ally, the inquisitor from the House of Questions, torturer and investigator, rack adept and nail puller. Master Darjeeling had warned him of the ghost. While the ghost didn't have the power to affect him in the real world, on the other side it would be different. If Aileen sent him through, then this ghost could be quite the challenge. Aileen had sent a spy and he needed to neutralize it before it reached Aileen's side.

He immediately turned from his course and began to run towards where Darjeeling should be. If all went well then Darjeeling could interfere with Aileen's plans before his doom was sealed.

The shape of a man came into view as he turned the corner, unseen by Franz. He was tall and wore a long cloak wrapped closely around his body. It looked to be soaked with water as if protecting the wearer from the smoke. A hood hung over the man's head. Master December strode purposefully after Apprentice Franz, eager to see what Master Darjeeling, his White Hand brother, had been up to.

ALL THE BLOOD

A wave of excitement passed through the Rat. He could sense something was in progress, something important. Pausing in his inspection of a newly ripened fruit, its green and yellow surface striped with the promise of fall flavors, he tried to fully understand this feeling of change that had descended on him. Normally he would stop and ponder the miracle of a fruit that grew until the first snow, but he had the feeling there wasn't time.

Bowing to the farmer, he returned the fruit and walked away through the busy market without a word. He needed to get a sense of what was happening, and what the Friends wanted of him. Spying an open table at a half-empty beer tent, he briskly walked past a small gaggle of a half dozen people. Navigating around them, the Rat moved past to get a table with a single chair. He pulled out the seat and sat down. It sat next to a waist-high table whose dark walnut surface was barely large enough to hold a mug of ale. He doubted that anyone would be interrupting him here.

"Sir? What will you be having this fine morning?"

A server interrupted him. The Rat exhaled in agitation, then thought better of it. He offered a smile, more to himself than to the server. "I'll have a dark beer, and whatever bread you have about."

As the server nodded and immediately walked off, The Rat positioned himself at the table. He placed his head in his hands to cover his forehead and eyes. He began taking inventory of the urges that had suddenly arrived. Something was calling him toward the center of Home's Hearth, pulling him there. It must be the Friends, but the feeling didn't give him any information, just a sense of urgency.

Luckily, he was already at the Market, only three blocks from the city center. He wondered what had gotten the Friends excited. Hoping it wasn't something that could ruin all of his carefully laid plans, he tried to get a sense of what particular thing was happening. The Friends weren't very good at providing details. He tried to reach out through their group mind, to find another of his allies who could see what was happening, to get a human being's point of view.

Shouts erupted from the edge of the Market.

An older man with a paunch belly stood and pointed across the market toward the road, "Look! They are marching!"

A young lady with a twelve-year-old girl at her side shouted back to him, "The 'Vard! They're back! Does the goddess know?"

"What is happening? Why are they here?" came from the crowd. The crowd in the marketplace surged toward the road, attempting to see the spectacle.

It looks like I'm in the right place at the right time, the Rat thought excitedly. He stood up from the chair he had so recently conquered and moved toward the edge of the market. The Rat wasn't the only one. The entire marketplace paused in an effort to see what was happening. He joined a cluster of fifty people standing by the side of the street, the market at their back.

It was a parade. White flags snapped above the tops of the five spear men leading a procession. Their black emblems stood out plainly against white shields and cloth. The Rat felt surprised, it looked like an Eisenvard parade. The procession seemed to number only a few dozen but the crowds surged about it making it seem like hundreds. The Eisenvard had come out of their little keep, peeking out to see the light of day. For a second The Rat wondered what had driven them out, then he felt the Friends trepidation. In the midst of the wizard-hunting, witch burning, spear-wielding armed squad walked a Master of the White Hand. The Friends drove his attention to him, then to the woman that followed behind. The Rat felt something from her, a familiar touch as if she too had been touched by the Friends. Something blocked him from making a connection with the woman.

"Faa," The Rat swore as he had his entire life, without vulgarity. Watching the way the procession was deployed to protect her, he decided it must be the woman they had kept in the inn. The White Hand master must have found a way to shield her. The Rat knew that a spell would not be good enough to guard her. With enough time the Friends could break through that barrier and reclaim her, with or without his potions.

But that wasn't the point. The White Hand had captured one of them. They now had someone to experiment on, someone that could put the White Hand on a path to discover a weakness in the Friends. The Rat remembered that they had done it before just three years ago. There was an apprentice walking behind, speaking calmly with a woman dressed in the Eisenvard's colors. The masks seemed to be coming off, he thought excitedly.

The Friends had been right to be concerned. The Rat knew about their captive woman already. He had received reports from other Taken almost as soon as she had entered the city. Now White and their Eisenvard allies escorted the Taken woman through Home's Hearth, directly toward the Gardens.

He didn't know what magical tools the Garden could offer the necromancers. It didn't seem to be a natural alliance to him; none of it did. The Garden normally didn't allow the White Hand to even enter their grounds, let alone use their arts. The Eisenvard alliance was an even larger surprise.

The Eisenvard had fallen into decline. The Gardens had become more tolerant after Phyllicitus joined forces with the necromancers as well. The entire world seemed to revolve around the White Hand right now. His plans to seize the temple and take the goddess seemed to be coming apart before his eyes. The White Hand had found a way to defeat the Friends during the previous incursion. He wondered if he was seeing preparation for that same defeat in front of his eyes.

The Rat knew what he had to do. He had to stop these necromancers.

There was nothing to be done by standing here. He reached down and pulled a leather flask from his belt. This flask was smaller than his hand, dyed red and decorated with an image of a snake drawn upon its rough surface. He drank the bitter juice that it contained. He felt the world lurch beneath him. He staggered, almost losing his balance before he recovered. The alchemical fluid he had swallowed worked to open his perceptions, to allow him to call to the Friends, and thus to every other Taken in the city.

He poured his will outward, even while crawling upon the ground. Half of his forces were to join near the temple and begin their true mission. The other half he called to him. He pressed every ounce of will to send a final clear message.

"Come! Now! Come! Bring your Blades!"

The Rat led his followers toward the Temple, toward the Taker's true goal.

Sunshine flowed into the room softly, filling the space with warmth and comfort. Phyllicitus stood on the balcony, its marble railings stood between her and the Garden filling her eyes with the beauty of expert cut stone-work. Periodically across the stone railing that an artisan had fixed cut gems. She delighted watching the light dance from their surfaces to form beams in the air and patterns on the walls.

The sunshine clothed her with its radiance, the morning sun complementing her beauty as it reflected off her perfect white gown. Her brown hair hung to the small of her back, natural ringlets gave it a somewhat wild look.

Phyllicitus loved everything beautiful. She loved to watch the sunrise every day. She loved to watch it set. She loved the stars at night and the clouds at noon. Life was like a harmony of perfection with music that penetrated into her soul.

But now there was a note of discord in that harmony. She stood still, soaking in the late morning light, desperately searching for where the poorly tuned note had come from. She could tell that something was wrong in her city. She hadn't felt a note like this for the past few years.

The bottle of wine tempted her with its full bouquet of flavors. It stood alone, half empty on a small round table tucked away in the corner of the room. The Gardens kept an excellent supply of her favorite vintages on hand, just for her. Sadly, she had the feeling that it wasn't time to indulge in that little pleasure right now. The wine would have to wait, a pity, she thought to herself.

Something was either happening now or preparing to happen. She needed to be ready. As much as she loved the Gardens, she knew where she needed to be, at her temple.

A small bell stood next to the wine bottle. Its dark bronze curves embossed with the etched leaves and trees. Small animals danced within the design, bringing the feeling of celebratory abandon and joy when she looked at it. The bell was an ancient thing left over from times-gone-by, back when the First Gods walked the lands, and the people worshiped them.

Of course, that was before people had understood that the First Gods really didn't care about them in any sense of the word. The First Gods were as much animal spirits as they were deities. Perhaps humans had learned of godhood from them, perhaps they had always had it inside themselves. In any case, the First Gods were only a note in history today. A thousand years ago they walked the lands, sometimes alone, sometimes with their herds of beasts, and sometimes with their human shamans. The First Gods had abandoned humanity at least five hundred years ago. While she couldn't ever abandon her people, they were close to her heart, she could understand why animal spirits might. Humanity had never done well in the care of animal spirits. Now that people had left behind the dark days of living in forests and worshiping beasts, humanity might just blossom into something truly amazing.

She hoped that was true. In her darkest hours, she had begun to doubt.

A powerful note of discord rang out from Home's Hearth, soundless yet its vibrations shook her heart. It was time to go. She picked up the bell and rang it three times. By the end of the third ring Sister Immaculate entered the room. The sister came in, glancing around at the room's unusual disarray, looking for some emergency.

"Goddess?" She asked, as she finally bowed low to Phyllicitus, keeping her eyes firmly locked on her feet.

"Don't you feel it?" Phyllicitus responded, "Something is about to happen. I need to return to the temple. Fetch my light blue dress, my small boots, and my silver headband. I'll need to get changed quickly."

"Changed? There were three bells. Shouldn't that be an emergency?"

"It is an emergency girl. I can't face the unknown looking like I just crawled out of bed. It simply isn't done."

Phyllicitus smiled as she saw the discomfort on Sister Immaculate's face. Sister Immaculate was always serious about her duties, sometimes Phyllicitus feared that her tolerance of missed schedules and overlooked details would give the poor woman stomach aches for a month.

Sister Immaculate regrouped, and simply stood up and acknowledged the order. "Yes, Goddess."

She walked from the room. Phyllicitus's silvery voice called from behind her. "Hurry now. This seems important. Let's not let all of Home's Hearth become discordant."

The sister hurried along, whispering to herself. "Discordant? What does that even mean?" She had served the goddess directly for the past year and had long ago stopped trying to understand everything she said. Some things, Sister Immaculate thought, were only comprehensible to the gods.

Twenty minutes later, after a quick change into a long flowing blue dress the color of a baby's eyes, and two shoe selection changes, Sister Immaculate, Goddess Phyllicitus, and three young neophytes from the temple stood before a waiting carriage. A broad-shouldered man dressed in the livery of the Garden stood waiting, holding the richly decorated door open for her. A small red stair had been swung down from the entry to give her easy entry into the interior.

Just before she placed her foot on the bottom step, she glanced up to the sky. Another note had sounded, although she was the only one who could hear it. A stream of black smoke had sprung up from over the Home's Hearth. A tower was burning on the other side of town, releasing a black smoke that had begun to stain the sky. It smelled sour, at once like lemons, then like burning meat.

There was no more time. She quickly stepped up into the coach.

Phyllicitus commanded the coachman onward, "Go! Now! Don't wait!"

The coachman was surprised. He tried to push up the stairs but was stalled as Sister Immaculate, followed by her three neophytes, charged onto the stairs. Then entered the carriage as the coachman swung the stairs up and secured them in place with a metal pin. He swung the door closed and leaped onto the coach, scrambling into the coachman's seat and grabbing the reins.

"Faster! Come on! Go!" Phyllicitus shouted, panic rising in her voice. She didn't know what was happening but knew in the depths of her soul that it was dangerous for Home's Hearth.

The coach surged forward, the horses picking up speed as they left the Gardens, dashing through Home's Hearth, racing against some unknown doom.

CRIES FOR HELP

A bolt of recognition went through the Rat's heart. He felt the Friends call out as one of their own was taken from them. It was more than just another victim. This time one of their own had been lost. Visions of fire danced in his thoughts. Somehow, he knew that a Taker had been burned to death, passing beyond the final black door along with the body of its earthly Taken host.

The Rat paused to think. He hadn't known that it was possible to kill one of the Takers, but he had felt its passing and knew what it was. He had no idea what could have done such a thing though, or who.

He opened his feelings to the Friends, exploring, seeking his family of Taken. He began to call out to each of them, seeking to confirm their safety. He needed everyone to accomplish his plans, at least over the next few months. After that, there would be room for a few absences. He already anticipated that half of them would die in the attempt.

Hazel didn't return his summons. When he reached out to

her through the Friends, it was as if she wasn't even there. It was a void in the continuum of life.

He arched an eyebrow, surprised at himself. He thought the days of caring about other people had been left far behind him and was surprised to find that not entirely true. He had to admit that he had grown fond of Hazel.

"Did you feel that?" Joaquin, another of his Taken family asked from across the workbench. A set of iron manacles, forged with rune-craft and embed with alchemical strength, lay upon the table. Pools of acid, proven incapable of dissolving any of its construction, streamed hand-sized clouds of stinking vapor into the air.

The Rat looked back at Joaquin, judging the craftsman as a dolt. A talented dolt, a useful dolt, but a dolt that would not be missed. "Of course."

"What does it mean?" Joaquin continued, trying to appear more informed and intelligent than he actually was.

Shaking his head in response, the Rat could not conceive of an answer. He found at such times that it was better to remain silent, but there was too much to do.

"It means that we need more information. You clean this up and prepare for your role. I will seek out some answers." The Rat blurted out angrily.

Joaquin reached down to pick up an oil-soaked rag from the floor. He laid it upon the bench then gently set the manacles on its surface. Once the chain had been collected between the two manacles, he rolled up the bundle and carried it into the depths of his shop.

The Rat stood up, adjusted his coat making sure to present an entirely respectable appearance, then walked into the street. A group of young men stood in the middle of the street. The youngest, a brown-haired boy perhaps twelve years old, pointed to the distance. The group spoke excitedly together, wondering at the source of the disturbance.

The Rat looked up as well, then froze. His alchemy tower was ablaze overhead. Black smoke curled up above Home's

Hearth, giving testament to his dying citadel.

The tower was his fortress, his place of safety, his laboratory, his refuge. Now it burned. Flames shot out of the upper story windows, engulfing the place, becoming a scene of hell.

His prisoner was held there too. He had left Hazel behind to guard to the White Hand's warrior slave and now he regretted it. The Rat quickly thought through all the details. It seemed clear to him that the White Hand had discovered his home. They killed Hazel. They burned his place of power. They would be coming for him next.

He would miss Hazel. She was going to die in any case, but he had grown fond of her. He let the feeling go as it was too late to save her now. The great plans were in danger. He needed to quicken his efforts. He felt a surge of adrenaline indicating agreement by the Friends. The Rat reached out through the Friends to Brother Quiet, busily toiling away at some useless task in the temple. He reached out through the Friends again, willing Brother Quiet into attention. The Rat had a special task for him.

Brother Quiet soon called back through the Friends. Quiet wasn't skilled using the Friends yet, but he improved every day. The Rat couldn't make out his words, they were garbled and sounded as if Brother Quiet was underwater. The Rat reached into his bag of potions and retrieved Guiliet's Syrum, a potion that would sharpen his will and mental acuity. Within a minute, The Rat could communicate directly with Brother Quiet.

"Do you see what is happening?" The Rat asked.

"I heard there is a fire." Brother Quiet responded.

The Rat paused a moment before he responded, "It's my shop. The White Hand found me."

"That isn't good. What do we do?"

"Can you find Phyllicitus? We need to move our plans up."

"Phyllicitus? She just returned to the temple. She has finally left the Gardens."

"At last, some good news." Said the Rat.

The Rat smiled. Perhaps this wasn't going to be a bad day

after all.

###

The carriage arrived at the temple amid a flurry of activity. A dozen priestesses rushed about with four young initiate priests following closely behind, desperately trying to make the temple ready for Phyllicitus's arrival. They had been told of her impending arrival only minutes before. A large burly priest carried a clay pot filled with perfumed oil the size of a small chest. The pot had just been cleaned and refilled. A small trail of soapy water and perfumed oil, along with a set of wet footsteps trailed behind him.

The carriage bearing Phyllicitus entered the temple grounds. Two brown horses pulled it along the flagstone carriage path. A graceful older woman stepped up from the temple doors as the carriage slowed to a stop. Sister Fidelity reached up then pulled the carriage door open as another of the sisters, a twenty-year-old brown-haired beauty, pulled the stairs from beneath.

"I'm glad to see you, Goddess." Sister Fidelity said as show bowed low.

Phyllicitus cut her off from with the carriage before she could continue. "Sorry, no time for playing catch-up. Something is happening in my city. I need to get inside."

The goddess stepped out of the carriage, down the stairs, and began striding off towards the interior of the main temple.

"What's the matter?" Sister Fidelity asked, alarmed at Phyllicitus's unusually brusque mood.

"Did you see the smoke?" Phyllicitus said, walking quickly through an open temple door. Two priestesses bowed as she passed, but she paid them no mind.

"Smoke? Yes. It looks like one of the crafting halls in the trader's quarter. I hope everyone is all right."

"Yes, indeed. Have you gotten any word whose house is afire?"

"Not yet. I sent two brothers out only ten minutes ago. They will return with word soon. I asked them to bring a few capable healers to help with wounded. I hope they won't be needed."

"I suspect they may not be sufficient," Phyllicitus responded, a worry plainly audible in her voice.

"Goddess?" Sister Fidelity asked as fear descended upon her. She had never seen the goddess nervous, or, as it looked now, frightened.

Phyllicitus ignored her and began climbing a circular marble staircase. It was wide enough for three people to stand side-by-side. She began putting on speed as she ascended, rushing to gain her apartments. Sister Fidelity followed behind as if on the end of a rope.

"I don't understand," Sister Fidelity continued to protest, "It's just a fire."

"No, it isn't. Home's Hearth is filled with discord. The fire isn't the problem, it's just a symptom. Now keep alert and stay ready."

Sister Fidelity bowed, lowering her head toward the ground. "I apologize goddess. I fear I had forgotten my place."

Phyllicitus motioned her onward but smiled back reassuringly.

"Don't worry, you haven't forgotten your place. Everything will become clear soon, I am sure of that. Right now, I need to get to my bath."

Phyllicitus climbed another stair, intent on her destination.

Sister Fidelity followed behind. Her mind overflowed with questions. "A bath? I thought there was a dire emergency, with the rush you are in?"

"There is. I find baths invigorating. They give me peace, power, insight. I've always had an affinity for water, you see. Even when I was young, I loved the water. Its peace clears my thoughts and helps me think."

Sister Fidelity struggled to keep up without breaking into a sprint. They left the circular staircase and rushed into an open hallway. A single red and gold carpet covered a white marble floor. Gold etching stood out in relief against the walls, writing

Phyllicitus's name over and over as if announcing the goddess to the world. There was a time when this place gave her comfort, now it simply created fear. She was no longer a young goddess recently come into her power. Now she was at its height, but it all felt at risk.

"Before I ascended, I was a priestess myself. Did you know that?"

"Yes, Goddess. Your histories are well known to us."

"The histories I tell you are, anyway. There are only a few alive who could add much to my words. But in any case, I was a neophyte and servant to the Water Mother, a goddess who had ascended as I eventually did. I had the dire misfortune to watch her fall, and against a terrible enemy as well. The world lost its heart that day. It lost the Water Mother and an entire city in one blow."

Sister Fidelity gave a sharp intake of breath. "What could do that?"

"A war. The Order of the White Hand tried to enforce its vision of order. A First God had little patience for their maneuvers. In the end, the Raven God sent an avatar. The city had two human gods then. Both gods of the city were thrown down and the city burned. Now it is nothing but a curiosity on an old map, only unmarked sand dunes abandoned by time. That could happen here."

She turned right, passing through two open doors. A priest stood aside, holding one open, their red lacquered surface and gold trim stood out against the white marble floor.

Brother Quiet stood in front of them. A massive pool of water stood behind him. The stone pond had been built into the temple, thirty paces wide and forty long. Brother Quiet was accompanied by six priests and priestesses. Three of them flanked the pool on the right side, the other three on the left. The priests and priestesses looked young, newly come to the temple and serving in a place of great honor. All seven bowed their heads deeply as she entered.

"Disrobe me, I must bathe," Phyllicitus commanded

hurriedly. She could feel something wrong in her city, it was crawling through her consciousness like a worm. "Quickly Please."

Brother Quiet raised his head, then gave his hands a single clap. The attendants raised their heads as well and positioned themselves around Phyllicitus. It seemed like a dance, where each move took away an article of clothing then took it to the side and laid upon a pink marble bench. One piece at a time, the priests disrobed Phyllicitus. Within two minutes, Phyllicitus stood nude, her beauty radiantly displayed.

Standing as still as stone, Brother Quiet tried to think about Phyllicitus's beauty and her love. The Takers quickly silenced those thoughts. Unlike The Rat, Brother Quiet had no illusions. He knew that Takers were not his allies, but they had him in their clutches now and he had already lost that battle. If all turned out well, they would simply discard him later. He doubted it. Eventually, he would either die violently or by his own hand.

He started to think about Goddess Phyllicitus, and how important she was to him and to the city. Since she had returned Home's Hearth had regained its soul. The people who lived here had regained their hope. Now she stood surrounded by enemies. He had a single thought. Couldn't he do something about this? Couldn't he at least leave her a clue?

He didn't have time. It felt like a gate of thoughts slammed down to blanket his mind. He began to move through his motions as keeper of the bath, standing aside and allowing Goddess Phyllicitus to enter its warm waters. She walked forward, not pausing to speak with any of them, moving down the marble stairs into the pool's embrace. She walked out, sinking to her hips, then to her breasts, then to her neck. She launched forward, turning on her back so she floated, free in the weightlessness of the water. Phyllicitus gazed at the ceiling with her eyes, but her concentration was on the water, on the pool, on its connection to all other water in her city, on its connection to her beloved people who drank the water every day.

She reached out to find them, and to find the cancer that had invaded their midst.

Brother Quiet bowed left, then right, signaling the attendants to back away from the pool. He turned and walked across the open room until he stopped in front of a light red clay jar. It was plain, decorated with only a circle that had been baked into its surface to mark it. He picked it up in two hands. It wasn't heavy but he wanted to be sure not to spill it. In his arms it weighed less than three stone, in his heart it seemed a boulder.

Sister Fidelity raised an eyebrow at this new addition to the ritual bath. The six attendants passed by her, passing left and right, but stopped only a few paces away. "What is this Brother Quiet?"

Brother Quiet kept walking toward the water. Phyllicitus floated atop the pool, lost in her search, even though the cancer was in her city, she could still give her servants attention. Brother Quiet opened the jar and began to slowly pour a red powder into the water, careful not to pour too fast. The Rat had instructed him how to avoid clotting.

"What are you doing?" Sister Fidelity asked, anger and fear mixing into her voice. This felt wrong to her, more discord, more danger.

Then she felt the knife. It was cold, and it passed through her lung. She turned her head. A young priestess, barely past her maidenhood stood there holding its handle. The blade jutted out of her chest. The other attendants, all Taken, descended upon Sister Fidelity, stabbing, cutting, killing.

Sister Fidelity screamed as she fell on the marble floor. Blood began to pour out of her body, pooling, trailing toward the pool where Phyllicitus swam. It poured into the water and mixed with the pool of floating powder turning water red, like blood.

Phyllicitus felt Sister Fidelity's death like a hammer. She willed herself upward away from the pool. She willed herself out of the water, hovering a few feet above. The water began to rotate, pushing the foul invading powder away from her. Her eyes went wide as she saw what her attendants had done to

Sister Fidelity. She could feel their stink, their cancer. They had been infected by the Taken.

Phyllicitus wondered why she hadn't noticed it before. Aileen and Easter had distracted her. She had been concentrating on bringing Aileen the peace she so desperately needed, and lost track of her own home.

Using her power, she connected with the flows of water, pushing them, commanding them to form into a wave and knock away the Taken. She hadn't known rage in three hundred years, but now it rose up in her chest. She felt her heart breaking, watching those who once served her becoming monsters.

The water churned, swirled, and became a vortex. It called up waves that spilled over the edges of the pool. They were only three feet high now, but in moments they would grow to encompass the entire room.

Brother Quiet reached down into his robe, pulling a white silk bag from beneath. He jammed his hand into the bag and pulled out its contents. A single chalky ball emerged, another gift from The Rat. He didn't hesitate. He threw the ball into the pool of water.

The pool had formed a protective vortex around Phyllicitus. She levitated above it, untouched by the red poison. She saw Brother Quiet throw the chalky ball into the water, and her heart broke again. The water touched the chalk ball then exploded.

The sound of thunder filled the room. The swirling vortex erupted into a powerful spray, showering everyone within the room with a mist of red-tinted water. Phyllicitus screamed as she felt her connections to her god-powers dissolve. She fell back into the now-shallow pool, landing on one leg, then collapsing. Water began to pour back in from the sides of the pool. She tried to swim but her body wouldn't obey. She reached out to her core, where her goddess powers lay, they would not answer.

She felt herself being lifted, but she couldn't see. A haze of dark red had covered her vision.

The Taken kept silent as they performed their task. Phyllicitus's screams seized up in her throat. Her chest pounded, gasping for air yet gaining little. The room began to spin as they lifted her from the pool.

She felt someone grab her by the hair and pull her head up, allowing a small bit of air to fill her lungs. Her goddess powers had deserted her.

Another thunderclap sounded from within the temple. It sounded like a war had begun within her halls.

It had, after all.

RALLY

Chamise jogged ahead of the procession. Four Eisenvard followed six paces behind by Brita. Brita's raven-black hair lay limp on her shoulders. Its shine had dulled over the weeks spent in captivity. Mistress Storm followed behind with Master Easter close by her side. Three more Eisenvard came after, ensuring that no one cut into their procession. Members of the Garden, rich in their display of jewelry and wealth, paused to stare at the parade marching through ornate halls. Their footsteps echoed through the chamber.

Chamise led them straight to the library, then beyond to the pattern room. The room stood unchanged since they left it only two days ago. She remembered when she and Miller had last met here. Chamise had been happy the way lessons had progressed, even if most of it was learning the mental disciplines of the White Hand and being a spare source of energy for Miller to tap. She had seen new ways of thinking about magic, crafting, and the variety of casting disciplines scattered across the world.

Miller knew a lot about the disciplines and how they could improve magical flows, but he knew precious little of this pattern. Chamise didn't understand what fascinated him about this place. He had referred to it as primal magic, whatever that was.

They stopped as the lead Eisenvard came into contact with the edge of the pattern's pit. The moment seemed solemn; they stood in the presence of history. It felt as if they were preparing to dip their cup into the mysterious unknown and drink it fully. The group paused a moment before Tabor spoke up. "Are we there yet?"

Miller burst out with a hearty laugh. Tabor was always the joker, though mostly on the Nets field. Even Master Easter offered a grin. The bit of humor was the perfect medicine to overcome the gloomy nature of their quest.

"What's so funny?" Brita asked.

Miller erupted in laughter. His earlier mirth unleashed by a battering ram of humor.

"Nothing really," Miller managed to choke out, "We stand next to a pattern of life. I think it may reflect, or even govern, how all magic works in the world. Most people would be impressed. Not Tabor apparently."

"Er, sorry." Tabor stumbled with his words, completely unaware of the gravity of this room and what it connected to.

"Enough already. Can we get this little party started?" Chamise demanded, tiring of the laughs.

Miller nodded, then took Brita's hand as he walked forward. He had cast protective crafting on his gloves, but probably not enough to stop the Takers. Here, of all places, he felt like he had to take a chance. He was out of options and only had one lead to follow. The Takers could communicate without magic. They infected people without magic. The Takers even traveled between worlds without magic. He had only seen that impossibility once in his life, and it wasn't on this world. It was between the worlds, in that strange place that seemed unique to itself, possessing no magic yet imbued with all of it.

Miller had thought long and hard about what that meant. He pondered how the Takers could move in and out of this world and decided that the only logical way he knew of was using the place-between-the-worlds.

The place between worlds could be wholly unique in the way magic flows within its boundaries. Its magic could have changed or died long ago from some metaphysical disaster. It could also be missing a component part that allows magic to flow as they do here in this world. The last idea he had was the most alarming but seemed to make the most sense.

The place-between-the-worlds could be the baseline ingredient for all other worlds and all other magics. Miller didn't pretend to understand the theory of worlds. In the White Hand library, he had read about the idea of worlds, where each world was a place that was a mirror of another, and each had its own unique reality. Worlds were larger than nations or mountains. They stood alone, isolated within their own realities. Only the most powerful magic of legend could form a bridge between them. Some famous scholars of the past thought that perhaps this was where the secret to godhood lay. Others dismissed that idea entirely, pointing to the fact that it could take strength beyond a god to tap into that kind of channel, and if someone wasn't a god then they would not have the strength to even attempt it.

Others subscribed to a different idea. Instead of there being bridges between worlds, they supported the idea that the worlds were all connected on a more basic level. Each world could be a distorted reflection of another world, and perhaps even a third or more. When viewed from that aspect, what the White Hand thought of as magic could be viewed as a force that had mutated and changed as it passed through different reflections. This place-between-the-worlds that the White Hand referred to had always been there, would always be there, and was perhaps the originating world where the first reflection was cast from.

These thoughts boggled his mind. None of his theories agreed with each other, yet all satisfied the evidence he had available to understand the problem. Miller had talked to all the masters in the cabal about his theory. The only one who took him seriously was Master Darjeeling, and that didn't give him confidence given Darjeeling's suspect behavior lately. Easter has been missing and Aileen had been distracted with Phyllicitus. Miller suspected that the Takers were indeed coming into their world from the place-between-worlds and that the force they used wasn't the same magic that the White Hand knew and understood because it was based in the world of the Takers, not on the world that mankind inhabited. Any number of weird mutations of world and force may have resulted in a hive of insects who were composed of universal forces.

If they faced the same problem using their powers between-the-worlds, Miller theorized that the Takers should be equally challenged in the environment of the place-between-worlds. If true, it would make that place ideal for a battleground.

Since the pattern connected his world to that place-between-worlds it made an excellent opportunity to conduct an experiment. When he had passed between-the-worlds, he had lost his channels, his perceptions changed, yet his heart continued to beat. The Takers could pass through as well, but in order to survive the journey he expected that they could not rely on magic, it must be some other force. If he exposed an infected person like Brita to that world, Miller expected that they would lose a majority of their power. It might even immobilize a Taken victim like Brita and allow him to remove the infection from her. The trick would be determining how to access his own flows like he was accustomed to, yet ensure the Takers were prisoners of the lack of powers from the place between.

The pattern was the answer. Instead of pulling Brita to that other strange place, he would open up a small gap in the world and allow just a bit of that strange place to seep through. He thought about how the Pattern used its own identity as a source of power, thus, he concluded, all things that exist might do the same thing. Once Brita was exposed to to that power of identity, he would use his channels to identify all of her natural essences, then remove anything that seemed to be a foreign presence. He didn't intend to identify and force out the Takers, instead, he would search for the gaps in her and push those away, back through the opening and back between the worlds.

He shook his head in disbelief. The intimidated him. If it worked, he would have found a cure to the Takers. If it didn't then he would most probably send Brita between the worlds, and probably in hand-sized pieces. Magic tended to do that when it wasn't fully understood.

Miller held her hand in his gloved hand. He hoped it would protect him long enough for this to work. "Are you ready?"

"I guess I need to be," Brita responded, her voice quavering.

She looked up into his eyes. The deep green caught him momentarily off guard. Her eyes were lovely, her face, a beauty. He wanted to reach out to her, to touch her, to comfort her.

"Mistress?" Miller called to Mistress Storm at the front of the procession, trying to disconnect from the emotions and get some guidance.

Mistress Storm stood at the side of the pool talking with Master Easter. She turned around. "I think I see a place that might work." She pointed at a broad arc that swiped across the center of the pattern. "That might be the touch point. Do you agree?"

Easter continued staring down at the pattern for a few heartbeats before he spoke, "I'm really not confident in any of this, you know? I've read more Stevenson than either of you. He talks about touch points but never describes how to spot one. Essentially, he just said that you know one when you see one, and there is always only one. If I had to bet, I would agree with you on the arc. There is only one in the entire pattern. That doesn't make it an obvious choice, as any marking down to a hair's width might be unique. We just might not be able to see it with our limited sight and knowledge."

"We are betting though, aren't we?" Mistress Storm countered.

"I guess we are."

"Not really." Miller disagreed. "We don't have much at stake. If this doesn't work, then we try a few more experiments. If that doesn't work, then we just go back to the New Pony no worse off than we were this morning. We aren't betting because we've got nothing to lose and everything to gain. Yes, it's a dice roll, but not one that we will lose our shirt from."

"You're making a lot of assumptions." Master Easter countered, more nervous about what he didn't know than what he did.

"We've got to start somewhere." Miller pointed out. It seemed to be pithy logic, but that was all he had.

"Let's try it, please," Brita said, her nervous words echoing in the room. "I've been under their heel for so long. Anything we can do is better than nothing."

Easter shook his head. "You have no idea. None of us do. Doesn't that frighten you?"

"Worse than I already am? No."

Master Easter turned to Mistress Storm and shook his head up and down, deep in thought, and beginning to agree. "It's your life, I guess. I would hate to see something terrible happen to you. These patterns, they have a history of unreliability. The texts have reported everything from complete success to all the people within a three-league distance being cut in half. The only reason I would ever even try this is that we are in Home's Hearth and the goddess's power tends to stabilize chaos and preserve life. Otherwise wouldn't dare."

Miller didn't have any other path forward. He looked at the White Hand Mistress who had so recently been called Aileen and pleaded to her with his eyes. Miller felt changes in her after she had announced her new name. He hoped their old connections would survive, but he feared they would not.

"Yet here we are, in the protective bosom of the goddess's power. It's here or nowhere. It's now or never. Let's not fool ourselves. This is our only option." Miller said.

Easter replied, staring over at Brita. "I see. Well, don't let it be said that I didn't try to warn you. If you are committed to this, then let us begin."

"Yes. I want this." She said, fear and excitement mixing in her voice.

"You are a brave girl." Easter's words seemed like praise, but they sounded sorrowful as if resigned to some terrible fate. "Let's get started then. You're up, apprentice."

Miller sat down at the pool's edge and dropped his legs down, then pushed off to fall the few inches onto the pattern-decorated floor. He held on to Brita's hand, helping her descend as well. His channels were calm. He felt no outside forces acting on him. It was like the calmest of ponds, just like the place between worlds. When he first felt it, it gave him some comfort, but now that he understood its connections to that place between the worlds, it filled him with trepidation.

He led her to the center of the pit, stopping directly on top of a broad finger-wide arc that crossed over most of the pattern. The arc sprung forth an arm's reach from one corner of the pool then traversed the entirety of the pattern. The pattern's chaotic swirls and lines mixed together beneath the arc then emerged at the opposite corner of the pool.

Miller began to channel power. He set event triggers and tied channels to them. He formed emergent fates then used a thin needle to sew them into Brita's flesh. Her body channels resisted his demands until Easter added his energy and they both bore down, breaking through Brita's defenses. An hour of casting passed before Miller had completed his network of magic. Miller held Brita's hand one more time and took a few moments to stare kindly into her eyes.

"It will be alright. It doesn't work then we just go back."

She smiled back. "I trust you."

He let go of her hand and walked back to the side of the pattern. The waist-high pool wall stood between him and the room above. Chamise stood there glowing down at him. "Are you done with all your lovey-dove handholds? I've got other things to do if you aren't."

247

"Don't be like that. I leave you with the Eisenvard for a few days and you get all evil on me. Have a little compassion. What we are doing is dangerous."

She held out her hand, helping Miller from the pit.

Easter walked up beside Miller and set his arm on his shoulder. Normally Miller would be terrified, but something about Easter made him feel a little more human than usual. It was as if he could feel Brita's fear, and Miller's as well.

Easter moved closer so he could whisper. "Have you tested this at all? You've done some reading on your own. Storm may know how to activate the pattern, but she doesn't know what will happen when it starts.

Miller shook his head. "The Takers are in motion. If we don't try soon, I don't think we are going to get another chance."

Easter patted his shoulder. "I've lived seven hundred years, and there is never enough time."

Taking two steps backwards, Easter announced called out loudly. "Let's get started then."

A moment passed in silence, then another. Brita nodded encouragement at Miller.

"We are ready, go ahead and activate it."

"Have you memorized the pattern like I told you to" Mistress Storm asked, the question sounding like an incantation rather than a simple query.

"I have."

"Can you see the lines, the shapes, the patterns when you close your eyes?"

Miller closed his eyes, envisioning the swirls and cuts of the lines that cross crossed the floor. "I can."

"Look closely within your mind. Seek out the line that feels stronger than the others. It will pull you toward it, and probably feel a little frightening.

It didn't take long for Miller to find it. The line, a ragged thing, stretched diagonal across the pattern. It was more an arc than a line. He concentrated on it, and a feeling of dread filled his heart.

"Found it."

"Great. This is the easy part. Keep looking at the line in your imagination. When the fear becomes unbearable, open your eyes and find the line outside of your imagination. Just touch it. That will be enough."

"Me?" Miller asked surprised. "I thought you were going to open it."

"I'm not touching it. This is your insane idea. You are playing with the primal force of all primal forces. With one mistake you can erase yourself from reality. I'm not confident enough to try that." Mistress Storm replied.

"But it's fine if I do?" Miller responded.

"I recommended against it. You told me that this was the only way. Do you want to back out now?" Mistress Storm said.

Brita stood on the pattern. She felt desperate to be freed. Miller knew that this was her only hope. It had to work.

"I understand." Miller's heart began to beat wildly. Mistress Aileen, now Storm, had never hesitated to put herself in danger when lives were on the line. Miller could see her face, completely resistant to the idea of touching this with her own power. Something had changed within her. She seemed afraid of the pattern.

"Can you guide me through it at least?" Miller asked.

Mistress Storm's voice grew soft. "I doubt there will be enough time for it to matter. When the pattern does whatever it does, it will happen quickly. Master Easter and I will be watching Brita. We will try to keep her away from whatever comes through."

"You won't have time to watch me then. Understood."

"That is the price to those who face the Takers." Easter said, almost to himself, as if reliving some moment long past.

Miller waited as the minutes passed, each second seeming

longer and longer there, surrounded by the pattern. His eyes moved across Brita's figure, pulling the vision into his warming heart. Soon, he thought, she would be free. He tried to get his hopes under control. They might free Brita, but they might also end up in the middle of a fight that could span between worlds.

He paused a moment. Miller wasn't sure what would happen. He had been between-the-worlds once, and it had been confusing as well as terrible. All the laws of reality seemed subject to change when he passed through last time. He wondered what would happen in his world when the two realities met.

He heard footsteps pounding across the marble floor above.

Shouts came from near the entrance to the room. They echoed across the marble floors and walls, filling the room with its shrill warning, "Alarm! We temple is invaded! Takers!"

The librarian called out the alert loudly, breaking any hope of silence. Miller's eyes flicked between each of them, Easter, Mistress Storm, even Brita. He didn't know who to look to, but he knew that he was in the right place. Master necromancers surrounded him. Eisenvard guarded the doors.

"What? Explain yourself!" Eater barked. His command penetrated the librarian's frenzy.

"I just got a message. The temple has been attacked. Dozens of priests have been killed. The goddess has been seized. I don't know how. Some of the priests seem to have been Taken."

Chamise turned toward Miller.

"What can we do?" She asked.

"Do? Nothing. All of Home's Hearth is doomed. Without the goddess, they will rip into our people and burn us to the ground." Fear filled Miller's voice. His eyes seemed to search for an idea but could not find any inspiration.

Before the full import of those words could sink in, Miller heard a new set of words. These were not something understandable, or even knowable. The syllables were not pronounceable by a human mouth, the ideas they held seemed too large for a human head. Easter called out, pouring power, will, and ancient arts into his crafting. A giant black gap opened in mid-air. It stood there only a moment before Mistress Storm leaped through, her deadly sword held in one tight fist. Easter's dogs sprinted as fast as they could to join her. After all the dogs had gone through, Easter turned to enter the gate as well.

Easter paused before he leaped through. The strain of casting showed on his face. A crack had appeared on his cheek, splitting his skin as if had dried in the sun like cheap leather. Small droplets of blood seeped through and dripped down onto his chin. Whatever he had done had cost him.

He called out behind, "Anyone who wants to be a hero, now is the time!" Then Easter jumped.

Brita continued to stand in the center of the pattern, frozen in place. Miller called out, "What do I do?"

Thoughts rampaged through Miller's mind. The Takers were kidnapping a goddess? How could this even be possible? Miller felt panic rising in his heart.

No one remained that could answer those questions.

"Well Apprentice, you need to make a decision." Chamise's voice rang through the room like a clear bell. "Stay here and wait for the Takers or go forward."

The portal stood open, urging him forward.

"Are you insane? If I go forward, I won't have anyone to pull me out."

Chamise responded coldly, "If you stay here, the Takers will come, eat your girl, and probably the rest of us as well. Are you looking forward to becoming some kind of puppet for them?"

Miller thought he detected a hint of scorn in her voice as if accusing him of cowardice.

Only one thought came to his mind. The Eisenvard had never left her after all.

But she was right, Miller admitted to himself. There was no time to prepare. The entire city could be engulfed by Takers if they didn't find a way to stop them. Even if they lost Home's Hearth, the Order would still fight them somewhere else, and to do so, they needed to understand this newly transformed threat.

"Ready?" Those words were all he could utter.

"Don't worry. Do it. I believe in you." Brita pleaded, panicking as her only chance at escape seemed to be slipping away.

Miller began to follow Mistress Storm's casting instructions. It was odd, he reflected, how easily her name had changed in his mind. Chasing those distracting thoughts away, he focused on the single arcing line that cut through the pattern. It was easy to find again. More thoughts invalided his mind, interrupting his concentration.

Were the Takers coming here?

What could stop them?

He called on the discipline of focus, slowed his beating heart to a calm level, clearing his mind, and then pushed on. He cast emotions aside as he stared deeper and deeper at the arc.

His eyes began to hurt. It felt like someone had sprayed sand in them. The pain crept behind his eyes into his forehead. He kept staring, trying to find the bottom of the line as Mistress Storm had instructed him. He had no idea what he was looking for but kept on. The discipline of focus complete, he embarked on the discipline of piety. He felt his confidence rise and fear lessen as the discipline cleared his emotions. The line was all that mattered. His life, his existences, were all immaterial to him as the discipline completed.

The discipline of Piety removed his egotism and substituted a cause, to save Home's Hearth, no, to save the world. He no longer mattered in the greater scheme of things, but the pattern did. There was only the line. His connections to the world, to his friends, to himself faded away. It was all background, everything but the line.

And there it was. It wasn't a thing that could be sought out and discovered. The critical piece of the pattern had to make itself seen, and now he could not unsee it. He felt it enter his consciousness. Miller could see the line's name etched in his own heart. He knew the line and its identity better than he knew his own himself. The line wasn't a line, it was a connection. It had a function, to join things, to join worlds. It had been carved here to allow explorers to investigate a thousand spells, to poke and prod at reality itself. Now it lay before him, ready for his attention.

All of those explorers were gone now. Some died at home in bed, others to violence, but more than half never returned from their journeys. Now it was time for his journey.

Miller opened the gate between the worlds.

The carved arc spanned the pattern. Orange light began to glow from the arc, first softly, then growing into a burning curve. A new design of orange and red cuts blossomed across the surface of the ancient pattern cutting new routes and paths onto the surface.

Brita began to scream as the pattern's attention began to encompass her. She could feel things happening to her. Brita saw memories come into, then leave her mind. A bright orange stain had appeared on her arm, then it began crawling as if it were a spider living beneath her skin. Intense light began emerging from her skin. Other stains appeared, each like a star of lava surrounded by diffuse blobs of lesser red. One appeared on her face. She began to rip away her dress, exposing her breasts and hips. Three more lights had emerged on her chest, on her breasts, and across her stomach.

Ripping away the last of her garments, she began to claw at herself. She dug her nails into her own belly, trying to cut through her skin, to dig out lights. The glowing aura seemed to detach itself from her left breast. It moved on its own, leaving her skin and floating in the air above it, spreading like an oil drop on water. The other spots changed as well. Within moments the only thing left in her skin was the glowing stars. Halos of orange light floated above them attached with tendrils of a magic that Miller didn't recognize.

"What is going on?" Chamise Screamed.

The other Eisenvard raised their shields and swords. "Should we attack it?" Schaller asked loudly, battle lust mixing with confusion in his voice.

"Attack what? Brita? How would you even do that?" Miller replied, "Hold your blades. Let's see where this goes."

Miller had no idea if it was even possible to harm these glowing things. They appeared to be made of some kind of magic. Moment by moment the creatures grew more solid, as if the light from the pattern granted them mass as well as power. They were emerging into the world and Miller was seeing it firsthand.

The spots floated in the air,\ yet remained tethered to Brita's skin. Miller tried to open a spirit channel, to view in the spots in their entirety, but his channel fought against him. His magical flows became sporadic, jetting on and off as his heartbeat.

Miller realized that the arc in the pattern wasn't a marker for a place to begin exploring between-the-worlds, it was a crack between-the-worlds. That crack could be pried open. When it opened, the powers of the worlds would mix, forming some new kind of magical reality, one that existed nowhere but right here, right now.

The crack between worlds widened. Miller felt magic breaking, but at the same time, he sensed new powers, new flows, new potentials. The pattern was merging his world with between, bringing Takers into a place where he could see their true form, and showing them his.

Miller shook his head wondering if any other person had ever seen such a thing. Not the White Hand, not even the gods. He stood witness to it in awe and terror.

Brita began to scream. The Takers had become truly physical. He watched in horror as a Taker disconnected itself from her forearm, ripping a fist-size hunk of flesh out as it pulled away. She fell onto her knees screaming in pain, blood pouring from her wound.

Chamise Screamed out. "Swords! Cut them down!"

The Eisenvard rushed into action. Schaller sprinted forward

with his shield held high above his head. As Schaller approached, one of the Takers, looking now like a brown and orange worm, turned its head and spit a brown paste into his face. It covered his eyes and nose in brown mist. Tendrils of sticky goo stretched from the Taker, covering his face and eyes. Schaller screamed as he brought is sword down, slicing through the Taker and spraying brown effluent across the room. It fell from midair onto the floor, wriggling in death throws.

Miller realized that they might not win this fight. In a normal world, Takers could travel into people through food or blood exchange. Here, the Takers could become physical. They could fight with every weapon at their disposal. He knew that had to close the door between worlds before they were overcome. The Takers would lose their form and return to invisibility, but he had to shut it anyway.

Brita began to writhe on the floor, contorting in agony. Two more wounds had appeared on her. He didn't know how to stop the Takers or to restore the barrier between worlds. He needed to come up with a plan, fast. Slamming down his willpower, he embraced the concentration discipline to drive the chaotic scene from his mind. Calmness descended as he watched Schaller fall to the ground as he began ripping at his own eyeballs, desperately trying to scrape away the Taker's poisonous bile. Miller wished he could do something to help, but in his calm, he was all too aware of how much danger they were all in. He needed precise and speedy action.

Two other Eisenvard joined Schaller, ripping at their armor and clothes where they had been sprayed. He didn't care. It didn't affect him. The concentration discipline shielded his heart from the pain around him.

Miller focused his mind on finding a solution to all of this. He thought about the pattern and how it stood unique in the world, with only the arc seeming to tie it to a normal geometric shape. Miller wondered if uniqueness could be a magical property, much like a name or a soul. The arc was a thing, it had a name, it had an identity, he could change it. He just needed to find its core again, and pull it shut.

He watched impassively as Brita began to scream louder. An orange dot had emerged on her chest, directly between her two breasts. The glowing light surrounding it started to grow. Miller watched as a dark orange bubble formed above her heart, seeping out of her skin and taking shape upon her chest. It was worm-shaped and smaller than the others. It had dozens of small finger-sized legs that skittered as the worm took shape in the world, no longer a worm but a centipede. The Taker rose out of her heart and emerged into the world. It wasn't as large as the others. This taker was dark gray and smaller than his hand. It twisted as it floated above Brita. His analytic mind, deep in his disciplined thoughts, recognized it immediately.

A Taker had just been born into the world. Implications of such a thing, newly hatched from its larvae were clear. The Takers didn't attack humanity to take them over. They didn't attack humanity to conquer them. They did it to lay eggs, grow larvae, and consume them all as meat for their nests.

He had a vision of maggots feeding on a rotting corpse. The Takers had something in common with insects. Three years ago, the only spells that showed any promise against the Taken were from the most unusual of magical schools, farming and insect control.

Ideas, like pieces of a puzzle, clicked together in his mind. He was following the logical conclusions to a final end. The White Hand had always assumed it was facing some force with an agenda, something with human-like goals and habits. Nothing could be farther from the truth. The White Hand wasn't at war with an enemy army, it was defending against an insect swarm. It was a sea of locusts, and mankind was its wheat field.

Something moved in the peripheries of Miller's vision. His eyes went wide as he recognized what was happening. He had been deep in the trances of the disciplines and missed just a few moments. The bubble that had formed atop Brita has begun to pull away, its long tendril stretching out between its floating worm-like body and Brita's chest. Miller scrambled across the patterned floor desperate to reach Brita's side, remembering how the other Takers had tended flesh when they emerged.

Brita screamed. He heard ripping. Blood spouted from her chest, spraying the ceiling and falling in droplets across the floor. Miller felt the warm blood sprinkle across his exposed arms and face. Brita stopped moving, her body curved outward, splayed open like a hunter's trophy.

Miller saw the crack between the worlds. He screamed as he bore down on it with all his anger and despair. Brita had fallen to the Takers long ago. He thought that he could save her. He hadn't. He had killed her.

Her body lay discarded on the floor. The glow from the arc began to fade and narrow. Finally, the crack-between-the-worlds sealed shut, the Takers faded to nothingness. He didn't know where they went, but right now he didn't much care.

He fell to his knees beside Brita. Picking up her head, he held her against him. She didn't move. She had gone beyond the final door.

The only marks of her passage were her own blood and Miller's tears.

LOSS

The crowd of Taken sprinted down the marble staircase. They spoke no words. It would be too easy to alert the temple with careless shouts and war cries. They passed the body of a slain priestess. Her blood puddled the center of the hall. The Taken splashed through it, tracking blood down the hall and casting the blood across the white walls. One of the Taken slipped on the slick marble floor, falling down and losing his grip on Phyllicitus's prone body. The other Taken kept the goddess from smashing her head onto the hard surface.

Phyllicitus had been immobile since the red powder had touched her, soaked into her skin, and invaded her blood. Even now she was little more than a rag doll in their grip. The Rat looked on, a hint of anger crossing his face. The red powder would wear off soon. He didn't relish the idea of being around the goddess when it did. The Rat decided that he didn't need to scold the clumsy fool, the Takers would do that for him.

The taken men kept rushing forward, losing no time in their effort to escape the temple before the alarm was raised. The group had been broken in two, part rushing forward with the goddess, the other part dragging their fallen member behind. The fallen man rolled over and scrambled up as the others released him. He seemed off balance and a little shocked by the experience, his head had impacted the floor and he had not fully recovered.

The Taken, spurred on by their internal masters, quickly forgot about the lone straggler and sped on. Six of the Taken reached the twin outer doors and scrambled to a halt. Five more Taken followed behind carrying the goddess. The Rat, in the lead, stepped forward and grasped the handle of the right door, shoving it open in a rush. He knew that time was of the essence. If the priests and priestesses who knew crafting found them before they could escape, this entire endeavor could end badly for all of them. Luckily, Phyllicitus had banned her followers from practicing violent magic; all their efforts focused on peaceful use.

The Rat watched one of his men, Cadwell he remembered, grab the left door and push it open exposing the wide passageway beyond. Bright morning light shone into the temple lighting the hallway and illuminating the faces of his men along with the prone body of Phyllicitus. Light bathed them, showing every detail to the five people standing outside unaware of the approaching Takers.

Three priestesses and two temple servants stood gazing down at a bloody form sprawled upon the ground. Blood soaked into a fallen priestess's temple robe. Stab marks coated the robe where red mixed with pure white. Blood dampened her long black hair, fresh, almost warm. Shouts of alarm rose from the priests. The Taken didn't pause. Five of them rushed forward, bloody swords ready to continue their morning's work.

The Rat spurred them on, urging them to kill the followers of Phyllicitus. Screams came from two servants as they fled.

"Alarm!" One of the priests screamed.

A young priestess called out, "Taken! The Taken have come!" Cadwell rushed at her with a short sword and jammed it through her stomach. Blood poured out of the wound coating her belly and Cadwell's hand. He pulled the sword out, allowing the priestess's lifeblood to pour out.

Five more Taken rushed in. One of the Taken closed on the lead priestess, swinging his sword with all of his might. She tried to call out, to use prayer to protect her, but her goddess was unaware of her plight. There was no power for the priestess to beg for. The sword cut into her arm. Skin parted as blood sprayed out from her veins. The arm bent at an angle where the bone had been smashed. The Taken swordsman didn't say a word. He raised the sword and slammed it down on the priestesses wide-eyed face, splitting her skull and embedding the blade between her eyes. Brain matter splattered across the ground in chunks.

The other two priestesses saw what would soon befall them. A red-haired priestess abandoned her friends. She turned abruptly to the right and began to sprint away, cutting through the flowerbeds and fleeing to toward the temple gate, hoping for protection from the townsfolk.

A priest called out words of power. Opening his heart to the universe as he had been taught, he sent will into the world. Light flashed. It exploded brightly across the entrance, burning into everyone's vision. A ball of flashing light hovered above the ground spraying painful bright light into the eyes of Taken and priests alike. The Taken screamed, covering their faces with their palms. White hot pain shot into their eyeballs like hot fishhooks.

The Rat could no longer see. The flash blinded him. The world had transformed into a white burning mass. Everything seemed to stab into his eyes, cutting, impaling, burning. His alchemist mind tried to stay calm, tried to think about a way to cast the spell off. This was only the pain, he thought, nothing had been done to him other than a strong flash of light. He could hear voices calling out as his Taken men tried to strike back, or just to simply walk.

He opened his inner voice to the Takers. Make the pain go

away. Please make it go away, he pleaded.

The Takers responded. They reached into him and began their work. Within a few heartbeats, the pain faded then disappeared. He felt the Takers communicating, passing the knowledge of how to recover from Taker to Taker. The screams stopped. The Taken men removed their hands from their eyes. He saw the caster standing in front of them, his triumphant smile melting from his face.

"What a pity. You actually thought that you had won." The Rat said as his men began to rush toward the priest. He spun and bolted away, trying to follow behind the red-haired priestess that had just left. One of his quicker Taken, a man by the name of Felder, leaped at him then grabbed. With a shove, Felder pushed hard, forcing the priest off his feet and smashing his face into the stonework. The priest's face bounced against the hard surface, smearing blood and shattering his nose. A tooth shot out of his mouth, crushed beneath the heel of the next Taken.

The priest screamed. The Rat smiled with rare joy. It felt delicious to him. The pain rendered the priest desperate as his instincts turned to survival, surrendering any hope of divine rescue. Beyond the screams, The Rat heard the clarion call of horns alerting the temple, and all of Home's Hearth, to their danger. The Takers wanted to continue their raid, to rend, to kill, to take. The Rat knew better. Any delay would spell their doom.

'No! Don't waste time with the lesser folk!' The Rat called out to his Takers.

'We need to get to the pattern. There is only one sure path to escape, and it is closing soon! Follow! Follow!' The Rat urged the Taken on, desperate to escape with his prize.

He felt the Takers urging him back, calling on him to attack the temple, to mix with the populate, to spread their blood around and create more Taken. His men began to break up, seeking victims. The six carrying Phyllicitus tossed her to the ground without ceremony, then began to move back toward the interior of the temple.

"You can't take them here. Their spell crafters have prepared for you." The Rat yelled, abandoning the easy communication offered by the Friends.

The Taken didn't listen. They pushed him onward. They wanted death. They wanted victory. He struggled with his large pouch, opening the white binding rope and thrusting his hand in. It came out with a metal vial. He didn't hesitate. Pulling the cork out with his teeth, he spit it on the ground and quickly drank the mind-discipline potion. At the first swallow, it hammered into action. He felt his awareness expand, his thoughts speed up, and his willpower harden. He pushed with his mind against the Takers, shoving the idea into them.

"To me! Follow me!" The Rat called out.

He knew that true victory was close and true defeat was even closer. The priests weren't the enemy to worry about, it was time. He began to slowly jog away, hoping to lead them on.

"Bring her with us! He screamed with his mind. The way is open! Follow!" He ordered.

The Rat felt the urges lessen from the Friends. His men stopped their attack and returned to the scene, disorganized and still attempting to obey his wishes. Six of the Taken picked up the body of Phyllicitus and began to jog behind him.

The Rat felt relieved. Not only had he saved their evening and their lives, he had found a way to manipulate the Friends themselves. The mind-discipline potion seemed to give him some influence over them. He could feel it work, connecting his will with their collective goals. Once Phyllicitus had been dealt with, he would revisit this and see how far this power could be used.

He called them onward, leading them as he urged speed. The Rat guided them through the garden and into the old section of the temple grounds. The first cloister, an original building from the first days of the temple stood in front of the Taken. The building seemed lonely. Its vine-covered gray stone walls hadn't been painted in decades. A stout black door stood closed. It would not open when Felder tried.

"Swords! Axes! We have no time!" The Rat ordered his Taken followers.

Within moments all of the Taken were pounding on the door with any weapons they could hold. Wood chips flew, iron hinges bent. The Taken inched closer to their goal.

A cold burst of air passed over the Rat. He looked up. A black line stood in the center of their path. Only moments ago, he and his group of Taken had stood in that place. Now the line grew, then widened into a patch of absolute blackness. It formed into an oval, blacker than night and taller than the tallest Taken. It appeared like a hole in the world. A man walked from the darkness to stand in front of the gate. The Rat recognized him. It was a White Hand master.

"Get that door open!" The Rat screamed, abandoning any attempt at stealth.

Another black shape appeared out of nowhere directly next to the new visitor. It stretched into an oval, upward until it matched the first. A woman stepped out, her elegant black dress trailing behind, fluttering in the cold wind.

Then the dogs emerged. Easter's pack came rushing out of both black gates, one after the other. The dogs rushed at the Taken, eager to bite, rend, and devour. Finally, a single person stepped through. He wasn't tall or muscular. He dressed in the finery that a successful merchant might wear. His hair was cut in a commoner's style, the front of his hair cut flat like the ancients once preferred.

The Rat recognized her as well. Mistress Storm called out an unintelligible word into the room. A curtain of sparks rose up like a wave in front of her, spinning in a tornado of sparks and small lightning. Dogs began to sprint forward, their jowls dripping with drool, snapping as they chased behind the moving curtain of lighting.

The Rat recognized Master Easter and wondered where the rest of his cabal was. The woman must be Aileen, he thought. The Rat hadn't anticipated that the cabal could react so quickly. He hadn't known they could cut a hole through reality then transport themselves directly to him.

He had made plans and formed contingencies. None of them included a wall of blue lightning that stretched from the floor to the ceiling, covering the width of the room and charging toward him. He didn't have time to make more plans, only to run.

The Rat jumped back and grabbed Phyllicitus's body. He urged the other Taken carrying her on, pushing against their will. He used his arms to take up some of her weight in a desperate attempt to move faster. With every ounce of will, he pushed his men forward, to run for the pattern, to their last and only hope of escape. The wall of blue lightning began to move forward. It closed on them quickly. Sparks crackled and shattered against the walls and ceiling. He could hear Aileen calling out magical words of power behind him. Doom was closing in.

Surprise filled the Rat's mind as he considered the risk the White Hand were taking. He had assumed they would not endanger Phyllicitus. He realized that he had assumed wrong. The White Hand would clearly risk the goddess by sending a lightning storm against all of them. Phyllicitus was divine right now, but in her current state, she could be injured or killed by such a thing. He wasn't surprised that the White Hand would use such a weapon against him though.

He jammed his free hand deep into the belt pouch he had used just moments ago. There were three remaining vials. One of them would protect him against lightning and fire, one would transform him into a bird, and the other would heal any wounds he suffered. He grabbed the protective vial, seized the cork with his teeth, and pulled it out.

He continued to urge the men forward as he drank the potion.

His mind raced, urging him to run faster. More! Faster!

Almost there!

The pattern stood only five steps ahead of him. Carved hundreds of years ago and forgotten, it looked ready to welcome him with open arms. The Rat had never used a pattern before, but the Friends had shown him how it was done. It was a door into another place, a place where the Friends could pass easily. He would be safe there, he thought, at least momentarily.

He felt Phyllicitus's body jerk downward. One of his Taken, Gronian, a physically impressive man that was recently turned, calling out through the Friends just before he heard him hit the floor.

Another clumsy idiot? The Rat thought.

Then he heard another one of his men hit the floor. He looked back. Black sinuous hands reached through the floor. It appeared as if the floor had grown human arms. The arms seemed to be made of shadow and yet solid. A dozen arms jutted from the floor, grabbing legs, seizing clothes, slowing the group. Cold emanated from the floor beneath him. It looked like a gate had opened through the final black door and it was pulling them down to the realm of death.

These were necromancers, the Rat thought, perhaps it was.

He felt the Friends panic. They didn't know what to do. Only two steps from the pattern, the wall of lightning hit. Screams erupted from his Taken. They lost their footing, fell to the ground, and began to shake within the waves of lighting that flowed over their bodies and burned through their veins. Even Phyllicitus shook and gyrated beneath its chaotic power.

The Rat didn't though. Abandoning all of the other taken raiders, he screamed with effort and seized Phyllicitus's body by the shoulders. She wasn't heavy, and he had enough panic-fueled strength to drag her the last two paces.

The lightning disappeared as his foot stepped onto the pattern. Circles, ovals, curved lines, and the shapes of stars decorated the floor in a pattern drawn by an ancient priest two hundred years ago. The Rat didn't know what the purpose of this pattern was, nor even why it was carved into the stonework of this floor. He didn't care. He knew the pattern was his only chance of survival.

Dogs ran forward. They passed over his fallen men like wind blowing over long grass. They didn't slow for a moment. Just as the first paw touched the patterned floor, The Rat opened the way between-the-worlds.

.

A DECISION

Chamise claimed down and stepped onto the pattern. It lay dormant now, partly drowned out in blood. Miller held Brita close, whispering to her over and over.

"I'm sorry. I"m sorry. I'm sorry. I had no idea they could do that. I'm sorry."

She walked over and touched his head. Miller looked up, tears streaming down his face.

"What have I done?" He said, his voice cracking with sorrow.

"You? You tried to make a difference. It isn't over yet though. You are still in the battle." Chamise snapped back, anger flowing into her voice.

Miller looked down at the ground. "I'm done. I can't do it. I failed her."

Chamise's grip tightened on his head, pulling his hair tightly into her fist. "You aren't done yet. You haven't even started. The goddess is in danger. Your masters have left to help. You need to support them and get into the cursed fight."

"I'll just fail." He said.

Chamise replied coldly, "Of course you will, but you'll try. Don't sit there blubbering. Brita died to give you something to use against the Takers. Did she succeed? Did you learn anything?"

He nodded up and down. "But at what price?"

"The price she agreed to pay, her life. It's the same price all of us agreed to pay if we must, or didn't you notice that detail. Here's my question to you though. Was it enough to make a difference? Can you use it against them?"

He nodded cautiously. "I think so. I'll need to do some more work."

"There's no time for work. You're at war. Get your work done between the battles when you have time. Right now, it's time for fighting. Get ready to get bloody. People need us. They need you." Chamise said, urging him on.

"What about Brita?" Miller asked.

"Brita is finished right now. She will meet us beyond the last door. Someday we will all pass through, even your necromancer masters. Right now, our job is to send these Taken through that door, preferably in small pieces."

Miller nodded. Somehow her Eisenvard-fueled speech motivating him to get back into the fight. They had lost Brita, but they had gained insight into their enemies' nature, and perhaps their goals and plans. He knew where they must be heading.

He gently Brita's head on the floor, bending over, he gave her a final kiss on her forehead. Then he leaned away from her and stood.

"Let's go." He said, steel in his voice.

He started walking toward the portal that Master Easter had left, its black maw open before them. The rest of the Eisenvard fell in behind to form a column of iron wielding men, and a woman, filled with battle rage.

Miller stepped through.

Chamise leaped through the portal, emerging into a catastrophe. Screams of pain and despair filled the aged stone-walled room. A pack of dogs surrounded a Taken man who lay on the floor screaming, trying to crawl forward and away from the pack of dogs. A pattern lay carved on the floor in front of her. The pattern lay filled with geometric shapes similar in purpose to the other pattern, but this one had been made with a very different purpose.

Miller emerged from the portal. He rushed forward to take his place by her side.

A voice rang out across the room, filled with urgency.

"We've got to get her!" Mistress Storm called out, desperation in every word.

Master Easter stood hard-faced looking on. Chamise had never seen such emotion from him. His face wore a look of horror, yet he steeled himself as if expecting the end of the world.

Easter spoke, "We don't know where she had gone. Even if we open this pattern, there is no way to know if it leads to her. We need to regroup. We need a plan that won't get us all killed."

"We're necromancers damn it!" Mistress Storm screamed, anger filling her voice. "We will come back! Our lives are less than worthless if we don't save her."

Easter pointed back at her, cutting her off with a sharp motion of his hand. "Yes, we will come back to our bodies months later. We will be lost and eternally cast adrift in the kingdom of the Takers. It won't take long before we beg for the final door. We won't receive it though. We will live on in torment for an eternity, just us and the victorious Takers. Is that really your plan?"

Mistress Storm would not accept that. "The goddess, we have to save her. We can't leave her to that."

Easter shook his head side to side. "She doesn't have a black ring. Gods have come and gone through the ages. It just might be her time." Easter's voice cracked as he spoke, betraying the battle within his own soul.

A deep note of sadness rang in his voice as he addressed the woman who once been Aileen.

"Mistress Storm, you aren't Phyllicitus's servant anymore. You left that behind with your old name. Now your duty is to the order, not to her."

Without announcing his order, three of Easter's dogs responded. One loped up to Mistress Storm's side and took her black dress between its drooling jaws. Two others approached, preparing to block Mistress Storm from the pattern.

Mistress Storm surged forward, trying to escape the clutches of Easter's dogs. Cloth ripped and she slipped out of the dog's grasp. She scrambled forward toward the pattern, reaching out to open it, daring Easter to stop her.

Easter didn't hesitate. The dogs leaped. One seized her ankle in its drooling jaws, another her forearm. They pinned her down.

Chamise spoke quietly to Miller. "Should we help? If so, then which one?"

Miller thought hard. He tried to puzzle out a way that he could bring peace between Easter and Storm, and still rescue Phyllicitus. He had no idea. He tried to think through what little evidence he had. Someone had gone through the pattern, and it was probably Phyllicitus, judging by Mistress Storm's reaction.

"We help the goddess. Follow me." Miller said.

Miller ran forward, his boots stomping on the rough stonework floor. Two of the giant mastiffs looked up, recognized him, then let him pass. He ran through them, not stopping to talk with Easter, not stopping to help release Storm. Chamise sprinted alongside him, a grim look of determination on her face.

"What are we getting into?" Chamise asked.

"Nothing that will work out well for you. Fall back, let me go in the front." Miller replied.

Chamise called back, "No way, not gonna happen."

"I'm going through," Miller responded.

"I know."

"I don't know how to get back."

"I figured."

"Still coming?"

They arrived at the edge of the pattern. Defiantly, Chamise called out the ancient battle cry of the Eisenvard.

"Sans Humanitia! By the sword!"

Miller scanned the pattern and found the key point. He set his hand upon a circle the size of his head. A line cut through its center like a knife wound.

He reached forward with his channels, with his mind, and found its core.

He opened the crack between worlds. Miller felt reality shifting around him. A black gate opened up. Before he could decide what to do, the blackness grew and enveloped him. True to her word, Chamise charged behind, hefting her mace in preparation for battle.

He emerged in dim lighting. The new place felt like the inside of a cave. Plants grew on the walls and ceiling. The plants had broad leaves and a slight illumination glowed from their edges. The cave looked to be taller than a two-story barn. He could fit twenty horses in here without a problem.

The problem was all the Takers waiting for him. The room was swarming with Takers. They floated like a swarm of fish circling their prey. Dull orange mixed with gray and sick-brown. Miller stood momentarily stunned as he looked at a Taker. Their forms resembled worms. Each one of the writhing forms stretched between an arm's length, and a man's height. Tentacle-like appendages hung from several points on their bodies.

Some Takers had only one tentacle. Others had more than a dozen. Then only common feature was the slime that dripped from their twisting feelers.

Phyllicitus lay at the center of the room surrounded by

Takers. She seemed to be groggy, not completely aware of her situation. Four of the Takers had connected their tentacles to her, trying to inject something into her. Phyllicitus looked confused, aware that she was in danger but not why.

Chamise didn't wait. She called out her battle-cry again, then charged into the swarm. The Takers moved toward her, reaching out with their slime covered tentacles as they sailed through the air. Each one in the swarm attempted to touch her, to connect with her skin, to invade her soul.

Miller stood rock solid in place. He wanted to jump into the fray, to unleash his channels and destroy these things. Right now, the Takers were more vulnerable than they ever had been in his world. They could be seen here between-the-worlds, and they could also be cut and burned. But he also knew his magic would not work here, at least not as he intended. Master Easter had once told him that the hardest thing to do was to wait for the pieces to be in place. So, he waited. He held the way back to his world open and waited. He knew that if he let the core of the pattern out of his mind then the way back would close, trapping all of them there forever.

Three seconds later the first Eisenvard arrived. Screaming in a battle frenzy, Ulf emerged from the gate, a long sword held in his right hand, pointing forward like a spear. Den and Gable followed after. In a few moments, the rest of the Eisenvard arrived in force. The Eisenvard chopped, cut, and smashed at the Takers as they floated through the air. The Takers moved quick, but not so quick that trained fighters could not counter them.

"Fetch the goddess! Pull her back through!" Miller shouted, afraid that the Eisenvard would spend all of their valuable time trying to kill the Takers instead of rescuing Phyllicitus.

Tabor surged forward, ignoring the Takers. He allowed them to score touches on his body. They connected to his skin. The long worm-like appendages wriggled as they penetrated into his skin. Tabor sprinted to Phyllicutus's side, picked her up in a protective embrace, and fled back toward the crack pulling three

Takers behind him.

Tabor only made it halfway. Two other Takers connected to him. One sent out a gray tendril and touched his left leg. The tentacle slid beneath his armor. Blood splattered out as the thing gained entry into Tabor's body. Another touched his legs, then his face. All Tabor could do was try to shield the goddess from the fall. He spun as he fell, releasing her.

Chamise was there. She pulled the goddess away from Tabor as he fell and dragged her back toward the gate. Chamise dropped her mace then drew her long knife, stabbing at the Takers as they approached.

"Go!" Miller urged.

Chamise picked Phyllicitus up by the waist and ran back toward the crack. Miller looked on in excitement. He knew this was the moment where they would rescue Phyllicitus or they would all die.

"Everyone back! The gate is closing!" Miller screamed.

Chamise slowed, looking back at him.

"I've got to keep it open. I'm the last one through."

She nodded, understanding the danger he was in, and moved quickly through the gate they had emerged from. Miller saw her and Phyllicitus step in, then wink from existence.

Just before they disappeared, he saw the shadow on Phyllicitus's chest. One of the Takers had positioned itself between her breasts, over her heart.

The other Eisenvard, almost as if they had practiced it, turned as one and fled back through the gate.

He counted them as they passed through. The last one through was Ulf, carrying the Tabor's prone body.

"Last One!" Ulf shouted as he passed by.

Somehow there were even more Takers in the room now. Miller hadn't seen them arrive during the battle. The glowing leaves that decorated the walls snapped and writhed excitedly as the Takers passed by as if they could sense their otherness.

Miller was amazed they had made it through this ordeal. He stood alone in the room, facing more than fifty Takers. Miller had no idea what to do so he offered mocking grin, then turned and walked through the gate. His last thoughts before he passed through were of Aileen and Easter. He wondered if he would be praised or scolded when he returned. He decided that he didn't care in the least.

The darkness didn't go away. He didn't emerge into the old temple or see the old pattern. He simply felt the crack between worlds fade, dissipate, and go away, leaving him here.

He stood alone, with no way home, between the worlds.

The Takers began to circle him.

A MASTER'S RING

"Easter was right" Miller spoke out loud what might be his final words. There was nowhere to go, nothing to do. That didn't stop panic though. The cave opened up into a long cavern that stretched beyond where the gate had once stood. Miller began to run. He didn't know where the cave would leave him, or if any exits actually went anywhere. It didn't matter, he just needed to escape the Takers.

He fled down the broad cave. His feet hammered on the cave's spongy surface. The ground wasn't stone, it was something else. It had the consistency of a pile of wet leaves. He knew this feeling. He knew what it was like to be between-the-worlds. He had been here before.

He had only one thought, that was to run.

His feet pounded hard across the cave's spongy surface. The Takers began to follow him. Even though they seemed to lazily drift through the air, the distance between Miller and the Takers shortened with his every breath.

Miller wanted to embrace the disciplines, to find the calm

that would allow rational decision making. He didn't have time for rationality. He sprinted faster. His chest pounded as he fled down the cave. It began to narrow, the leaves growing closer. They moved in cutting motions as if they were the butcher preparing to cut meat.

He felt a sting his back. Glancing back, he saw a tendril stretching from his back and dragging a single Taker behind. He swept his arm back, breaking the connection. A finger's length of gray tendril remained attached to his back. It leaked clear slime onto his shirt. Where the slime leaked through to touch his skin, Miller felt his nerves go numb.

More Takers came, rushing down the cave.

He saw a tunnel entrance to the right. He turned into it, hoping to put more distance between him and the Takers. Miller felt another sting, this time at the base of his neck. He swiped at it, breaking its hold, ripping the tentacle in half.

At a full run, he turned another corner and rushed directly into a patch of waist-high plants. Their cutting leaves slashed as he ran into their midst. They weren't sharp and didn't cut through his pants, nor did they cut his skin, but they stung when they touched flesh. His legs erupted in pain as if someone had poured boiling water on them.

He could barely breathe, his chest pounded, his abdomen began to cramp in pain. The leaves grew taller, stretching up to cut at the center of his chest. Soon they would be slashing at his face.

Miller knew that he was doomed. He could see no escape. He thought about all the good advice Easter had given him over the years. Easter offered him advice before he began this journey. Easter had said that as long as he paid attention to his inner voice, then Miller would have no problems. Now that last piece of advice was the most critical, it led him to his doom but may have saved Phyllicitus from the Takers. He smiled softly as he thought about recovering Phyllicitus and about the fact that he had discovered things about the Takers, secret things.

Sadly, Miller realized, he would be dead before anyone could hear those secrets from his lips. He hoped that he would go through the last door peacefully and that Easter and Aileen would pull his soul back to talk to him. Miller knew the truth. Death here between the worlds would not work the same way. He would never be brought back from the dead to speak those secrets. Here, between the worlds, there may not be any final door for him, only long decay and rot until the end of time.

He tripped. His face went down to the spongy floor. The impact didn't hurt, but a dozen stings he received on the way down did. Tentacles ripped free only to be reattached with new tendrils. Before he could scramble up, the Takers were on him.

He felt the Taker connect to his lower arm. Another on his leg, a third to his hip. He could feel the blood flow from the wounds, sucked into the Taker's floating worm-bodies. The Takers bore through his clothes. The tried to roll around, to break the connection.

He felt a pull on his neck as if one of the broken tendrils was pulling against him. He dared a look back. Smaller pustules had formed on the ends of those broken tendrils. The Takers had begun to grow back!

He began to crawl. He had no goal. He moved on instinct, desperately trying to preserve his life, if only for a second more.

Miler grabbed at the plant stalks, trying to use them for leverage. The broke off easily in his hand.

Hysteria began to seize him. Out of desperation, he dove into his mental disciplines. The concentration discipline had always been easy for him. It was comforting and safe. He could think of no better place to be for his final breath. He embraced it.

Calm fell upon him. He was aware of the Takers. They were connecting to him, drinking from his channels and his veins like leeches.

Excellent, he thought, I've just learned something more about these Taker things. Come on Easter, you've got to find my soul when this is done.

But the Takers drank from more than his channels. They

drank his essence, his soul.

But Miller knew there was no use worrying about it now. He knew that life was done for him. He might as well relax and finish up the experience. It hadn't been a great life, but it had been well-lived.

Then he saw it. On the ground, the plant stalks looked like a forest. A path stood open between their shifting branches and cutting leaves. Directly in front of him, less than an arm's reach away stood single plant. This plant looked different, it was jet-black and stood alone. A ring the color of night floated above it. A necromancer's ring.

He stared at the ring. He could snatch it, seizing a master's power. The ring would change him, change is very identity. It would make him invulnerable to the Takers. His soul would become poison to them, to all living things.

Then Miller thought about the other masters, about Aileen who just took a new name to match her new identity, about Easter and his long journey through loneliness, about Darjeeling who had sacrificed his sanity to the cause long ago. Even Master Hermagon had embraced desperation over love.

Miller shook his head, realizing that the cost was too much. He didn't want the power to fight. He wanted to make the world a better place. Another master necromancer wouldn't do that. It would make the world worse. He spoke a few words from the writings of Phyllicitus in an effort to seek a bit of solace in his final minutes.

"Peace is the only goal that contains virtue. All others are hollow beside it."

Miller thought about Phyllicitus as the tentacles crawled beneath his skin, and how Aileen couldn't truly grasp Phyllicitus's peaceful nature. The human gods were embodiments of forces and human aspects. They could not change who they were. If the gods changed, they would simply cease to exist. There is no constant like change, so human gods came and went. Miller had a stray thought. The First Gods were not human, they didn't have that problem. They seemed to be eternal.

A light began to shine atop the black plant. Miller could feel the tendrils digging deeper into his skin as he looked up again. The black ring continued to float. It had begun to rotate. A thin shaft of silver light shone out of the ring where a crack had formed, splaying light upon the surrounding plants. Their leaves bent toward it as if feeding from it-s natural light.

Miller screamed in pain as the tendrils dug deeper. He felt them eating their way into his muscle. There, at the end of his life, deep in the discipline of concentration, all Miller could think about was the plants.

He thought about how the plants may have never seen direct sunlight, but they knew something healthy when the felt it. Miller watched in amazement as black fragments of ring began to fall away. Each sliver of black that fell away revealed more shining silver and created more light. Soon the entire ring stood bare. Where there was once a dark ring of death, a brilliant silver ring of hope stood in its place. The aspect of doom and dangerous secrets was gone from the ring. Miller opened his channels and found the ring's core. He knew instantly that the ring before him emanated some kind of universal truth. It promised knowledge without strife, influence without power. This ring wasn't made to command the world, it was made to be part of it, to dance with it in a close embrace.

Miller could see a vision of how such a ring could be used. The discipline of concentration added detail to his vision. The black ring, with its snake-like shape, had fallen away to expose this new right. It was a simple design, a plain silver band with the shape of a complex knot. It reminded Miller of a horse's mane, waving as it galloped across the plains. Free.

Pain exploded from his neck. The Taker had found his spinal cord. He felt it cutting into his back, chewing through his bone. Miller knew that there was nothing left to do but die.

He remembered something Easter had told him once. "In the absence of a plan, any plan becomes the best plan," Miller smirked at the nonsense of it all, but he finally understood. He didn't have a plan. He didn't have a way out.

But he did have a ring.

He crawled forward another pace. Pain ripped through his neck. He began to cough. Blood sprayed out of his mouth to decorate the ground. A tendril jutted into his throat, choking him. He didn't know how the tentacle managed to attack so quickly, he just knew it would not matter soon, one way or another.

Miller reached and took the ring in his hand. It felt warm to his touch. Light began to shine from it, spraying beams of intense silver across the room. The dark plants reacted. They began to dance in its luminous joy, weaving back and forth as if to music. The plants didn't seem dire or murderous anymore, only excited by the light, and happy to be fulfilling their part in this world.

Slipping the silver ring onto his finger, Miller watched in amazement as his vision changed. The light didn't emerge from anywhere, yet he could see things perfectly. He felt the pain lessen as the Takers began to disconnect from him. More Takers arrived, hovering over his prone body. None would come near him.

'Am I poison to them?' He thought,'Maybe not. Maybe I'm just something they don't understand.'

He pushed up with his hands, regaining his feet to stand in the center of the dancing plants. Taking a moment to get his bearings, he began walking back toward where the gate had been. He arrived in moments.

A half-dozen Takers remained. Their worm-like bodies floated about. They reacted with curiosity to him, orbiting him from above, but not coming within reach. He stood for a few long moments. Easter and Aileen hadn't come through to fetch him yet. He didn't know if they would. Aileen hadn't embraced the dark pragmatism of the order fully, at least until she had changed her name. He hoped that a trickle of humanity would motivate her to reopen the gate.

He decided to sit and wait for her until then. He stared down at the ring. It was a master's ring, yet it wasn't. It was a ring of magic, but not a ring of death. The master's ring was flawed, without blackness or fear. Its silver shone in a testament to it's new form. Miller could not have been happier for it. He had not pulled a ring of death from this place, but a ring of life.

REQUIEM

When the Eisenvard returned to the world they interrupted a screaming match. Mistress Storm stood, regally pointing her finger at Easter.

"You black-hearted bastard! We could have saved her! Why didn't you save her?" She choked on her tears.

Easter pointed at the newly arrived Eisenvard, interrupting her verbal assault.

Mistress Storm looked back to see the Eisenvard. She stared in disbelief as they pulled Phyllicitus back through the gate. One after the other Eisenvard came through. Chamise set Phyllicitus down then help carry Tabor. Phyllicitus had recovered somewhat and was able to raise her head to look around.

"Miller. They left him behind." Chamise said. Her eyes looked hollow.

Mistress Storm shouted back at Easter. "See? I told you we could do it. Are you ready now?"

Easter nodded. "Let's go get him."

She ran to the pattern's side. Mistress Storm looked down at it, seeking the key point, the place of opening.

An ugly tear had appeared on the surface of the pattern. Its surface was marked with an ugly disfigurement. The pattern would bring no one back.

"It won't open." Mistress Storm said, her voice falling to a whisper.

Easter joined her and stood by her side. He set his hands upon the pattern, searching, feeling for any crack, any place where he could open the barrier. There was none. The pattern was gone. It had reverted into a simple collection of symbols. The crack between worlds had been sealed.

Miller had waited days. He hadn't tracked the passage of time, but with the concentration discipline still upon him, he found it easy to calculate it.

He had been here days. He thought about all of the things that had clouded his mind. He explored his own heart. He knew that his love for Aileen was a real thing and that it didn't have to be returned. He knew that his failure at Brita's side was a necessary piece of the journey but regretted it. Brita had wanted to be released, no matter how. He knew that Chamise was growing fond of him, and he was strangely happy with that. Someday they would both find a happy place to find comfort in. For now, the Order of the White Hand had its jealousy, Chamise had the ghosts of the Eisenvard, and he had a puzzle to solve.

The order had to learn that the rules had just changed. He thought about the order a for long spans of time. The order's central task, their reason for being, had transformed from a collection of evil death-eating necromancers bent on gaining power into heroes. They willingly took on the cause of defending the world from the Takers. The change was so profound that even the order didn't understand it. The order thought about the Takers from the point of view of an enemy or a rival. Nothing could be more incorrect. The Takers weren't rivals, they were carnivores and humanity was their meat.

To keep busy during the days, Miller spent time constructing thought experiments. He built mental models using the discipline of concentration. He spent long periods of time connecting theories and thoughts together to form original ideas. He tested them in his imagination. Some passed the test, but most did not.

He reasoned that if the pattern could open a crack so he could slip between-the-worlds to come here then that meant that the pattern could open a crack to return. He had no idea how to do such a thing, but if it could be done one way then perhaps it could be done another.

Patterns were an invention of man, he reasoned, they did not occur in nature. Men had used the truths of the universe to trick it, using patterns to capture the fates and destinies of the worlds and modify them.

Patterns were a primal force, if not the primal force. It was the power of being, of identity. He needed a power of that caliber, something greater than the machinations of wizards or of mankind. He needed something stronger than flows, and more resilient than disciplines.

There was only one such force that he knew of, The First Gods. They were the embodiment of animal spirits. Perhaps this wasn't because they were magic, but because they were reflections of the different aspects of his world. The First Gods could not be summoned. They could not be controlled. The bards sing of elder days when the First Gods walked the earth, human friends beside them. They could not be commanded, but they could be spoken to.

The legends of man said that the First Gods had gone from the world. Years ago, when he spoke to them about the First Gods, both Aileen and Easter had disagreed. When Easter spoke of an encounter he had with the Raven God a few hundred years ago, he was artful to only talk about the Raven God in respectful terms. That First God clearly had Easter's respect. Aileen had told stories of fighting against the followers of the Stag God in the north, back when she led expeditions to hunt down necromancers, and Phyllicitus had not yet returned to Home's Hearth.

The First Gods were present in the world, only quiet and unconcerned with the business of humanity.

Yet somehow, he had been given a Great Horse to come on this journey. He thought about that horse for hours. Great Horses were wonderful things. They lived in the tales of legend, assisting great warriors with fantastic quests. Great Horses were prized above all possessions by the very rich and could not be kept because they could escape any time they wished. Legends tell of such horses where they would be found, captured, and disappear as soon as their captor's eyes left them.

Peasants say that Great Horses were the foals of the Horse God. They believed these horses could understand the speech of men and could serve their cause.

Some tales even described them as leading a cause, saving villages, people.

The thought struck a chord in his mind. Miller felt like a hundred pieces of a puzzle had just assembled itself in front of his eyes. If the Horse God would allow him access to one of its children, would it not help him now? Could he call a First God at all, even between the worlds?

His analytical mind, now deep in the discipline of concentration, answered back. 'Why not?'

He had no spells, no channels, no secrets to do it. He did have a ring. The ring seemed to find connections to the world, to unify him with it, and everything within.

The First Gods were part of the worlds too, just not this one.

Miller reached to his belt-knife. It's thick utility blade perfectly cut into the soft yielding surface of the cave floor.

He began to draw his pattern. Starting with the hoof print, he expanded the drawing with the shapes of blowing grass, the arcs of sunlight, and distant hints of mountains in the background. With his eyes, it appeared chaotic and without purpose. His ring chimed with purpose, guiding him through the process of drawing shapes and embedding wishes into them.

Two days later, he finished his pattern. He had been here without food or water for an amazing period. Miller wondered at is newfound resilience. He knew that he should be laying on the ground dehydrated, but he wasn't. There was no food in his stomach. He should be hungry, but he wasn't.

He had drawn the pattern. He found the key point and put flowed his will into it. The pattern didn't split the world, it merely issued a call. It wasn't a commandment though. It was a plea for help.

He felt a presence come into the room, first as a weak heartbeat, then it grew into an overwhelming emotion. It was wild, filled with excited joy. He couldn't help but soak in the elation. The presence wasn't in his body as much as in his spirit. It wrapped him, embraced his soul, and called out for him to come along.

Joyously, he did.

The place-between-worlds faded away. He found himself riding a horse along the open hillside. Home's Hearth stood in the distance, its craftsmen's forges sending smoke into the air. His mare, no, the Horse God's mare trotted beneath him.

He had come through. A shining silver ring encircled his finger. Its knotted surface shone in the sunlight. It could represent a horse's mane. It could represent an open field. It was definitely a pattern.

The concentration discipline continued upon him. He had never managed to use it more than a few hours at a time. Now it was natural, part of him. It no longer dominated his perceptions nor caused him to become emotionless. He had made it his own, or it had made him its own.

He rubbed the mare's neck.

"Thanks for coming for me."

Miller didn't know if he was talking to the mare, or to the Horse God himself. He didn't think it mattered either way. Both of them had his gratitude.

"Let's go back to Home's Hearth for a day. I want to check on Aileen and Easter."

He needed to make sure they knew he was back. He didn't want them taking risks to find him between-the-worlds.

Miller rubbed his ring with his thumb.

The Order needed to know that there was a new master in their midst, a different kind of master who didn't obey the old rules. They needed to know that their old ways of death had just changed.

A new day had dawned in this world.

NOTE FROM THE AUTHOR

Thanks for reading my third book, Flaw in the Master's Ring. This book has been both a joy to write, and a chore as it signaled the end of Miller's trilogy. There appears to be a bit more to this story yet to come. The Taker's true forms have been discovered, but they have yet to be defeated. Phyllicitus has been spirited into unknown worlds. A secret group of necromancers plot to release their own god. I am writing a prequel to this trilogy right now (working title *Avatar of the Raven)* that describes a place far away and hundreds of years ago, where the Order of the White Hand discovered how difficult it could be to deal with the powers of the First Gods.

Just a note - If you liked this book, please review it online! Also, look out for a prequel novella soon. *Avatar of the Raven* should be out by early 2020.

Best Wishes

Brian P

Brian@brianphillipswriter.com
http://whitehand.brianphillipswriter.com

ABOUT THE AUTHOR

Brian Phillips lives in Northern Virginia, writes books, plays games, and lives life to its fullest. He has been in turn a sailor, a student, a Doctor of Philosophy, an engineer, and an author.